Since the dawn of existence, war has raged between the forces of good and evil.

The prize: humanity.

Knowing they were fighting a losing battle, the pantheon of Gods did something they had never done before – they cheated. Blessing ten humans with the powers of the Gods, they created the Guardians to fight on their behalf. When the darkness eventually retreated into the underworld, they knew it was merely slumbering. So too did the Guardians go into a slumber, waiting for the day that they would be called forth again to battle for the souls of humanity . . .

THE MADEIRAN GUARDIANS

BOOK ONE

AWAKENING

AMELIUS MARIN

Cover art by sncinderart

ISBN: 978-1-7776811-0-4
Copyright © 2021 Amelius Marin
Niagara Falls, Ontario

Dedicated to Jasmine, my best friend,
And to Xander and Draven,
the next generation of storytellers

Part One

Chapter One

The morning light shone bright as the young, olive-skinned boy laying in the tall grass opened his eyes. He blinked a few times, his eyes adjusting to the light. Placing a hand on his forehead to cast some shade over his eyes, he squinted up at the cloudless, violet sky. Branches and leaves swayed back and forth in the cool breeze of the southern winds. He pushed himself to his feet, trying to look over the grass, though it still rose above his shoulders.

"Yukaio?" he heard a soft voice nearby.

Looking around to try and find the source, he noticed an indent in the tall stalks of grass. A young girl, his little sister, lay nearby.

"Terry!"

Yukaio ran towards his sister, crouching down beside her. His long, dark brown hair hung down around his face. With a flick of his hand, he threw his hair back over his shoulder. He looked down at her, his brown eyes sparkling in the light.

She lay in the grass and looked up at her brother. Taking a deep breath, she tried to sit up but winced in pain. Her brother brushed aside the locks of auburn hair that hung in tangles around her face so he could see her clearly. Her face was marred with pain. Yukaio placed a hand behind her shoulder to help prop her forward and leaned her against his side. She tried to smile, but the pain was too much.

"Yukaio, what happened?" she asked. "Where are we?"

"I'm not entirely sure," Yukaio admitted to his sister. "The last thing I remember is . . ."

He paused. He couldn't actually remember anything. With one quick movement, he looked away from his sister as he tried not to appear concerned. Yukaio closed his eyes and tried to remember. Before he woke up in the grass everything was blank. He knew the young girl in his arms was his sister, he knew her name was Terry. But that was it. The rest was a blank.

"I don't remember anything either," she said, trying and failing to hide the worry in her voice.

"It's going to be ok," Yukaio said. He gently squeezed her shoulder, reassuring her, and himself, that they were together, and everything would turn out alright. "We're together, and that's what matters. The rest we'll just have to figure out."

"I know, we just . . . ahh," she gasped in pain.

"What's wrong?" Yukaio asked.

Terry lifted her arm and placed her hand on her right hip, pulling up her shirt to reveal where she felt the pain. "Right here, in my side."

There wasn't any blood, but Yukaio could see a fair amount of bruising. With a gentle hand, Yukaio touched the bruise, and Terry closed her eyes, wincing in pain. Taking a deep breath, she raised her head to look up at her brother, who tried to smile back at her. Yukaio again looked away, trying to think of what he could do. His eyes landed on a nearby tree with low hanging branches, leaves swaying in time with the grass. *If I can climb up there, maybe I will be able to figure out where we are*, Yukaio thought to himself.

"Terry," he said, trying to hide the shakiness in his voice, "I'm going to climb up that tree over there and see if I can see anything."

"Are you sure it's safe?" Terry grabbed her brother's arm as he tried to stand up.

"Of course," Yukaio smiled, hoping he sounded confident.

Gently laying his sister down on the ground, he made her as comfortable as possible before walking towards the tree. Did he know how to climb trees? Had he ever climbed one before? Yukaio couldn't remember. Stepping into the shade of the great oak, he looked up at the towering trunk. Standing below it and looking up, at the branches, it seemed so much higher than before. He pulled a string from his pocket and tied back his long brown hair to keep it out of his face. Digging a foot into the ground he crouched, preparing to jump for the lowest branch to pull himself up. He sprang upwards, arms swiping the air, grasping for a branch still several inches above his fingers.

Yukaio fell back to the ground with a *thud*. He examined the tree for any other way to get up. Peeking out from the other side of the tree, he noticed a root sticking out from the ground underneath a branch that seemed to appear out of nowhere. *That might be just enough to help me,* he thought. Stepping up onto the protruding root, he again sprang upwards towards the branch. His fingers scraped the edge of the bark before again falling to the ground. The breath caught in his chest at the impact.

"One more time," he whispered as he rose to his feet. "I can do this."

Preparing to step back up, he lifted his foot and knocked the side of the root, losing his balance in the process. Propping himself up on his elbows, Yukaio looked at the root in front of him. He shook his head trying to remember, was the root that high all along? Or had it somehow moved? No, that couldn't be. He tried to put the crazy thought out of his mind.

Yukaio placed a hand on the trunk of the tree as he steadied himself on the root. He crouched and jumped as hard as he could. His hands clasped around a branch. Not the one he was aiming for, but the next one above it. Realizing what he did, Yukaio smiled as he swung his legs around the lower branch and pulled himself into a sitting position to catch his breath. He looked back at the ground below him, and then up towards the sky. Though he was high above the ground, the top of the tree was still much, much further.

His arms embraced the trunk of the tree to steady himself as he rose to his feet. Looking up, now the branches didn't seem quite as intimidating as when he was on the ground. Reaching up one hand, he grasped a branch to pull himself higher. Slowly, one branch at a time, he climbed through the tree. Finally reaching the top, he looked out and saw. . . grass. And more grass. Moving to the other side of the tree, he saw. . . even more grass. But beyond that lay a mountainous range, a thick forest of evergreen trees lining its base. There was nothing else to indicate where they were.

He gave a resigned sigh. That would have to do for now.

As Yukaio prepared to descend the tree, a glimmer caught his eyes. Nearby, deep in the thick grass, the brightness of the sun reflected off of something. Despite the shade cast by overhanging branches, Yukaio raised a hand to block the remaining sunlight from his eyes. The object, which looked quite small, shone bright in the gleaming sun. Letting his curiosity get the better of him, he quickly descended the tree, making sure to stay aware of where that shining object was. As Yukaio neared the ground and the grass began to obstruct his view, he decided to forgo climbing down the last several branches and leaped to the ground. Landing on his feet, he took off running toward where he saw the object.

Parting the grass as he approached, he could again see it shine in the light. A small orb, as brown as the dirt around it, lay before him. Reaching out a hand, he closed his fingers around it and picked it up for a closer look. Although the orb had a brown colour, it was opaque and perfectly smooth. Yukaio stared at it, transfixed by the small object. Though it was light, the weight he felt in his hand was immense. His breath grew faster the longer he stared at it, his mind entirely engulfed by the orb.

"Yukaio?" Terry's voice brought him out of his trance. Taking another quick look at the orb, he pocketed it in one swift motion as he took off back towards his sister.

"I'm here," Yukaio knelt beside her.

"See anything?"

She was hopeful he had found something, anything.

"There isn't much," he shook his head. "A lot of tall grass and a small forest at the base of some mountains. That's probably our best bet for now."

Yukaio extended a hand to help Terry as a strong gust of wind knocked them both back to the ground. The howling of the wind grew as clouds rushed across the sky, blocking out the sun. Shade moved over the grass like waves. Looking up, the siblings watched as shadows flew across the sky, circling above the area where they sat.

"What is that?" Terry asked her brother.

"I don't know, but I don't think it's good," he said.

Yukaio placed Terry's arm around his shoulders

and propped her up. Keeping low below the top of the grass, he guided her towards the forest. She whimpered in pain at each movement. Yukaio didn't let his worry show as he slowed their pace. The howling of the wind continued to grow above them, and the circling shadows drew closer. Looking back, Yukaio realized the howling moved not with the wind but with the swelling darkness - it was the shadows that were howling. Taking a deep breath, he picked up the pace again, pulling his sister along with him. His knees buckled as Terry collapsed, her weight dragging him down with her.

"I'm sorry, I can't go that fast." Terry apologized.

"It's ok," Yukaio tried to smile. "I'll carry you, get on."

He turned and helped her climb onto his back. Gripping her legs tight around his waist, he ran as fast as he could through the grass. Gasping for air, he didn't dare look back at the shadows to see if they were still following. With the forest in sight, he let out a deep, heavy breath. Terry closed her eyes and tucked her head against her brother's shoulders as the pines of the evergreen brushed past them. Finally, stopping at the base of a mountainous cliff, Yukaio set Terry down on the ground.

"There's more cover here, we should be safe," Yukaio said, looking for shadows above the trees.

"Were they following us?" Terry couldn't hide the concern in her voice.

"I don't know," Yukaio shook his head.

"What were they? What do they want?"

Yukaio shook his head. He couldn't help the growing panic and frustration that sounded in his voice.

"I don't know."

Terry gasped, her light brown eyes welled up with tears. With a gentle finger, Yukaio wiped them away. He placed a hand on her shoulder, giving it a light squeeze. Terry's own hand hovered over her side, her clenched fist slightly shaking.

"I'm sorry, I just wish I had some answers for you."

"You'll figure it out, right?" she asked.

Yukaio smiled and nodded before turning away. In the distance, the sun had begun to set, the last bits of light creeping through the trees. Gathering some fallen branches, he started a fire to keep them warm through the night. Laying Terry near the fire, he checked her bruising. It hadn't gotten any worse, but it wasn't getting any better either.

"Gaia root," Yukaio said after a long period of silence.

"What?"

"I should try and find some Gaia root, it might help with the pain."

Yukaio stood up, looking around the darkening forest.

"I don't want to stay here alone though."

Terry looked up at her brother, her soft brown eyes glimmering, still welling up with tears. Yukaio smiled softly as he pushed a strand of auburn hair back behind her ear.

"I'll be back really soon, I promise."

"No," Terry pulled at her brother's arm. "Please don't go. I don't need the roots, it isn't that bad."

"I'm sure they're nearby, just stay here and try to stay quiet," Yukaio reassured his sister.

After a moment of consideration, Terry nodded. She wanted to protest her brother leaving and going off on his own. As worried as she was for herself, she also worried about him. Despite her doubts, she knew that he wouldn't be doing it if he didn't think it was the best decision. Terry forced a smile at her brother as he turned away. Watching him go, her breath caught in her throat, the smile fading. He looked so confident, why couldn't she be like that, too? She laid her head back on the ground and closed her eyes, trying not to count the time passing.

Yukaio didn't turn back as he walked away from his sister. Yes, he wanted to find the Gaia root to help her, but he also needed some time. Time to think, time to figure things out. His fingers slipped into his pocket, wrapping around the small orb he had found in the grass. The warmth it emanated brought him comfort, and the frown on his face began to relax. Once he was sure that he was out of his sister's sight, Yukaio leaned against a tree and pulled the orb out to examine it once more. It seemed familiar somehow. Holding it up, he watched the fading light from the setting sun gleam through it.

As he stared at it, shadows began to pass over him, vanquishing the light from the area. Looking up, he could see the shadows swirling in the sky. They weren't clouds, they were something else - and they were getting closer. Instinct told him to run, but he forced himself to pause. *I can't lead them back to Terry*, he thought. Resolving himself to run in the other direction, he tried to move, but his legs failed him. Frozen in place, he watched the shadows surround him. As they touched the ground, they began to take form. They looked vaguely human-like but were much larger than any person. Their features were non-existent, only darkness emanated from them.

Yukaio looked back and forth between the shadows surrounding him. He counted at least a dozen of them. They bore no weapons, but with their size, he figured they wouldn't need them anyway. One of the shadows directly in front of him approached. Its steps made no sound on the ground, and the grass only just swayed as if a light breeze were passing over. Steadying his nerve, Yukaio put his hands up, ready to fight.

Swinging his fist toward the shadow, it passed through its leg without making any impact. Looking at his hand remnants of black smoke trailed behind it. Yukaio looked up at the shadow just in time to see its massive arm coming towards him. It struck him square in the chest, throwing him back, landing with a painful *thud* on the ground. Before he could move or brace himself for another impact, the leg of a second shadow scooped under his back, sending him flying into the air. As Yukaio tumbled back to the ground, he looked around. There had to be something he could do to stop them, some way he could fight back. He tried not to think of Terry alone. What would she do if these . . . things came after her? He shouldn't have left her, he should be there to protect her.

Struggling to get to his feet, Yukaio willed his legs to work, to run. He took off, away from Terry, hoping to find . . . he didn't know. But he believed, he had to; he still couldn't remember anything before waking up in the grass, his belief was all he had. Yukaio passed through the thick of the trees as fast as he could, only daring to look over his shoulder once to see how quickly the shadows were gaining on him. He looked up as the darkness around him increased, shadows passing over his head. He didn't have time to scream, or stop running, as they retook their form in front of him. Yukaio crashed into the center shadow, sending it tumbling to the ground with him.

Rolling away, he stood up. *What just happened?* He wondered, as the shadow also recovered and moved to strike him again. This time he was able to duck out of the way, the shadow crashing into a tree, cracking several branches and sending a flurry of leaves down around them. Yukaio turned to face the shadow again. As it lunged towards him, he threw himself at it, hoping that whatever happened before would happen again. The shadow, unable to move out of the way, was knocked to the ground. Yukaio smiled as he got to his feet, ready to pounce on the shadow again.

"Ahhh," he yelled as he leaped on the shadow. Black smoke curled around him, and the shadow below vanished. Looking down, all Yukaio saw amidst the disappearing smoke was a pike of burnt ashes.

The remaining shadows encircled him. He had taken one of them down, but no way could he take all of them on at once. His breathing was heavy, his heart pounding. One of the shadows made contact, sending him back into the tree behind him. Yukaio slid down the tree to the ground, rolling out of the way of another attack. He tried to scramble to his feet, but a stinging pain in his head caused him to sway. The wind left his lungs as another blow to the back sent him back down to the ground.

Looking at the strewn branches on the ground, Yukaio reached out for one. A small gleam of light made one of the branches shine. No, not a branch, he realized, a glaive! Pulling himself forward, Yukaio wrapped his fingers around the polearm, gripping it as tight as he could. Rolling onto his back, he swung the bladed end at the nearest shadow. It let out a howl as the blade cut through it, the smoke dissipating, and ashes falling to the ground.

Yukaio stared at the weapon in shock. He hadn't expected that to happen. Recovering, he slammed the end of the polearm into the ground, leaning against it to pull himself to his feet. Placing his other hand further down the polearm, he readied himself for another attack. A sudden focus washed over him, his feet moving into a proper battle stance, balancing himself and preparing to strike. His hands found their spot on the glaive as if it was an extension of his own body. As a shadow moved towards him, Yukaio ducked under its massive arm, swinging his weapon with great surety.

Moving through the shadows, swinging the glaive, he felt comfortable, confident. The pain in his head was the farthest thing from his mind, his razor sharp focus taking over. Around him, wasps of smoke dissipated into the air, and the ground became covered with burnt ashes. Soon a lone shadow remained. Yukaio turned to face it head-on, ready to attack. In a *whoosh,* the shadow vanished into the air. He watched as the shadow rose back into the sky and moved off.

He instinctively moved to run after the fading shadow when a far-off scream caught his mind. Snapping back into his mind, he looked at the disappearing shadow and began to wonder why he wanted to go after it. Looking in the other direction, he remembered his sister. Forgetting everything else, he took off at a run to find Terry.

Chapter Two

Terry lay on the ground, unmoving. The pain in her side was getting worse, not better. Each shallow breath brought a new sting of pain. Closing her eyes, she hoped Yukaio would be back soon. A noise in the distance made her open her eyes as she tried to prop herself up on her elbows. She looked off in the direction Yukaio had gone. That noise, it was a scream, she realized. But it didn't sound like a scream of pain. It sounded angry.

"Yukaio?" Terry called out. Only the wind blowing through the trees answered her call.

Leaning back against the ground, Terry placed a hand to her side. Moving made the pain much worse than it was a minute ago. Tears welled up in her eyes, rolling down the side of her face. Where was her brother? She stared at the trees above her. The leaves swayed gently in the wind, streams of light peeking through the dense foliage. As she stared at it, the light grew brighter and closer until it was near blinding.

Terry raised a hand to shield her eyes as she tried to see where the light was coming from. Squinting, Terry thought for sure she could see something emerging from the light, a figure of some kind. She let out a scream when she saw what emerged. Terry blinked a few times to make sure what she was seeing was real and not just a figment of her mind.

Before her, appearing out of nowhere, was a

large, winged figure. Pure white feathered wings spread out on either side, gently flapping, lowering it to the ground. Long, silver hair draped around a face with a soft, smiling expression. Its violet eyes looked at Terry as it spoke.

"You don't need to fear me, child," it said with a smooth voice.

"What are you?" Terry gasped between painful breaths of air.

"My name is Uaithiel," it said. "I am an angel."

Before Terry could respond, she heard rapid footsteps approaching. Turning her head to the side, she saw Yukaio emerge from the trees, holding a long pole with a blade at the end. Yukaio stopped running as soon as he saw the figure standing before his sister. Pointing the blade in front of him, the long pole tucked under his arm, Yukaio moved between the figure and his sister.

"Stay away from my sister," he said with as much force as he could muster.

"You have nothing to fear from me, Yukaio," it held up its hands in front of it. "I am only here to help you."

"How do you know my name?" Yukaio asked.

"I know all about you, Yukaio, and your sister, Terry," it said, nodding towards them. "My name is Uaithiel, and we are . . . friends of a sort."

"What do you mean 'of a sort?'"

"I am your guardian angel," Uaithiel said.

"You're my what?" Yukaio said in disbelief.

"Your guardian angel," Uaithiel repeated.

"Ok, then tell me what happened to us? Why can't I remember anything?" Yukaio asked, still pointing the glaive at Uaithiel.

"That's a rather long story, I'm afraid. But I am, of course, willing to explain everything to you, but first . . ." Uaithiel reached for a small sack tied to the belt around their waist. "I believe you had gone off in search of Gaia root before the Umbra attacked."

"Umbra? You mean those shadowy things?"

"Yes, they're called Umbra," Uaithiel said. "They are gone for now, but you will have to face them again in the future, I'm afraid."

Yukaio lowered the glaive and reached to take the bag from Uaithiel's outstretched hand. Pulling the root out of the bag, he held up the white, spiny root. He knew right away that this was the root he needed.

"Thank you."

Yukaio nodded towards the angel, still somewhat skeptical. He moved back towards his sister, glancing at the angel out of the corner of his eye. Setting down his glaive, he broke off a piece of the root and went to hand it to Terry.

"I also have some water if you want to boil it into a tea for your sister, it might be easier for her to take," Uaithiel said. "I've always heard that the raw root has a rather pungent taste."

He looked at the root in his hand and then back up at the angel. Their guardian angel. Could he trust this Uaithiel?

"Alright, but once I'm done, I want to know what is going on," Yukaio commanded.

Uaithiel nodded and placed a skein of water and a cup on the ground by Terry before taking a step back to give the siblings some space. Yukaio worked quietly as he gathered the branches to make a fire and started to boil the water. He leaned in towards his sister, keeping his voice low.

"Before I got here, what did the . . . uh, he . . . um . . ." Yukaio scrunched his brows and looked up at the angel. "They?" he asked.

"Angels have no gender," Uaithiel nodded. "So yes, they is correct."

"Right," Yukaio nodded, turning back to his sister. "Before I got here, what did they do? Did they hurt you at all?"

"No," Terry said. "I was just surprised when they appeared. I'm sorry if my scream scared you."

"Hey, you never have to apologize to me," Yukaio smiled as he placed a hand on his sister's arm.

Terry nodded, returning his smile. Crushing the root into a powder between a rock and the bottom of his glaive, he added it to the boiling water.

Terry looked at the glaive in her brother's hands. "Where did you get that?"

"I found it," he said. "When I was fighting the . . . Umbra."

Yukaio carefully took the cup of root tea, blowing on it to cool it a bit before handing it to his sister. He propped up her head with his hand and helped her take one sip at a time. Terry wrinkled her nose at the smell of it but drank the whole cup before laying back down.

"Ok, Uaithiel," Yukaio turned to face the angel. "Start at the beginning."

"I rather think starting at the beginning would be even more confusing," Uaithiel said. "I'll start with what just happened."

"Why don't you start with why I can't remember anything?"

"It's complicated. There is a lot you need to understand first before that will make sense."

"Fine."

"That glaive in your hands, it was able to destroy the Umbra." It wasn't a question.

"Yes, they turned to some kind of ash when I struck them with it," Yukaio confirmed. "But when I tried to hit them with my hand, I just went right through them."

"That is because the weapon you are holding, as

well as the one concealed in your pocket, are weapons of the Gods," Uaithiel said. The angel glanced towards Yukaio's pocket, as the boy placed his hand against his side.

"The Gods?" Yukaio repeated skeptically.

"The Umbra are phantoms, made of shadow and darkness. They are servants of the dark forces; they are not alive, so they cannot be killed. Mortal weapons are useless against them, but weapons of the Gods can return them to the ash from whence they came."

"And someone just left these lying around for anyone to find?" Yukaio asked.

"Not just anyone – you were meant to find them, they have always belonged to you."

"Why me?"

"Because you are a Guardian."

"I'm a what?" Yukaio scrunched his brow, trying to process what he was hearing.

"You are one of the Guardians of Madeira, protectors of the eight realms and humanity," Uaithiel explained. "You, along with several others, were chosen before you were even born. The Guardians are blessed with the powers of the Gods and the ability to fight the forces of darkness."

"Yeah, I think I would remember this."

"Unfortunately, the memory of this, and the rest of your lives is currently lost to you. I know that will make this harder for you to understand, but I assure it, it is the truth."

Yukaio looked at his sister. He knew that Uaithiel was right about at least part of it - neither of them could remember a thing. But that didn't mean that he had to believe this nonsense. Being a protector of the realm – no way would he have asked to be that. The only one he cared about protecting right now was his sister. Terry returned her brother's look. He placed a hand on her shoulder.

"In the last battle, you and the other Guardians were successful in banishing the forces of darkness back into the underworld. But the celestial host knew that they wouldn't be kept there forever, we knew that they would be back and that we would need the Guardians again. I placed your souls into a type of stasis, ready to be awoken when the darkness returned, but something went wrong," Uaithiel said. "You and the other Guardians were supposed to be awoken together, ready to resume the fight. But when . . ."

"Ok, I'm going to stop you there," Yukaio held up a hand. "This is crazy."

"As crazy as causing roots to rise out of the ground or branches to bend down?"

Yukaio stared at the angel in disbelief. "How did you know about that?"

Terry looked from her brother to Uaithiel and back. "What are they talking about?"

"Earlier, when I was trying to climb that tree, I stood on a root to give me a boost, but it wasn't enough at first. When I tried again, I could have sworn that the root moved further out of the ground," Yukaio told his sister before turning back to the angel. "But I imagined it."

"No, you didn't," Uaithiel smiled. "When you were born you were blessed by Gaia, the Goddess of the earth. Your powers are rooted in nature."

"Gaia? That's a root."

"Yes, but it is also the name of a Goddess," the angel explained. "She is the one who watches over you, the one that has watched over you your entire life. Your powers come from her. It's also why the first thing you remembered was Gaia root. The plant gives life, just as she does."

Yukaio stood up, shaking his head. He turned

away from his sister and the angel. Taking a deep breath, he tried to figure out if anything he was hearing made sense. It was crazy. It couldn't be right.

"Is Terry one of these Guardians too?" Yukaio turned to face Uaithiel.

"No," the angel shook their head. "She's a regular human."

"But there are other Guardians?"

"Yes, there are more."

"And what did you say we were Guardians of?"

"Humanity," Uaithiel explained. "Although, technically, the Guardians are also protectors of the eight realms. This realm, Madeira, has been the battleground between the celestial host and the forces of the underworld for millennia. Of all the realms, this one was chosen due to the inherent magic it holds."

"What are the other realms?" Yukaio asked.

"Well, of course, there's Madeira and the Celestial Cities, although many refer to it as Heaven. There's the underworld, which some also call Hell. Then there is the astral realm, called Summerland, and the enlightenment realm, Nirvana. There's the shadowy realm, Purgatory, and the void realm, Oblivion. And finally, there's Earth, the home of humanity."

"So, are some of the Guardians in other realms?"

"No, as the battlefield is here, so are all the Guardians. Though, at present, you are scattered across this world."

"How did we end up like that?"

"I'm afraid that is partly my fault," Uaithiel admitted. "While the Guardians are the protectors of the realm, my role is to be the watcher of the Guardians. I am the protectorate, the protector of the protectors, so to say. It was my job to safeguard all of your souls while you slumbered. But I was attacked by a demon named . . . well, it isn't really important."

"Why not?" Yukaio asked.

"All that matters is that he is a servant of the darkness, a general in their forces. He commands several armies of Umbra and other beings, all loyal to the darkness," Uaithiel said. "When he discovered I was guarding your souls, he attacked me. In the attack, I lost my grip on all of you, and you ended up scattered. You all emerged from your stasis before you could be properly prepared, that's why you have no memories."

"If Terry isn't a Guardian, why was she affected?" Yukaio asked.

"When you Guardians were set to go into stasis, we didn't know how long it would be for. You all spent years training and preparing for the war, and by fighting, you sacrificed much. When it was decided that you would go into stasis, many of you refused to lose what family you had left. At first, the Gods were unsure, but given all that you've sacrificed, and will sacrifice in the future, it was permitted. Those of you with siblings were allowed to have them join you in stasis."

"How long were we in stasis for?" Terry chimed in.

"Several thousand years."

"Wait . . . I'm barely sixteen! You say I've been fighting in a war?"

"You came to me when you were fourteen, and within a year, you were united with the rest of the Guardians and properly trained. However, you have had your powers since you were born. They have always been a part of you."

"Why should I believe any of this?" Yukaio crossed his arms over his chest.

"The orb in your pocket," Uaithiel said. "Take it out."

Yukaio reached into his pocket and pulled out the small brown orb. It felt warm in his hand. "What is it?" he asked.

"It's known as a meamina. It is the materialization of your soul," the angel explained. "It is what links you to your powers and your patron Goddess."

"What do I do with it?"

"The meamina will help you access your powers, especially now since you can't remember any of your training," Uaithiel said. "Hold it in your hand and focus. Feel the power flow through you."

Still unsure if he believed any of this, Yukaio clasped his hand around the orb. Closing his eyes, he tried to feel this power. The warmth of the orb spread throughout his hand, but nothing else. Yukaio opened his eyes and looked around, nothing had changed.

"You need to believe," Uaithiel said.

"Believe? How am I supposed to believe any of this? It doesn't make any sense!" Yukaio couldn't help but shout.

"Then believe in yourself. Believe that you are stronger than you know. That even without your memories, you know who you are. Be true to yourself."

Yukaio sighed and closed his eyes again. He did manage to climb that tree, and he did defeat the Umbra. Maybe he could believe in himself, even if the rest of this didn't make sense.

"Yukaio," Terry's soft voice called out.

"What is it?" he leaned down beside his sister.

"I believe in you too," she put a hand on his shoulder. "I'll always believe in you."

"Thank you, Terry," Yukaio set down the orb, leaning on his arm to get closer to his sister to whisper in her ear. "Do you actually believe any of this?"

"I don't know," Terry admitted. "But it does explain a few things. Nothing has made sense since we woke up, but if anyone is blessed by the Gods, it's you."

"Ok, I'll try for you," Yukaio smiled as Terry placed a hand on his shoulder.

Yukaio nodded as he moved to stand up. He could believe in himself, for Terry. Pulling his hand away from the ground, he saw a stem peaking between his fingers.

"What the . . ." he started to say.

Terry turned to look at where her brother's hand had been. Instead of a dry patch of dirt, a small flower peaked through the loose grains. Yukaio, unable to hide his surprise, looked up at the angel.

"You did that," Uaithiel confirmed what Yukaio was thinking. "Close your eyes, Yukaio. Connect with your powers."

Yukaio stood up, holding the orb tight in his fist. The warmth filled his hand, and he took a deep breath, letting the warmth spread through the rest of him. For the first time since waking up, he felt at peace, as if everything was right with the world. The power flowed from the meamina through his whole body, swirling and encircling him. A gasp from Terry caused him to open his eyes.

Looking around the forest, he could have sworn that his eyes were playing a trick on him. He couldn't believe the sight that greeted him. The ground around them had been barren with only sporadic patches of grass, but now it was covered in fully bloomed wildflowers. Vibrant blues and violets, reds and pinks, covered the ground all around. Yukaio bent down and plucked a single violet flower from the ground. Holding it in his hand, he looked at the fully formed leaves, the pollen from the core drifting in the wind.

"I did this." It was a question as much as it was a statement.

"Yes, Yukaio, you did. And there is so much more that you can do too," Uaithiel smiled at the young Guardian.

Yukaio looked down at Terry. She cupped a violet in her hand, gently plucking it from the ground. She pushed back her hair, sliding the flower stem behind her ear, a smile covering her face. Neither of them needed to say what they were thinking, they knew their thoughts were the same. Terry nodded at her brother. This was about so much more than just the two of them.

"So," Yukaio said after a long pause. "There are other Guardians too?"

"Yes, there are."

"Where are they now?"

"I don't know, unfortunately. All of you were separated, and you were the first that I was able to find," Uaithiel explained. "I will need to gather the others before the darkness is able to make a full return."

"Well then," Yukaio smiled. "Where do we start?"

Chapter Three

The full moon gleamed in the night sky. Rays of light peaked through thick branches, illuminating patches of earth around the campsite. Fireflies buzzed above the head of the young boy sleeping by the fire. His sister looked down at him as she poked the flaming logs with a stick. The fire danced in the night, light reflecting on her dark skin. Bracelets jangled on her wrist as she set the stick down. The howling wind and swirling shadows above gave her pause, but she knew that they were safe by the fire.

It had been over a week since they first saw the shadows take form. They were lucky to have escaped, only finding refuge in an open field engulfed with sunlight. The shadows had paused, and ultimately retreated, rather than following them into the light. Somehow, it made sense to her that the light of the fire would do the same to keep them safe at night. She watched her brother sleep, the light casting shadows on his dark skin. He was only a couple years younger than her, but she felt responsible for him, he was all she had left, all that she could remember.

She closed her eyes for a moment. Her mind floated back to when she first woke up by the side of the river, the water almost washing her away as she pulled her brother to the side of the riverbank. But what had happened before that? How did they get there? She couldn't recall. They had followed the river for a couple of days, but after coming across nothing and no one, they moved inland. It wasn't long before they realized that a shadow was following them.

A rustle in the bushes nearby caused her to inch closer to the fire. *Please let it pass*, she thought to herself. She repeated it in her head like a mantra.

Let it pass.

Let it pass.

Let it pass.

Keeping her breath silent, she continued to listen. The rustling grew closer and closer. Looking up, she could see the moon still high in the night sky, the dawn several hours away. Shoving the stick she was holding back in the fire, she let the end catch the flame. Pulling it out of the fire, she moved back towards her brother. Placing a hand on his shoulder, she gently shook him.

"Wake up, Tiergan," her voice was hushed.

"What is it? What's going on?" he said in a groggy voice as he rubbed his eyes.

"There's a noise out in the bushes," she said. "I think it's getting closer."

"Is it the shadows again?" Tiergan asked, his voice unsteady as he sprang up.

"I don't know," she shook her head as she passed him the torch. "But here, take this."

Tiergan reached out for the torch, holding it close to him. His sister grabbed another branch and lit it in the fire. She stood still as the rustling grew louder. Whatever it was would appear soon.

"What if it isn't the shadows, Sagira? What if it's something else?" Tiergan asked as he stood beside his sister.

"I don't know," she placed a hand on his shoulder. "Hopefully, whatever it is, the fire also scares it."

The siblings stood motionless behind the fire as they watched the bushes on the opposite rustle and eventually part. A short boy with olive coloured skin and long brown hair emerged. His light brown eyes reflected the fire as the light danced on his skin. In his hand, he held a pole nearly as tall as himself with a curved blade at the top. Sagira laughed in her mind, silently wondering if someone so small could handle such a large weapon.

"I'm sorry if I scared you," he said.

"Who are you?" Sagira asked with as much force as she could.

"My name is Yukaio, I've been looking for you for a while," he looked between them and paused a moment before continuing. "You're Tiergan and Sagira, right?"

"Do you know who we are?" Tiergan asked eagerly, looking up at his sister. This was the first time they had encountered another person in almost two weeks, since the day they awoke with no memories.

"Not really, just your names," Yukaio admitted. "But I've been told who you are by someone who does know you."

A howl from above caused the trio to look up at the shadows still circling above them. To Sagira it looked like more had arrived since the last time she checked. Glancing at the new stranger, Yukaio, she studied his face. There was a set determination as he watched the shadows, but a flicker of fear hid just beneath the surface. He must have encountered them before too.

"You've seen these before?" Sagira asked him.

"They're called Umbra, they're dark phantoms," Yukaio explained. "The fire is a good idea, the light tends to repel them."

"Yea, we figured that much out for ourselves," she said defensively.

"I don't mean any offence."

"Forgive my sister," Tiergan said. "It's just the two of us, it's been that way for a while."

"Let me guess," Yukaio said, moving closer to the fire. "Ever since you woke up a couple of weeks ago with no memories of anything."

"How did you know that?" Tiergan asked.

"Because it happened to me too," Yukaio said. "And my sister."

"Where is your sister now?" Sagira asked.

"She's back at our camp with a friend."

"This friend, the one that supposedly knows us?"

"Yes," Yukaio said. "They were scouting the area and saw your fire."

"If they're the one that knows us, why didn't they come?" Sagira questioned him.

"It's difficult to explain, but we figured it was better if I did it," Yukaio said. "Do you mind if I sit down?"

Sagira motioned to a log beside the fire for Yukaio to sit. After watching him get comfortable, she sat down where she had been before he appeared. Tiergan moved in closer to his sister, placing his torch back in the fire pit. He looked from his sister to the stranger and back again, waiting for one of them to speak first.

Sagira leaned forward to get a better look at Yukaio. His long brown hair was tied back with a simple string, leaving his face open and easy for her to read. "So, what's your story then?"

"A couple weeks ago, my sister, Terry, and I woke up with no memories of who we were," he started. "Not long afterward we were attacked by the Umbra. I was barely able to fight them off but did manage to get by alright. Then we were approached by an . . . by an angel."

"An angel?" Tiergan asked, skeptical.

"I know," Yukaio laughed. "It sounds ridiculous. But believe me, the next part is even crazier."

"Doubtful," Tiergan said.

"They told me that I was blessed with special powers, that I was given these powers to protect others," he continued. "And that there are others like me with powers."

"What kind of powers?" Sagira asked.

"Mine are earth-based, but I guess we all have different powers based on which God or Goddess blessed us."

"Now there's Gods involved too?" Tiergan said.

"I know how it sounds, I was doubtful at first too," Yukaio admitted.

"Yea, I don't buy it," Tiergan looked at his sister. "Right, Sagira? Sagira?"

"You've been awfully quiet," Yukaio commented.

"Could wind be one of these powers?" she asked quietly.

"I suppose so," Yukaio said. "I'm not really sure."

"Are you saying you believe this?" Tiergan asked his sister.

"Ever since we woke up, I've noticed, something . . ." she started. "I thought it was just a coincidence at first, but then it happened again."

"What happened?" Yukaio asked her.

"It was a few days ago, after the last big rain, and the sky was still really overcast," Sagira explained. "We had been running from those shadows . . . those Umbra, for a couple of days, and the clouds made it quite dark out. I just wished that the wind would come and blow those clouds away. And then it did."

"Yeah, that sounds like something one of us would be able to do," he nodded.

"So, this angel . . ."

"Their name is Uaithiel."

"Ok, this Uaithiel. Did they explain why we don't have any memories of getting these powers?"

"It's a long story, but the short of it is there's a war with the forces of darkness that has been going on for a very long time. In an attack, we were separated and injured, and that's how we lost our memories."

"So, what powers do I have?" Tiergan asked.

"Sorry," Yukaio started. "Uaithiel said only one of the two of you was a Guardian."

"A Guardian?" Sagira asked, raising an eyebrow.

"That's what we're called. The Madeiran Guardians, protectors of the realm," Yukaio explained.

"That's. . . intense," Sagira shook her head.

"I know, it takes a bit to get used to," he nodded. "Uaithiel wanted me to ask you, do you have anything like this?"

Yukaio pulled the orb out of his pocket. Reaching across the fire, he placed it in Sagira's outstretched hand. Three silver bracelets jangled at her wrist as she pulled her hand back. She looked at the small object and instinctively put her free hand to her pocket. Sagira glanced up at Yukaio, trying to determine if she could trust him. His eyes fixated on her, watching her every move. She slowly reached into her pocket, grasping the orb, she tossed it to Yukaio. Catching it with both hands, he held it up by the fire to examine it. Hers was an opaque purple, but the same size and shape of his own orb.

"What are they?" Sagira asked him.

"It's a part of who you are, it links you to your powers," he explained, tossing it back to her as she returned his. "Uaithiel said it's called a meamina."

"So, these powers," Sagira started, twirling the

orb around in her hand. "I'm guessing that we're meant to use them to fight those."

Sagira looked up to the sky, shadows still swirling overhead, and then back to Yukaio. Taking a deep breath, he nodded.

"With Uaithiel's help you should be able to learn to control your powers soon," Yukaio reassured her. "I've been with them barely a couple weeks, and I've made a lot of progress."

"Well, no offence, but I think I've got a pretty good grasp of my abilities already," Sagira said.

Sagira stood up and raised her hands. Closing her eyes, taking a deep breath, she waved her hand in a circle. Opening her eyes, she looked up at the trees above them. Yukaio and Tiergan followed her gaze. Despite the stillness of the night, a breeze began to pick up, turning into a howling wind. Leaves began to tremble as branches shook back and forth. Sagira looked down at Yukaio and smiled as the wind whistled around her.

Tiergan watched the flames of the fire flickering as the wind around them picked up. "Sagira, be careful of the . . ."

"The fire," Yukaio finished as the flames snuffed out, smoke rising from the fire pit.

"Oh, no . . ." Sagira said.

A howl from above caught their attention as the swirling shadows started to move closer.

"Was that fire the only thing keeping them away from us?" Tiergan asked, his voice shaking.

"I'm afraid so," Yukaio said. He rose from his spot, holding his glaive in front of him.

"I . . . I didn't mean to," Sagira said. "Can we get the fire going again?"

"Not likely," Yukaio said. "But we should at least try."

"We can make a run for it. You said your camp is

only a couple miles, right? You have a fire there, I assume," Sagira rushed to gather their belongings.

"No, we won't make it," Yukaio shook his head. "They're too fast and too strong."

"Then what do we do?" Tiergan asked.

"We fight," Yukaio raised his grave, watching the advancing shadows. "Do you have a weapon of some kind?"

"I have this," Sagira picked up an axe. Its long narrow blades protruded from both sides of a cherry-coloured handle, one blade ending in a broad curve and the other in a fine point. Both looked equally as sharp.

"Nice axe," Yukaio said.

"It's a nzappa zap," Sagira smiled, holding it up for Yukaio to see. As he scrunched his brow at her statement, she sighed. "Yes, it's a type of axe."

"Right, Tiergan, get behind us. You won't be able to do any damage to the Umbra, but they will be able to hurt you," Yukaio explained. "The best thing you can do is try and get that fire going again. Stay low and stay quiet."

Tiergan stumbled over the smoking logs, rushing to get behind Yukaio. Sagira strode over gracefully, swinging the axe in her hand. As she positioned herself beside Yukaio, she glanced sideways at him. Though there was fear in his eyes, he hid it well. He looked comfortable holding the glaive as if it was a part of his own body. Sagira raised the axe in front of her, trying to look as comfortable with her own weapon.

"That axe was a gift from the Gods," Yukaio said, watching the Umbra take form in front of them. "It will protect you from the servants of the darkness."

As he finished speaking, Yukaio leapt over the empty fire pit, swinging the glaive at the first Umbra that appeared. Sagira froze, watching the speed of the shadow as it took form and moved to react to Yukaio's attack. As fast as it was, he was faster. His glaive sliced through it, reducing it to a pile of smoking ash with a ghoulish howl. In the same move, Yukaio turned on the next one and struck. The Umbra was prepared and blocked his attack, countering and sending him flying into a tree.

"Sagira!" Yukaio gasped as the blow knocked the wind from him.

Shaking her head, Sagira composed herself and ran towards the Umbra. The one closest to her was smaller than the rest. *I can do this,* she told herself. Raising the axe, she readied herself to strike as the Umbra lunged towards her. It struck her square in the chest, knocking her to the ground. Looking up at the figure, Sagira saw a shadowy arm pummeling towards her. Kicking her feet into the air, she used the momentum to roll out of the way. Tightening her grip on her axe, she came out of a roll and sprung up onto her knees, swinging her arm towards the crouching shadow. Sagira felt a rush of heat as the blade sliced through it.

Her heart pounded as she looked up at the remaining Umbra. The night was too dark, and there were too many for her to count. Yukaio didn't seem to notice, but if he did, he didn't care. He took on one after the other, his pace and breath steady. Sagira stood ready to continue the fight, no way was she going to be shown up by a kid. Raising her axe, she ran towards the nearest Umbra.

Tiergan, crouching behind the fire pit, watched his sister fighting. She moved swiftly between the Umbra, taking them out one by one. His breath was quiet as he tried with all his might to get the fire started again. Striking the stones again and again, he looked up for fear of the noise attracting the

Umbra. As hard as he struck the stones, they wouldn't spark. Rubbing the dust off with his shirt, he tried again. Tiergan gasped as a large spark flashed before quickly going out.

"Tiergan!" Sagira screamed.

He looked up just as a shadow passed before him, the Umbra now aware of his presence. Tiergan hastened his movements, striking the stones as quickly as possible, watching the Umbra move towards him. Sagira chased after the Umbra, but he knew she was too far away to reach him in time. Hovering above him, the Umbra was much larger up close. He drew in a deep breath as it completely covered him. A howling shriek pierced the air as the shadow around Tiergan dissipated into swirling smoke, leaving him covered in ashes, a small fire burning on a pile of twigs before him.

"I'm ok," he said.

Sagira sank to the ground in relief, her chest heaved as she gasped for air. She nodded at Tiergan, who smiled back at her, before she rose and turned to continue the fight. Swinging her axe at the Umbra in front of her, she made her way to Yukaio. The pair covered their ears as a blood-curdling shriek filled the air. Looking around, it appeared as if the amount of Umbra doubled. Yukaio stood back-to-back with Sagira as the Umbra circled around them.

"There's too many of them," Sagira said.

"The sun will be up soon," Yukaio reassured her. "We just have to last a little bit longer. How's Tiergan doing with the fire?"

"He has a small flame, but it's nowhere near big enough to scare off this lot."

"We can do this," Yukaio repositioned the glaive in his hands. His skin burned as blisters covered his fingers from holding the polearm.

"Right, so you take that half and I'll take this half?" Sagira tried to force a smile.

Before Yukaio could answer, a flash of light from behind caught their attention. Tiergan waved a flaming branch in front of him as he ran towards the others. The Umbra shied away as the flame passed by them. Reaching the center, he stood by his sister.

"Maybe this will help," Tiergan said.

"You should get out of here," Sagira warned him. "That flame is barely big enough to hold off one or two of them."

"No, I'm not going anywhere without you," he said sternly.

"Please, Tiergan," Sagira pleaded. "It's my job to look out for you."

"I'm not a child anymore."

"You'll always be my kid brother."

"We're in this together."

"Tiergan, please, just go."

"Your sister is right," Yukaio added. "You've got the fire to protect you, you should run. The Umbra won't be interested in you on your own."

"And what about the two of you?" Tiergan looked at the shadows that were now wholly encircling them.

"We'll find a way to manage," Sagira said.

"We do this together," Tiergan stood his ground, holding the flame in front of him.

He looked at his sister with a stern expression. He wasn't going to run, not now, not when his sister needed him the most. Sagira glanced at him and forced a smile, hiding the pain she felt inside. She took a deep breath and nodded at both of the boys.

"Together then?" Sagira asked.

"Together," Yukaio and Tiergan concurred.

Raising their weapons, they watched as the Umbra shifted around them. Their forms becoming less rigid as they melded into each other, a blanket of darkness around them. The darkness rose above them, blocking out the light of the stars and moon. They gasped as the air was sucked from their lungs, and the fire was reduced to a wisp of smoke.

"Now what?"

Chapter Four

"Kalida, please be careful," the tall, slender girl with the long black hair called after her younger sister. She sighed as she watched the young girl swinging from one tree branch to another.

"You needn't worry so much," her twin placed his hand on her shoulder. "Kalida has Mitesh to look after her."

"You do know he's also swinging through the trees like a monkey, right, Sethos?" she glared at her twin.

"Iisha, all I'm saying is you can relax," Sethos smiled. "They're going to be fine. They're always like this."

"Yes, and while they're off playing, you're carving arrows, leaving me to make sure that none of you starve to death."

"And we appreciate you for it," he hugged his sister.

"Enough to help me with the stew?"

Sethos gave his sister an awkward smile, making her roll her eyes. "If we run out of arrows, then hunting tomorrow's dinner will be a bit difficult."

Shaking her head, she bent down to stir the stew. She flicked her long, black hair over her shoulder with a smooth wave of her delicate hand. With her other hand, she lifted the ladle from the stew to her full lips, taking a sip. Her soft blue eyes gleamed amongst her dark skin as she smiled up at her brother.

"The stew will be ready in ten minutes," she said. "If you aren't going to help, at least make sure our siblings are here when it's ready. This is too good to let it go cold."

Sethos leaned down to kiss his sister's cheek before walking away. She watched as he ran a hand through his hair, pushing it back out of his face as he unsheathed a small knife from his side. Picking up the wood he had been working with earlier, he continued to carve out the point of what would become another arrow in his quiver. His hazel eyes shone in the sun as he noticed his sister watching him and returned her smile. His calloused hands gripped the wood firmly as he ran his knife down the side of it in steady, even strokes.

The sound of their siblings' laugher made Sethos smile as he looked up to see them hanging from a tree branch. Both were scrambling to climb higher than the other. The large maple trees that lined the far edge of the village were popular with many of the children for climbing, though few dared reach the heights that the young twins did. Branch after branch, they rose higher and higher until Sethos could no longer see them through the waves of large green and brown leaves shaking in the wind. Iisha tapped her ladle against the side of the pot when Sethos turned her way, reminding him of the time. Placing his tools on the ground, he strode over to where his younger siblings were.

"Kalida, Mitesh, it's time to come down for dinner," he shouted into the maze of branches above his head.

Silence was the only response he got.

"Come on, you two," he shouted again. Silence.

Sighing, he reached up for the first branch. He was tall enough that he didn't even need to jump as he grabbed onto the branch and kicked his legs off the trunk of the tree to propel himself upwards. A few branches up he could see the twins. They had stopped climbing and had tucked into a small, curved branch, practically hiding them from anyone who would look for them.

"I can see you, Mitesh, Kalida," Sethos said, pausing several branches below them. "Your sister says it's time for dinner."

"Aww, do we have to?" Kalida moaned.

"Yea, I'm not even hungry," Mitesh agreed.

"Get down here now, I won't ask you again," he said sternly.

Both of the younger siblings began to scramble down the branches. As different as he and Iisha were in appearance, Mitesh and Kalida were near spitting images of each other. Their builds were both the same, and their hair was identical. At a quick glance, even their own siblings could mistake one for the other, especially when they were practically joined at the hip.

Sethos made his way back to the ground, watching the younger twins race back down. Mitesh, attempting to show off, tried to jump from one branch to the next without holding on. Landing on the first branch, he waved his arms, struggling to keep his balance, brushing his fingers along the trunk of the tree for a bit of extra stability. Once he regained his footing, he smiled at his twin, his brown eyes shining with excitement. She merely rolled her eyes at him as she descended to the branch below him. Pushing off the branch with his feet, Mitesh made to jump to the branch where his sister was sitting.

Sethos watched from the ground, judging the

distance of each jump that his brother made. He watched as Mitesh went to push off, his foot slipping on some leaking sap, causing him to fall. Sethos's voice failed him as he tried to scream for his brother, about to fall from at least thirty feet in the air. Mitesh swung his arms, trying to find anything to grab onto, before a firm hand wrapped around his wrist. Looking up, Kalida was lying on her stomach, both legs wrapped around the tree branch, her arms outstretched, holding onto her brother.

Both boys breathed a sigh of relief as Kalida swung him towards another branch. Mitesh wrapped an arm around the branch as he let go of his sister's hand and pulled himself onto the branch. Positioning himself to continue descending, he paused for a moment to catch his breath - all the air had left his lungs in the brief few seconds he was falling.

"Don't you even dare think about doing that again," Sethos bellowed from below, glaring at his younger brother. "And definitely don't tell your sister."

Sethos watched the two of them quickly descend the rest of the tree, one branch at a time. Ushering them over towards Iisha's stew, he rubbed his temples. *Why do they have to be such children?* He smiled at Iisha as they approached, and the young twins sat as close to the stew pot as they could.

"What happened?" Iisha asked.

"Believe me when I say that you definitely do not want to know," Sethos said, picking up a bowl.

Iisha ladled some stew into bowls for each of her siblings and then for herself. They ate silently as Iisha watched other villagers nearby preparing for the night ahead. She mentally counted how many there were - less than 20 of them. Barely half of how many there had been a month ago.

"Do you want any more?" she offered each of the siblings. Sethos was the only one to take a second serving.

Iisha placed her half-empty bowl on the ground and stood up, grabbing the handle of the pot, she walked towards the nearest hut. From hut to hut she went, offering each of them some of their stew until it was empty. The same as she did every night because of the generosity of those in the village for taking them in. She knew it was the least they could do. When they showed up with nothing to offer, they had been given refuge. None of the siblings could remember back more than a month or so. When Iisha tried, all she found was a headache. So, when they had come across a village, despite some of the inhabitants saying it was cursed, they were welcome to take one of the empty huts. That family had left a few months prior, as had many of the other villagers. Stories of shadows that lurked in the night were told in hushed tones, some merely claiming that they were the spirits of those who passed on, others claiming they were demons here to drag the damned down to hell. Iisha tried to ignore the rumours as much as she could, but it was hard when she had seen the shadows herself.

The last night they spent on their own outside of the village the rain had smothered their campfire, and the wind howled at them as shadows descended. She shook her twin awake as quickly and silently as she could, placing her hand over his mouth when he went to speak. Raising her other hand to her lips, she put one finger in front and then pointed up to the approaching shadows. Grabbing what little belongings they had, they scooped up their siblings and began to run. With the younger twins faces buried in their shoulders, they shielded them from seeing anything. They ran for hours until the sun started to peek over mountains and the shadows began to fade. When they stopped running, they found themselves at the edge of the village and had immediately asked for sanctuary. Despite everything, the villagers welcomed them with open arms.

Iisha returned to her siblings with the empty pot, setting it on the ground. Kalida threw her empty bowl inside and smiled at her big sister. Picking up her own bowl, Iisha finished the rest of her stew before placing her bowl on top of the pile. She rolled her eyes at her younger brother, Mitesh likely had more stew on his face than in his stomach. Kalida stifled a laugh at her twin.

"Do you have to be that sloppy?" Sethos asked, to which Mitesh just shrugged.

"Hurry up and finish Mitesh so you can get ready for bed," Iisha urged her brother as she watched the setting sun.

"We're fourteen, Iisha, we don't need to be tucked in," Kalida sighed.

"Oh, so I guess that also means that you don't need a song tonight then?" Iisha smiled at the young twins.

Mitesh and Kalida exchanged glances. Kalida urged her brother to quickly finish his stew, to which he replied by forgoing the spoon and tipping the bowl directly into his mouth. Broth dribbled down his chin, dripping onto his shirt as he slurped the rest of the stew before tossing his bowl with the others. The young twins ran towards the hut, racing each other.

"It's always a race between those two," Sethos commented.

"Well, if it gets stuff done, then that's fine," Iisha began to gather the discarded utensils. "Speaking of being done . . ."

Sethos tossed his spoon into the empty pot and tipped his bowl into his mouth, the same as his brother had done. He then threw the empty bowl into the pile with the rest.

"You're just as sloppy as he is sometimes," Iisha said, wiping broth off her brother's chin.

Iisha picked up the pot and headed towards the brook trickling around the edge of the village.

"No, here, let me," Sethos stood and took the pot from his sister's hand. "You go sing them a song, help them get to sleep before it gets too dark. I'll take care of these."

"Make sure you're back inside before the sun goes down," Iisha reminded her brother.

He nodded as he walked away to go wash the dishes. Typically, Iisha was the one to take care of the chores like that, but they had eaten later than usual today. The game in the forest was scarce, and it had taken far too long to hunt down the rabbit that stared in their dinner that night. Sethos glanced at the half-carved arrows on the ground as he passed - he would need to finish those soon as his quiver was starting to get too light for comfort.

Inside the small hut, Iisha strode over towards the bed shared by the young twins. They pushed at each other as they fought for the blanket. Sitting on the edge of the bed, Iisha pulled the blanket up and covered both of them equally. Looking at them, she couldn't help but smile. Despite everything they had been through, her siblings still seemed so young. They never let their lack of memories diminish their spirit, and each day, she reminded herself, they were making new memories together.

Together. That was the important part.

Iisha took a deep breath preparing to sing. It was the same song that she sung every night, the only song that she knew. She couldn't remember where she was from, what her parents looked like, or anything else about their history. But she could remember this song, remember a soft voice carrying the tune to her whenever she needed it. It was timeless, the song, as if it had always been there and would always be there.

Starlight shine bright on me
Shining stars from sky above
Bright stars ever guiding
Starlight shine bright on me
Starlight shine down on me

Reach your branches higher
Burrow your roots down deep
Grown in darkness around
Grow in light above

Moonlight shine bright on me
Smiling down on all below
Pale moon ever watching
Moonlight shine bright on me
Moonlight shine down on me

Ride on the night's wind
Float above the meadows
Drift farther than the sea
Dreaming for a new day

Sunlight shine bright on me
Lighting the path far ahead
Glowing sun ever reaching
Sunlight shine bright on me
Sunlight shine down on me

Starlight shine bright on me

Shining stars from sky above
Bright stars ever guiding
Starlight shine bright on me
Starlight shine down on me

Iisha's voice floated around the twins as they both drifted off to sleep. She looked to the window, the setting sun hung in the sky. It looked like it hadn't moved at all in the time it took the twins to fall asleep as if it waited for them to go to sleep before succumbing to darkness itself. Iisha gently stood up and quietly walked out of the hut, looking back only once to make sure the twins were actually asleep and not just pretending.

She leaned against the frame of the hut, watching her brother return with the now clean dishes. He discarded them by the fire pit, embers still glowing against the darkening skyline. Sethos picked up the stack of arrows he had been carving earlier and made his way over towards his sister.

"We're still low on arrows," he said by way of greeting.

"You'll manage to make more."

"It would be better if I was able to catch a decent amount of game at once," Sethos stated. "Or if we were able to make the food last longer."

"We're not having this conversation again," Iisha looked away.

"Iisha, I know you want to help these people," Sethos moved in front of her. "But we need to make sure that we're taking care of ourselves too."

"I know," Iisha said. "But these people, they took us in. They've helped us despite . . . despite . . ."

"That wasn't our fault," Sethos said as his sister's voice failed her.

"Wasn't it?"

"We've done all we can to stop it for now," Sethos

said. "Let's just focus on one thing at a time, ok?"

Iisha looked at her brother, her eyes heavy with worry. Slowly, she nodded in agreement. Sethos placed a reassuring hand on her shoulder before sitting on the ground by the doorway. He pulled one of the half-carved arrows towards him and continued to shape it with a small knife. Iisha knelt down and sat beside her brother, leaning into his side and resting her head on his shoulder.

"Tsuna told me she and her boys are leaving," Iisha said quietly.

"When?"

"First light, tomorrow," Iisha said. "Right after I gave her the last bit of stew, she told me that with everything going on in these woods lately, it was wiser to leave."

"Do you want to leave, too?" Sethos looked at his sister. "We don't have anywhere else to go."

"We could find somewhere, we found here."

"I don't think we would get this lucky again."

"No, you're probably right," Iisha said. "But maybe there's more I could do."

"You already do too much," Sethos said. "You do all of the cooking, the cleaning, you're practically raising Mitesh and Kalida."

"Maybe I could help you hunt," Iisha offered. "We have two bows."

"I appreciate it," Sethos said. "I really do, but we're low on arrows as it is. For now, I think it's best to keep one quiver stocked, rather than having two nearly empty ones."

"I'm just as good of a shot as you are, maybe better."

"That's cute that you think you're a better shot than me."

Iisha punched her brother in the arm.

"Besides," Sethos continued. "If you came out

into the forest with me hunting, who would watch the twins?"

Iisha sighed. She knew her brother was right. Iisha peered through the doorway back at the sleeping twins. This wasn't about what she wanted, what she felt she needed to do. No, this was about keeping her family safe. The only family she could remember. Silently, leaning against his muscled shoulder, Iisha watched as Sethos carved another arrow. They were a team, their skills complementing each other. Sethos took care of providing the food, and Iisha took care of everything else. Though she let her brother win the argument, in her heart, she knew she could shoot even better than him.

"We should get inside," Sethos said as the moon began to rise. "Just in case."

"It's been four nights since the last attack," Iisha said. "Do you think we still need to worry?"

"It's better to be safe," Sethos said.

Sethos looked at the moon rising behind the trees in the distance. His gaze lingered on the large one in the center, the one his siblings had been climbing earlier. Its branches swayed in the night's wind, almost as if they were dancing to a melody coming from deep beneath the earth. Sethos pulled his attention back to the arrows around him. He gathered up the ones he deemed were sharp enough for hunting with and placed them in the quiver that he swung over his shoulder. The rest he piled against the side of the hut to be continued in the morning. As he followed his sister inside, he looked back at that tree one more time before turning away from it.

Chapter Five

Terry sat by the fire, her legs curled up into her chest, head resting on her knees. She watched Uaithiel standing on the other side of the fire, a hand resting on the hilt of the blade strapped around their waist. Uaithiel stared off into the distance as if they could see what was happening to her brother miles away.

"You should get some sleep," they said without turning around.

"I'm ok," Terry knew that despite how tired she was, she wouldn't be able to sleep without knowing her brother was safe. "What about you? You've been standing there for hours."

"I don't sleep."

"Ever?"

"No," they laughed. "One of the benefits of being a celestial creature, we don't need to sleep."

Uaithiel turned to face her and smiled. She tried to return the smile but ended up wincing. The angel turned back to stare off into the distance. Terry looked up to the sky, the stars shining through the treetops comforted her. *Yukaio is looking at the same stars,* she told herself. Despite there only being a few miles between them, it may as well have been leagues. He had always made her feel safe when he was around.

"Shouldn't they be back by now?"

"It may have taken some time to convince Sagira

to come back. Or he may have chosen to stay there until sunrise," Uaithiel said. "The Umbra are always nearby hunting the Guardians, staying there might have been safer than trying to make it back here in the dark."

Uaithiel let out a soft sigh, resisting the urge to look back at the young girl, to show any sign of uncertainty. But they knew that Terry was right, Yukaio should have made his way back by now with the others. It's possible it could have taken some time to convince Sagira to come back, but it shouldn't have been this long. Although they didn't like lying to Terry, it was necessary to keep her from worrying further about her brother. Closing their eyes, Uaithiel could still feel the presence of the Guardians. It was impossible to know if they were ok or not, but they were alive, that was certain.

Shifting their weight from one leg to the other, Uaithiel grew impatient as the night dragged by, the moon crawling overhead. They had been silently counting the minutes, and then the hours, as each second seemed to move slower and slower. Not daring to look back at Terry, as she might take the indecision for worry, Uaithiel kept staring straight ahead. Uaithiel reached out their mind, searching for the Guardians. The souls of the Guardians shone as bright in Uaithiel's mind as the stars above. Ahead there were two lights together - Sagira and Yukaio. They shone bright in the darkness, their wills strong and their hearts true. But something was wrong, Uaithiel could sense it.

A shriek rolled across the air, bringing Uaithiel back to reality. Their eyes snapped open as they willed the rest of their body to remain as motionless as possible. Instinctively, they tightened their fingers around the hilt of their sword. A sound like that could only come from the Umbra.

"Uaithiel, what was that?" Terry asked, rushing to their side.

"The Umbra," they said calmly. "Don't worry, Terry. Your brother knows how to fight them, and he isn't alone. He will be fine."

"Are you sure we shouldn't go find them?" she begged.

"No, child," they smiled down at Terry. "It is better for us to wait here. Go, sit by the fire, close your eyes and try to get some sleep."

Terry hesitated before giving up and strode back over towards the fire. Uaithiel watched as she sat down, pulling her knees into her chest again.

"Close your eyes," they repeated.

"I'm not tired," Terry said.

They knew she was lying but turned away to stare off into the darkness again. Uaithiel wanted to fly through the forest, find the Guardians and protect them. But doing so would mean leaving Terry behind, unguarded. Even if she was okay, Yukaio would likely never forgive them for potentially endangering his sister. The other option was to take Terry along - but that would slow them down, and again put her in danger. No, the only option was to wait for the sun to rise. Looking at the moon and gauging its position, Uaithiel guessed it would be a little less than an hour until the sun began to peek through the trees. Keeping their breath steady, they watched the moon slowly descend behind the trees. After what seemed like an eternity, the first rays of the sun's light began to shine between the trees.

A rustling noise caused Uaithiel to turn back towards Terry. She stood by the fire, packing up their belongings and snuffing out the flames. Swinging the sack over her shoulder, she marched up towards Uaithiel and looked up at them. Their long silvery hair shone in the morning light, their violet eyes matching the cloudless, morning sky. Uaithiel's soft face conveyed a confused expression.

"Sun's up, let's go," Terry said bluntly.

Uaithiel nodded in agreement. Without hesitation, they motioned for her to lead the way through the forest. The angel knew that Terry was too determined to be told to stay behind, doing so would only waste precious time. The pair followed the footprints Yukaio had made in the soft ground the night before. Before long, they came to a log blocking their path. Stepping over the log, Terry looked around - the footprints just ended.

"I don't get it," she said. "The tracks stop here, where is he?"

Uaithiel stepped past the young girl and surveyed the area. A small pile of logs littered with twigs and leaves indicated that someone had made a fire here. Crouching down by the fire, they extended their hand. The fire pit was still warm, someone had been here recently.

"Where's Yukaio?" Terry's voice grew louder as she tried to keep it from shaking.

"I don't know," Uaithiel shook their head. Their chest tightened with panic, they should have come sooner. If anything bad had happened to the Guardians . . . No, they couldn't think like that. "They must have moved on last night."

It was a lie. Uaithiel knew it was a lie before the words passed their lips. They didn't dare glance at Terry - did she know it was a lie too? Staring around the abandoned site, Uaithiel pondered their next step. Taking a few steps forward, they studied the ground, there were markings in the dirt. Following the lines, they realized it formed a circle. In the center, three sets of footprints were squished together.

"Amatheon," Uaithiel said under their breath.

"What was that?" Terry asked, following the angel's footsteps.

"Nothing," they lied again.

"Yukaio wouldn't have just left," Terry insisted. "What aren't you telling me?"

"If Yukaio and Sagira are not here and did not come back to our camp last night, they must have had an excellent reason for doing so," Uaithiel avoided the girl's question. "We will find them."

"How?" she asked.

"One of my gifts is the ability to sense the life force of all the Guardians, no matter where they are. I can feel the presence of their souls in this realm and seek them out," they explained.

"And you can use this gift to find my brother?"

"Yes, and no," Uaithiel continued. "The gift isn't that specific. I can feel their souls, but I can't tell them apart. I can only tell where a Guardian is, not which Guardian they are though."

"So then, what are you waiting for?"

Uaithiel nodded in agreement, closing their eyes once more. Letting out a deep breath, they reached out with their mind. Letting go of the physical world, they moved through the empty space of their mind. Flickers of light in the distance were all around, some near, some far. Most were alone, but there, to the north, there were two together. Uaithiel guessed the distance was several leagues. How had they travelled so far in such a short amount of time? The angel didn't let their mind ponder the possibilities. Instead, they focussed on the light of the Guardians. The two lights together, that had to be Yukaio and Sagira. But the distance it would take to get there, especially walking with Terry, it would take days. Reaching out once again, Uaithiel found another light, in the same general direction, but far closer. A single light. It could be worth it to detour to the other Guardian first, especially if their suspicions about what had happened there was true . . .

"We need to go due north," Uaithiel looked down at the young girl. "But it's a long distance to travel."

"Well, then we better get started," Terry pulled a long stick free from the ashen firepit. Her face was set with determination.

"There is something you need to know," Uaithiel began as they started through the forest.

"What is it?"

"We aren't going directly to your brother, at least not right away," they said hesitantly.

"What?" Terry shrieked, stopping in her tracks. "Where else would we go?"

"We will make our way to where I think he is, but there is another Guardian much closer. We should stop there first to get them . . ."

"Because you think something bad has happened to Yukaio."

"I don't know anything for certain," they placed a hand on Terry's shoulder, urging her to start walking again. "But it would be better to be safe than sorry. We need to gather all the Guardians regardless, so it makes sense to find the other Guardian first."

"But you don't know which one it is, do you?"

"No, I don't. The way that I perceive their souls, it's all the same. I can't tell them apart."

Terry nodded, accepting their answer. Uaithiel's wings twitched with anticipation. They wished they could just fly away, leave Terry somewhere safe. What was coming would be dangerous for both of them. The sooner that they found the other Guardians, the better.

"Are there others like you?" Terry said after a long silence. "Are there other angels?"

"Yes, of course there are."

"Are they also looking for the Guardians?"

"No, that's my job, and mine alone."

"Why is that?"

"While they are the protectors of the realm, I am the protectorate of the Guardians."

"You're the Guardian's guardian angel?" Terry smiled.

"I suppose you could put it that way," Uaithiel returned her smile. "Technically, I'm referred to as the protectorate."

"But why just you?" Terry prodded.

"That's a long story."

"We've got a long walk."

"It's a story for another time," Uaithiel said flatly.

"Fine," Terry conceded. "Can you at least tell me more about how we lost our memories?"

Uaithiel stared at her with a wordless expression.

"I'll take that as a no," she rolled her eyes. "You know, this is going to be a very long walk if you don't talk."

"You're welcome to find a place to take shelter," Uaithiel offered.

"You wouldn't happen to be trying to get rid of me, would you?" Terry smiled up at the angel. Uaithiel's expression told her everything she needed to know. "Wait, you do want me gone, don't you?"

"It isn't that I want you gone," the angel explained. "But the path ahead is dangerous, and it would be remiss of me to put you in unnecessary danger, especially without your brother around to protect you."

"I can look after myself, thank you very much," she said sternly, standing as tall as possible.

"You have no idea the dangers that lie ahead," Uaithiel shook their head. "It would be safer for you to stay behind."

"Well, that's just too bad," she continued walking ahead of the angel. "Because I'm never, never, going to abandon my brother. And he would never abandon me. We're a package deal."

Uaithiel continued the trek, occasionally glancing down at Terry, but remaining silent during their walk. It wasn't that they didn't like her, she was particularly good company despite the circumstances, but she was slowing them down. The angel wished they could just get in the sky, it would be much faster than walking. They also knew what dangers she was walking into if she kept going. Uaithiel realized her strong will wouldn't let up as she continued walking even as the sun drifted across the sky. The day had passed far quicker than they would have liked, and the coming night would be dangerous.

"We should stop for the night and make camp," Uaithiel suggested as the last rays of sun danced over the trees. "You should make a fire."

"Because of the Umbra?" Terry asked. "I haven't seen them all day."

"No, the Umbra won't bother you tonight, they are only after the Guardians," Uaithiel explained. "But there are other dangers in the dark. Without any other weapons, at least having a fire might offer you some protection."

"What are you worried about?" Terry began to unpack her bag, preparing to make the fire. "Amatheon?"

"Don't say that," Uaithiel said sternly. "How do you even know about that?"

"I heard you say it this morning."

"I didn't think you heard me say that."

"Well, I did," she stood to face them, crossing her arms over her chest. "Now what or who is that?"

"He is someone very dangerous. He is a servant of the darkness," they explained. "He controls the Umbra."

"I thought you said we didn't have to worry about the Umbra since none of the Guardians are with us?"

"We don't have to worry about the Umbra, but we do have to worry about . . . him. Or rather, I do. He would have no interest in you. From his perspective, you're just a little human girl."

"But you're the protectorate of the Guardians," Terry continued as Uaithiel nodded. Terry turned to continue making the fire.

"On second thought . . ." Uaithiel started. "If you're not cold, it might be best not to make a fire tonight. The flames won't scare him away, and they might actually attract him."

Putting down the striking stones, Terry pulled the blanket from her sack. Leaning against a tree, she wrapped the cover around herself and closed her eyes. Uaithiel sighed a breath of relief when they noticed she was drifting off to sleep. She hadn't slept much the night before but didn't let it stop her from walking all day. *She might not be a Guardian, but she is just as strong-willed as they are*, Uaithiel thought.

As soon as Uaithiel was certain that Terry was asleep, they silently stepped away from her. Walking a few paces through the trees, they made sure to stay close enough that if Terry woke up, they would be nearby. Stretching their wings out behind them, they pushed off the ground, flapping hard to gain momentum. Branches shook as the angel shot up through the trees and emerged high above them. Hovering above the spot where Terry slept, they looked for a sign of any of the Guardians. Closing their eyes, Uaithiel reached out their mind only to find darkness.

«‹«◌»›»

Uaithiel reeled from the wave of darkness that encircled them. They looked up at the darkened sky – even the moon struggled to shine against the shadows.

"You're not doing a very good job, you know," Amatheon taunted the angel.

His black wings were almost invisible against the night sky, shadows blocking out the faint starlight above. Black eyes stared at Uaithiel from amongst a face as pale as the moon behind him. Amatheon held no sword in his hands, and Uaithiel knew that he didn't need one. The demon's power surged around him like black lightning, ready to strike.

"I will reunite them, despite everything that you've done," Uaithiel said. "And I will defeat you."

"Well then, you clearly don't remember our last battle," he flapped his wings, rising high above Uaithiel. "You lost to me; you will always lose."

"I won't lose again."

"Of course, you will. You've already lost everything else. You lost your home, your family. You lost your Guardians. Then you lost one of them again," Amatheon smirked as he looked past Uaithiel. "You could lose her too."

"Don't you dare touch her," Uaithiel moved to block his view of Terry. "I won't let you harm her."

"Oh, don't make me laugh, you can't defend her, and you know it," he said. "I could take her right now, and you would be powerless to stop me."

Uaithiel spread their wings and rose up to face Amatheon in the air. Drawing the sword at their waist, Uaithiel readied for battle. Amatheon shot through the air sending a flurry of leaves falling to the ground as he passed through the treetops. Uaithiel wasn't far behind him as they both emerged into the clear of the night sky.

"I will defend the Guardians and all that they stand for," Uaithiel held their sword up as they flew towards Amatheon.

"Oh, you'll defend the Guardians all right," Amatheon said. "And it will be the end of you."

Uaithiel swung the blade at Amatheon. "As you said, I have nothing left to lose."

In a flash, black lightning surged from Amatheon's outstretched hands, Uaithiel's sword acting as a lightning rod. With an intense flick of his wrist, Uaithiel turned his sword, flinging the lightning to the ground. A loud *crack* sounded as it split a branch from a large oak tree below. Whirling their sword in the air, Uaithiel again took aim at the demon. Wings flapped as they charged forwards. A smirk spread across Amatheon's face as a single beat of his wings rose him out angel's path. As he turned, the power around him again surging, he threw the black lightning towards Uaithiel's back.

"Ahhh!" Uaithiel screamed as the feathers on their pure white wings ruffled.

The blow sent the angel spiralling down towards the trees, their breath heaving in their chest. Moments before crashing, Uaithiel spread their wings and soared above the treetops, rising and turning to face Amatheon once more. They let out a deep breath of relief.

"Your tricks haven't changed, even after all this time."

"Oh, those *tricks* are nothing, I promise you that."

Holding up a hand in front of him, black lightning crackling in his palm, he threw his arm out to the side, pointing towards the ground.

Uaithiel watched in horror as the black lightning raced away from them, towards a large thicket of trees. The ground shuddered at the impact as sparks flared. A small flame emerged from the impact site and quickly grew as an unnatural wind swept through the area.

"Have fun finding your human," Amatheon smirked as he flapped his wings, backing away from the area.

Uaithiel looked down at the ground, horror-stricken, before looking back to the now-empty sky beside them. They could chase Amatheon, likely catch him fairly quickly too, and maybe, *maybe*, find out where the other Guardians were taken. But down on the forest ground below, somewhere, Terry was likely still asleep. And now there was a fire leaping from tree to tree, burning everything in its wake. There was only time to do one - chase the demon or save the human. Uaithiel knew there wasn't time to debate the choice in their mind before acting.

Chapter Six

The pale light of the moon barely broke through the swirling darkness as if it were alive. Sagira sent a gentle breeze outward from her palm. It floated past Yukaio and Tiergan into the void. The cool breeze washed over them before it faded away. Sagira sighed. Nothing she or Yukaio had done helped to alleviate the darkness around them. Even when the sun was in the sky, the darkness around them held firm. She had lost count of the days and nights since they had been taken, and the little food in the bag her brother had carried was nearly gone.

Yukaio had tried to use his powers as well, summoning up roots from the ground, something for them to grab onto. But as hard as he tried, nothing sprouted. At first, he wondered if his powers were failing him, but as the first day had turned to night, they realized that they weren't on the ground. The Umbra encircling them carried them, moving through forests and fields, taking them to - who knows where. Yukaio tried to watch through the small cracks in the darkness, to see if he could recognize any of their surroundings, but after a while, the branches and shrubs and streams all began to look the same.

"Is there anything left to eat?" Tiergan asked quietly.

Yukaio looked into the bag that now sat at his feet. Barely a handful of berries, some dried meat, and a few roots were all that was left. He glanced up at Sagira, who returned his gaze. Though they didn't speak, he knew that she understood and that she agreed. Despite his height and stature, Tiergan seemed so young to Yukaio.

"Here," Yukaio said, passing him half of the remaining meat and a couple of berries.

"Thank you," Tiergan said as he shoved the berries into his mouth, the colour staining his lips purple.

Sagira strode over towards Yukaio. Moving inside the darkness felt like floating – it was a strange sensation to get used to.

"How much is left?" she whispered.

Yukaio turned the bag so she could see inside. "Not much."

"We need to do something."

"We've been trying," Yukaio said. "I've been trying to grow something to stop us, you've been trying to break it apart with wind."

"Yeah, all I've done is send it a gentle breeze, maybe made it a little chilly."

"I think it's being in here. It's messing with our minds, our powers. Every moment we're in here, I'm feeling weaker and weaker."

Sagira motioned towards the bag. "Maybe you should eat something."

"No, it isn't that," Yukaio said, shaking his head. "It's like I can feel my powers being drained."

"I know what you mean," Sagira said. "I don't know how much longer I'll even be able to produce that breeze."

"Maybe conserving our strength would be better," Yukaio said. "This has to be taking us somewhere, maybe once we get wherever we're going, we'll be able to fight back."

"I doubt it. We don't even know where we are

anymore," Sagira said. "Your sister and that angel could be miles away. They probably don't know where to even start looking for us."

"Uaithiel has a vague sense of where all the Guardians are," Yukaio said. "They'll find us, eventually."

"Eventually might be too late," Sagira said, her voice rising louder than she wanted. Tiergan looked up from his food for a moment. Sagira offered him a reassuring smile and a nod to continue eating. "I shouldn't have dragged Tiergan into this."

"You didn't, he wanted to stay and fight."

"And now he's trapped. We all are."

"Maybe we should get some sleep."

"I'm not tired."

"Me neither."

Sagira studied the expression on Yukaio's face through the shadows covering them. She could see in his eyes that he was tired, of course he was, he hadn't slept since they'd all been taken. But then again, neither had she. There was something about the darkness that drained her but at the same time kept her alert. Her hand reached for the axe at her side. She had tried using it the first day they were captured, but the darkness was too strong. Where she struck and Umbra faltered, more appeared to fill the gaps.

"Maybe it works both ways," Tiergan said.

Both Yukaio and Sagira turned towards him as he approached.

"What do you mean?" Sagira asked.

"You said Uaithiel can sense your presence, right?" Tiergan asked Yukaio.

"Uh, yeah . . ." he stammered. "How did you know?"

"This place isn't very big, and the two of you aren't good at talking quietly," Tiergan said. "Well, either that or I have unnaturally good hearing. I've heard almost everything you've said."

"I'm sorry," Sagira said. "You . . ."

"It's ok," he said, cutting off his sister's words.

"What's your theory?" Yukaio asked.

"Well, you said Uaithiel can sense the Guardians. What if it works the other way around too? What if you can sense their presence, or even each other?" Tiergan asked.

"I don't know, they never said anything about us having that kind of sense," Yukaio said.

"But could it be possible?" Tiergan asked.

"It could, I suppose," Yukaio said. "I mean, we are Gods-blessed, so I guess anything could be possible."

"How would we do it, though? I don't even know where we would start," Sagira admitted. "Do you know how Uaithiel found us?"

"Not exactly," Yukaio shook his head. "But I did see them do it a couple times. They closed their eyes and then . . . I don't know, just stood there, I guess."

"Like a meditation?" Sagira asked.

"Maybe," Yukaio said. "I'll try it."

Yukaio took a deep breath and let it out slowly. Closing his eyes, he repeated the breathing, trying to clear his mind. All around him, the darkness roiled, invading his every thought. He imagined Sagira's wind pushing it away. He imagined floating above the darkness, leaving it behind. The clear sky above him, solid ground far below. He reached as far as he could, branches stretching across the world. And at the end of it, he found - nothing.

Opening his eyes, he silently shook his head.

"You tried," Sagira sighed. She placed a reassuring hand on his shoulder.

The darkness around them shook, knocking all of

them to their knees. Yukaio felt a light glimmer briefly before fading away. Felt, more than saw, as the darkness still encompassed them.

"What was that?" Tiergan asked.

"Give me your hand," Yukaio reached out towards Sagira.

"Why?" she asked.

He grabbed onto her forearm. "Trust me."

The darkness around them recoiled again. Yukaio felt the light once more. Looking ahead, as if he could see through the darkness, it called to him. His name whispered by the earth itself. Sagira followed his gaze as if she too could see it, could hear winds calling her.

"What is it?" Tiergan asked.

"You don't see that?" Sagira said.

Tiergan shook his head.

Yukaio and Sagira looked at each other, a silent understanding. Alone they were strong, but together, they could be unstoppable.

"One more try?" Sagira asked.

"Once more."

"What's that?" Tiergan asked.

The Guardians looked down at Yukaio's pocket, where Tiergan was pointing. A light shone from within. Yukaio grasped the meamina and pulled it out into the open. The light emitting from the orb shone brightly in the darkness. As Yukaio held it in his hand, it began to grow. Sagira stared in awe before placing a hand in her own pocket. Her own meamina shone bright.

"Did you know they could do that?" she asked.

Yukaio shook his head. "No, I didn't."

"What exactly are they doing?" Tiergan stepped in closer to get a better look.

"No idea," Sagira said.

"Uaithiel said these are a reflection of our souls

and they link us to our powers," Yukaio said. "What if they link us to each other too?"

Sagira motioned for Tiergan to back up. She shifted the orb into one hand, its size now completely filling her entire palm. As she balanced it, she reached out for Yukaio with her other hand. He copied her actions and grasped her hand.

Sagira lifted her hand and the orb, summoning the winds around her, pushing back against the darkness. Yukaio placed his orb on the ground of darkness, feeling for the earth below. The life that flowed through roots deep beneath the earth sang to him, called to him. He reached for them, pulled them with all his might. Sagira's wind, surging around them like a funnel, tore through the side of the darkness. Moonlight and starlight broke through, illuminating the roots growing in front of them. Yukaio pulled with every inch of himself, unsure if he was screaming in his mind or out loud, as roots, tree roots, lifted above the ground.

"Jump," he said.

"What, are you crazy?" Tiergan cried.

"Trust him," Sagira said, reaching for her brother. "Trust me."

Sagira clasped her hand around her brother's wrist, holding him as tight as she could. She summoned the winds once more, pushing them from behind as they leapt through the air. The trio fell through the darkness into the night. The wind guided them through the freefall until they were surrounded by branches. Yukaio gasped as he saw the tree pull its roots out of the ground and swing them at the darkness. He grabbed for the branches, ending up with a handful of leaves as they tumbled through the branches of the tree, now shielding them from the darkness. Yukaio looked at the meamina, now shrunken back to its normal size.

They had never seen the likes of it before. A tree literally standing up out of the ground, as if stretching after a thousand years of slumber. The earth shook as its roots pulled free, attacking the floating darkness. As Umbra dissipated around them, the tree's branches surged towards the glow of life, the trio now ensconced within its grasp. A shriek pierced the air as the Umbra disappeared into the night, leaving only moonlight and starlight to shine on the tree. Branches swaying in the wind, the dance of victory, the roots returned to the earth.

Chapter Seven

The sun was blazing down on Terry as she lay in the grass. How long had it been since she had time to relax? She couldn't remember, she couldn't remember anything. Scrunching her nose, she thought about it before a voice in the distance made her smile. The light-hearted voice of her brother ran through the ground around her. Rolling over to look off into the distance at her brother, she smiled.

He was far away, barely more than a shadow in front of the sun moving quickly through the sky, an orange ball of flame surrounding her brother. The sun grew brighter and hotter as it moved, as if it were getting closer to them. Terry opened her mouth to shout towards her brother, but no voice came out. Placing a hand against her tanned throat, she tried again to scream. Her breath quickened as panic flowed over her like a wave. The distant shadow of her brother turned to smoke as it moved towards her, surrounding her, suffocating her. The blaze of the sun now encompassing everything around her.

Terry awoke with a start, sweat sliding down her brow as she sat up. The forest around her glowed – no, not glowed – burned. The flames licked the side of the trees near where she had made camp hours earlier, the smoke near suffocating. A *crack* sounding above her head made her look up in time to see a flaming branch falling from the treetops.

Terry scrambled out of the way, her lungs burning at the rapid movement as she choked down plumes of smoke. She looked back to see her blanket catch fire as the branch landed where she had been sleeping only moments before.

Panting, her breath heavy in her chest, she looked around. The fire was everywhere. But where was Uaithiel?

"Uaithiel?" she called out as loudly as she could. Her voice strained as the air in her lungs grew thin.

Turning and looking in every direction as best she could with smoke filling her airway, her eyes watering as she blinked rapidly. She called the angel's name repeatedly as she tried to move through the forest. The flames swept and danced around her, making finding a safe path nigh impossible. Stumbling through the woods, nearly blind despite the light of the flames, Terry fell to her knees. Her breath caught in her throat as she choked, trying to get any bit of fresh air that she could. The watering in her eyes turned to tears.

The trees rustled around her, their life being choked out by the smoke. Branches fell to the ground along the path in front of her, their flames fighting to stay lit. The branches cracked and groaned as a shape emerged above them. Looking up with wet eyes, Terry saw two figures ensconced in darkness, cloth covering most of their faces. The taller of the two moved towards her. Trying to back away, Terry's legs gave out as she crumpled to the ground.

"I'm not here to hurt you," the figure's voice was deep beneath the cloth covering his face. "Let me help you."

He reached down and scooped her into his arms. Without the energy to fight back, she buried her face in his shoulder, the cloth of his tunic blocking some of the smoke as she swallowed small breaths of air. His companion nodded to him as he turned, with what Terry thought was a long knife in his hand, he started swinging at the branches. Clearing a path amid the falling branches, he didn't look back at Terry or the one who now carried her. His movements were swift and sure despite the growing heat. Droplets of sweat landed on Terry's cheek, falling from the brow of the man now carrying her.

Terry didn't have the breath to ask them who they were, but she was glad to be moving away from the center of the flames. As they moved through the forest, Terry began to breathe easier where the smoke thinned and the fire became more distant. The figure in front stopped as they cleared the last of the flames and looked around.

"We should keep moving," the one carrying Terry said. "The fire will likely continue to spread for a while."

"I know," the other responded. "Which way should we go?"

"Over there," he nodded in a direction that Terry couldn't see. "Back beyond the river, we should be safe there."

"What about her?" the figure with the long knife said quietly.

"We bring her with us, for now," he started moving again, still holding Terry close to his chest. "It isn't safe to leave her here."

The first figure nodded in agreement. With the flaming branches now behind them, the first figure hooked the handle of his knife to the side of his belt. Looking at Terry, he smiled as he noticed her attention on the weapon. Without the smoke clouding her vision she could see it more clearly. The long handle was ornately carved with what looked like winged animals down the long handle. It would have reminded her of an axe if it weren't for the wavy blade that ended in a sharp curve. *No wonder it was able to take down the branches so easily*, she thought to herself.

The two figures walked in silence as the crackling flames behind them grew more distant, and the rushing of water approached. Terry looked up as they approached the bank. The rushing water looked as swift and violent as the flames they had just left.

"Can you stand?" the figure asked Terry.

She nodded and willed the strength to her legs as he set her down. Her breath caught in her throat as her legs faltered, giving out beneath her. The steady hands of the one who had carried her now gripped her shoulders, holding her up. Taking a deep breath, the clean air once again filling her lungs, Terry stood tall and stepped away from the figure. He released her and moved to take off the cloth covering his face. The fading darkness of the night gave way to enough light for her to see her saviours clearly for the first time.

The man smiled as he removed the cloth. His dark skin was smooth, and his smile was soft. She looked to the other as he also revealed his face. They both shared the same short, shaggy hairstyle, although the shorter man's hair was far lighter, almost a dirty blonde compared to the taller man's dark brown. Though he was a good half-foot shorter than the other, they looked like they could be brothers. The main difference was their eyes. Whereas the one who carried her had soft brown eyes, the others shone a bright yellow-green. The smile across his face made him look quite wicked with that complexion.

"Who are you?" Terry finally found her voice.

"My name is Tariq," said the one who carried her. "And this is my brother, Malik."

Malik nodded wordlessly.

"I don't mean to be improper, but we need to get across this river and quickly," Tariq said, looking back as the flames still grew in the distance. "There's a series of rocks over there. Do you think you can make the crossing?"

Terry looked at where the man pointed. A series of rocks spread across the width of the river, water splashing the sides and occasionally soaking the tops as the river rushed past. They were far apart, she would have to jump from one to the next, she realized. Terry started to nod before she remembered why she had been in the forest.

"Uaithiel," she said, backing away from the men and the river.

"We heard you calling that name in the forest," Malik said, reaching out towards her. "Whoever that is, we can try and find them later. Right now, we need to get to safety."

"No, no," she said, panic again filling her. "They're helping me find my brother, I need to go back."

"You can't go back," Malik grabbed her arm as she turned towards the flames. "You go back in there and you're as good as dead. Wait until the fire dies down."

"That could take days!" She nearly screamed at them.

"Please," Tariq said, placing a gentle hand on her shoulder. "Just come with us for now. Get across the river, and then we can talk about finding your brother, Uaithiel."

"No, Uaithiel isn't my brother. They're helping me to find my brother, he's missing."

Tariq only smiled and nodded at her. Terry

looked up at him, their eyes meeting. She could see his smile in his eyes, and it helped to soothe her. Taking a deep breath, she nodded back. Turning towards the river, she watched as Malik leapt from the riverbank to the first rock. He soared through the air, the axe-knife at his side swinging against his leg as he landed gracefully on the first rock. Though he made it look so easy, Terry knew that it wouldn't be. Tariq indicated for her to go next.

Placing her foot against the riverbank, dirt shifted beneath her toes, splashing as it hit the running water. *I just hope the next splash isn't me*, she thought. Willing all her strength into her legs, she pushed off and aimed towards the first rock. Her feet slipped on the slimy surface as she landed, her arms waving around her, trying to keep her balance. She looked over her shoulder back at Tariq, who gave her an encouraging nod. Terry smiled shyly and quickly looked to the next rock. It wasn't quite as far as the first, but with the slippery stones finding her footing, and keeping it, was going to be difficult. She scrunched her face in concentration as she leapt towards the next rock.

By the time she made it to the third rock, she looked up to see Malik landing on the solid ground on the other side of the river. He had moved across the rocks so quickly and easily. She didn't dare look back at Tariq again, he was probably getting impatient waiting for her to move across the stones. He had a firmer build than his little brother, and she was sure that he would be able to get across just as quickly as Malik. Putting the thoughts out of her mind, she tried to focus on one rock at a time. The slick rock bit at her knees as she collided with the last one. It had been the furthest jump so far, and she had barely made it.

Looking up at the riverbank, she saw Malik move

as close to the edge as he could and extend his hand. The distance between this last rock and the bank was even further than the jump she had just made. Terry pushed back against the fear growing inside of her chest, and she thought about Yukaio. *He wouldn't be afraid to make the jump*, she told herself. *Be strong, like him.*

Steadying herself, she looked at the distance and prepared to jump. Grunting as she pushed off the rock, her arms flailed through the air as she neared the riverbank. Her toes barely touched the dirt when Malik's fingers wrapped around hers, pulling her towards him as his other hand moved to her back to keep her from falling into the water.

"Thank you," she breathed as she knelt down on the dirt.

"I never caught your name," Malik said as he watched his brother move across the rocks.

"It's Terry," she said, following his gaze. She was right, his brother was moving across the rocks just as smoothly. "Have you two done this before?"

"Only once," Tariq admitted as he landed on the shore beside her. "But it's quite fun, I wouldn't mind doing it again."

"Minus the flames chasing us," Malik added. His brother smiled.

"Thank you, both of you, for saving me from the fire," Terry looked them both in the eyes. "But I need to go, I have to find my brother."

"Do you know where to start looking?" he asked.

"If I can find Uaithiel, they might be able to guide me to my brother, but they flew off in the night," she said.

"Flew off?" Malik asked.

"Yes, they're an angel," Terry explained.

"I've never met an angel before," Malik said.

"And with your winning personality, brother,

you're not likely to," Tariq smiled as Malik punched him in the arm.

"Thank you again, but I should go," Terry got to her feet and turned to walk along the riverbank.

"Wait up," Tariq called after her. "The forest isn't safe, especially at night, you should be careful."

"I appreciate the warning," she turned to face them. "But I've seen my own fair share of nightmares lately, that fire is the least of them. Although if I never have to see another fire again, I wouldn't mind. But once I find my brother we can continue on with our mission."

"And what kind of mission would that be?" Malik asked, crossing his arms over his chest. Terry watched as he surveyed her, likely assessing what kind of fighting skills she could possess.

"I'm not really sure I should say, I don't really understand all of it, and it isn't quite my place to tell my brother's story," she said.

"Fair enough," Tariq smiled. "We wish you all the best in your search. But I will leave you with a piece of advice if you will have it.

"Of course," she nodded.

"At night, be sure to build a fire. There is some type of demon spirits wandering these woods. They attack without warning, and it doesn't seem like anything can keep them away, except for the light of the fires," he explained.

"The Umbra."

"What did you say?" Malik asked.

"They're called Umbra," she repeated. "My brother and I have encountered them before. He was able to fight them off."

"Then your brother must be very strong. They nearly overpowered us a few times before we discovered that fire repels them," Tariq said. "Good luck in your journey."

Chapter Eight

The first rays of the sun's light reflected off the angel's wings as they soared through the sky. Uaithiel could see Amatheon ahead, had been chasing him through the night into the next day. Despite not turning around even once, Uaithiel knew that Amatheon realized he was being followed.

The cool air bit at their wings as they flew north. In the distance, despite the rising sun, Uaithiel could see the darkness of the Contenebris mountain. The angel knew that going there would not work out in their favour, nothing good could ever come from there. They prepared to make their move when, suddenly, Amatheon banked to the right and dove down towards the ground.

Uaithiel followed suit, landing in an open field across from the demon. They watched as the demon stood there, facing away from them, as he rolled his shoulders, stretching his wings. Pulling their own wings in towards their side, the angel stepped forward.

"You must really like me if you chose to follow me over saving the precious human," Amatheon said.

"You bastard," the angel shouted.

Amatheon turned around, grinning.

"Oh, that's right, it's not like you could have done anything for her. Leaving her might have been the kindest thing you've done so far," the demon said. "Unless of course it means she burns to death. What would her brother think?"

"What have you done with them?" they asked.

"Why, what ever do you mean?"

"You know exactly what I mean!"

"Oh, I'm quite sure I don't," Amatheon strode towards the angel.

"Where have you taken the Guardians?" the angel strode forward to meet the demon.

"I haven't taken them anywhere," the demon said. "Don't tell me you lost them again, and so soon."

Uaithiel drew their sword. "You will pay for what you've done."

"You do keep saying that. Tell me, the more you say it, does it help you believe it to be true?"

Amatheon drew the sword from his side, sliding into a battle stance. He twirled the sword in his hand, staring the angel up and down. The scene felt all too familiar. How many times now had he fought this angel? One way or another, the battle always ended in a draw.

The demon whispered under his breath. "Not this time."

As the two celestial beings ran towards one another, thunder clapped across the sky. Their swords clashed, echoing the rumbling over the grounds. Amatheon's face was set with determination as he stared into Uaithiel's violet eyes. He could see the years that the angel's face didn't show. The years and the fatigue that came with them, with living for so long.

Amatheon felt the weariness of the ages through his whole body, his sword arm dropping ever so slightly. At the brief moment of weakness, Uaithiel surged, striking hard and pushing the demon back.

Amatheon quickly recovered, poising to strike again, to meet the angel's attack.

Lightning struck the ground between them.

Amatheon looked towards the sky, the remnants of electricity jumping through the darkened clouds. Looking back at his enemy, he raised his sword. Thunder boomed above his head. A low growl emitted from his throat as he took a step back.

"I guess we'll have to finish this another time," Amatheon said.

"Afraid you're finally going to lose to me?" Uaithiel asked.

"Hardly," the demon answered. "But right now, I have much more important matters to attend to than you."

Uaithiel raised their sword and took another step forward. They would not just let Amatheon run off, not again.

"Besides," Amatheon continued. "Don't you have a human to go and find? If she somehow managed to escape that fire, I imagine she will be quite cross with you."

Before Uaithiel could answer, the demon shot into the sky. Lightning leapt through the clouds, blinding the angel. By the time they opened their eyes, Amatheon was gone.

The angel considered going after him once more. There was only one place he would be going with such urgency. But a thought tugged at his mind. The thought of a small human girl left all alone. Surrendering to their better judgment, Uaithiel took off into the sky, racing back down south.

Chapter Nine

Terry strode through the trees, leaving the two men behind. She had thanked them for their advice, regardless that she already knew everything they had said. She was eager to leave the burning forest behind her and find her brother. Despite their warnings, she knew that she would be fine, Uaithiel had told her as much the night before. The Umbra wouldn't be interested in her since she was only human.

A sudden realization made her gasp aloud as she stopped walking. She turned to look down the path she had just made, but the two men were out of sight already.

Her feet pounded on the ground as she ran back to the riverbank, hoping they were still there. But as she arrived, the area was empty. Looking around, she tried to see if there was any trace of where they had gone, but she saw nothing. Terry looked at the sun in the sky. It was barely midday, there was still plenty of daylight for her to go searching. Was one of them the Guardian that Uaithiel had sensed the other day?

Just as her thoughts shifted to the angel, a gust of wind wrapped around her. Looking up, she saw Uaithiel floating down to the ground. The feathers on their wings were ruffled, and their hair was knotted from the wind. They looked rough. Although she knew they didn't need to sleep,

Uaithiel looked ragged and tired. Despite their appearance, Terry smiled and ran to hug them. Uaithiel merely stared at the girl, caught off guard, before wrapping their arms around her.

"I'm glad that you're safe," Uaithiel said with a smooth voice despite their appearance.

"Where did you go?" she asked.

"There was something, or rather someone, I had to take care of," they said, looking back at the burning forest. "Unfortunately, it did not go as planned."

"Was it Ama-"

"Don't say his name," Uaithiel cut her off quickly. Terry scrunched her face and looked taken aback as the angel continued. "I'm sorry. I don't know if he can sense when his name is mentioned. Many demons can, and I think he is one of the ones who can. It's better not to risk it."

Terry nodded in agreement.

"We should move on from here," Uaithiel said.

"Wait," Terry said. "I think I found the Guardian you were looking for. He was here, but I don't know where he went."

"What makes you think he's a Guardian?" the angel asked.

"He and his brother rescued me from the fire, and then when we parted ways, they told me to stay safe because demon shadows were lurking in the woods. They were attacked by them and repelled them with fire. It sounds a lot like the Umbra."

"Yes, it does."

"And you said that they would only attack the Guardians," she continued. "So, wouldn't that mean that one of them is a Guardian?"

"It is very likely," Uaithiel concurred. "Do you know which way they went?"

"Not exactly," she admitted. "I know they didn't

go south along the river, that's the direction I had gone in. And I know they stayed on this side of the river, so either north or west, but I'm not sure. Can't you use that power of yours to find them?"

"Yes, I can," they smiled as they closed their eyes. Terry watched silently as minutes passed before Uaithiel opened their eyes. "They went west."

Terry let them lead the way through the thicket of trees. She ducked below a low hanging branch as she followed in Uaithiel's footsteps. She didn't think she had parted way with them that long ago. *They must have moved quickly to cover this much distance*, she thought to herself. While they walked, Terry told Uaithiel about what had happened, waking up in the fire, being rescued, and then parting ways after crossing the river. After what seemed to be an eternity, Uaithiel stopped walking.

"What is it?" she asked.

"I can sense him, just up ahead a bit."

"Are you . . . nervous?"

Uaithiel heaved a sigh and slowly nodded.

"Why?"

"Because there is a great deal of pressure on me to restore the Guardians and to defeat . . . him," Uaithiel looked down at the human girl. "You wouldn't really understand."

"Try me," she met his gaze and held it firm.

"Perhaps when you're 10,000 years old, I'll explain it to you," they smiled.

"You're how old?" she gaped.

"Well, I'm actually a bit older than that, but we don't count our ages as mortals do," the angel explained. "It's a celestial thing."

Uaithiel held up a hand as Terry opened her mouth to comment. Uaithiel turned away from her to look back down the path they had been travelling. Faint voices came from beyond the trees, they were speaking low on purpose. Uaithiel looked up at the sun and judged that they had only a few hours of daylight left before darkness resumed. Squaring their shoulders and puffing out their wings to make them look larger, the angel continued until only a few branches kept them hidden from the Guardian and his brother.

"Maybe we shouldn't have left her," Uaithiel heard Tariq say.

"We didn't leave her," Malik's voice was instantly recognizable, and Uaithiel couldn't help but smile. "She walked off on her own and didn't look back. At least we warned her."

"I still think she might have been able to . . ." Tariq paused.

"What is it, brother?"

"I thought I heard something."

Pushing the last of the branches out of the way, Uaithiel entered the clearing, immediately noticing the two men that turned to face him.

"Malik, Tariq . . ." Uaithiel said slowly.

"I'm going to guess you're Uaithiel," Tariq stood to face the angel. He smiled as he noticed Terry emerge from behind a pair of large wings. "I didn't think we would see you again."

"I didn't think I'd come back either, but I was thinking about what you said," Terry began to explain. "I think you should listen to what Uaithiel has to say, it might be important."

She looked up at the angel who nodded in confirmation. Yes, they had found the third Guardian. Uaithiel didn't let their face show the relief they felt inside. The fact that Terry had found him on her own, entirely by accident, it had to be a sign. Despite everything, it appeared that their luck was about to turn around.

"Terry tells me that you've encountered the

Umbra in the past few weeks," Uaithiel started.

"That's right," Tariq nodded. "But we didn't know that's what they were called. Or that they were called anything at all."

"There is a reason that they came after the two of you," they explained. "Have you heard of the Guardians?"

Both Malik and Tariq shook their heads.

"The Madeiran Guardians were handpicked by the Gods to defend humanity against the darkness, including the Umbra," Uaithiel looked both of them in the eyes. "It is why the Umbra are attracted to the Guardians - their instincts tell them to hunt and destroy the Guardians."

"And you think that we're part of these Guardians?" Tariq asked.

"Not both of you, just one of you," Uaithiel turned to face the shorter brother. "Just you, Malik."

"Me?" he said in disbelief. "That's doubtful."

"Let me ask you this," the angel took a step closer. "Did you wake up one day a few weeks ago with no memories of who you are or where you're from?"

"We both did," Malik said sharply.

"Yes, your brother got caught up in this because of his proximity to you when everything. . . happened," Uaithiel struggled to find the right words. "When you woke up, did you have a small orb with you?"

Malik hesitated, looking towards his brother. Slowly Tariq nodded once, and Malik removed an object from his pocket. He peeled back the cloth covering the smooth orb, glowing yellow in the light of the setting sun. Malik stared at the opaque orb in his open palm. The smooth surface reflected the light making it appear to glow.

"What is it?" Malik asked.

"It is a part of who you are, it connects you to the

powers given to you by the Gods," Uaithiel said.

"I find that hard to believe," Malik covered the orb and shoved it back in his pocket before looking to Terry. "Are you one of these Guardians too?"

"No, but my brother is," she said.

"The one that you're looking for?" Tariq asked. "Is he . . ."

"No, stop," Malik said forcefully. "I don't care."

"What do you mean you don't care?" Terry asked.

"About this. About these supposed Guardians," Malik held his hands out in front of him. "My brother and I have been fine on our own up until now."

"But you don't have any memories of what happened before, Malik. If you did, you would feel differently about fighting alongside your friends . . ." Uaithiel countered.

"Friends?" Malik cut in. "Tell me, where is Terry's brother now? This other Guardian?"

"We're searching for him," Uaithiel said. "We have a general idea of where to find him."

"Uh-huh, and why do you need to find him exactly? What happened?" he asked. "Why isn't he with you now?"

"Malik, try and calm down," Tariq approached his brother, placing a hand on his shoulder. "I know this is a lot to take in, but we should just listen for now I think."

"You have no idea what you're talking about, Tariq," Malik stepped away. "You aren't the one being told you're some kind of Guardian warrior. So, tell me, angel, where is Terry's brother?"

"We think he and another Guardian were taken a few days ago," they admitted.

"Taken where? By who?"

Uaithiel stood silently, contemplating how much to say. Scaring off Malik before he even joined would only complicate matters. The angel studied Malik's face, set with both rage and doubt. He was already so close to walking away, one wrong word could seal that fate.

"He was taken by an agent of the darkness," Uaithiel said. "But by working together, you and the other Guardians can get back those that were taken."

"I don't think so," Malik backed away. "My brother and I have been doing just fine on our own for the last few weeks. I'm not about to risk that for someone we don't even know."

"You're wandering around alone in the forest," Terry said. "Come with us and we can help each other."

"We saw a village the day before yesterday, nothing too big, but it looked like a good place to set up a home," Malik said. "We're going to head back that way and settle down for a while, right, Tariq?"

Tariq looked from Uaithiel to his brother and back. After a moment of consideration, he nodded. He and Malik had been a team for as long as he could remember. Even though he could only remember the last few weeks, he knew that he would stand beside his brother no matter what. Hiding the concern from showing on his face, Tariq considered what kind of powers his little brother might have as a Guardian, what responsibilities those powers might thrust upon him. But Malik was right, it wasn't his place to understand what was being asked of his brother. If Malik wanted to remain a two-man team, Tariq wouldn't argue with him.

"Please, reconsider," Uaithiel pleaded. "I can show you how to use your powers, how to fight against the agents of the darkness, how to protect those around you."

"The only one I care about protecting is my brother," Malik said. "I'm not interested in joining you, I'm sorry."

Malik turned away from them and bent over the fire pit, striking the flint to spark the first few flames.

"You know there's an easier way for you to do that," Uaithiel offered. "With your power . . ."

"Not interested," Malik repeated as he continued to strike the flint until the sparks caught and the flame started to take shape.

"What do we do now?" Terry turned towards Uaithiel, glancing towards the two men now sitting by the growing fire. "What will happen to Yukaio if we can't find him?"

"Try not to worry, Terry, we will find your brother," Uaithiel reassured her. "We may need to find other Guardians first, though."

"And if they don't want to join either?"

"Malik has always been . . . unique. Many of the Guardians are, come to think of it. But I feel fairly certain that I will be able to convince at least a couple of them to join us, both to rescue your brother and afterwards," Uaithiel tried to smile.

"You should at least stay the night," Tariq called over to the pair as they were about to continue down the forest path.

"Tariq!" Malik shouted.

"Just for the night, brother," he placed a hand on Malik's shoulder. "It's almost dark, and you look like you haven't eaten all day."

Terry placed a hand on her stomach as it growled. She hadn't realized how hungry she was until she watched Tariq take a small bundle of fruit from his sack. He removed the stained cloth from around the fruit, laying it out on the ground between them. Terry could barely contain herself as she raced towards it, grabbing the first one she could reach. Biting into the juicy apple, she moaned in delight. Licking the juices running down her chin and her hands, she savoured every last bit.

"Have some water too," Tariq tossed a skein of water towards Terry, who caught it with her free hand.

"Where was all of this earlier?" she asked, surveying the two packs that they had laid against a log near the fire.

"It was here," Tariq said. "We've been camping here for a couple of days, and we were just out scouting a path to take when the fire started. It was pure luck that we were there to hear you calling out."

"Speaking of scouting, that's what I should be doing," Uaithiel announced. "Malik, I know you've made your opinion regarding joining us very clear, but I would ask one favour of you. Watch over Terry, just for tonight while I am searching for the other Guardians."

Malik nodded silently in confirmation as Uaithiel's mighty wings surged, sending them up into the air high above.

"Wait, you're leaving me again?" Terry asked.

"I will return, I give you my word. You will be safe here."

"That's what you said last time."

Uaithiel looked towards Malik and Tariq. Malik was purposefully ignoring them, staring intently at what was apparently a remarkably interesting piece of grass. Uaithiel's gaze landed on Tariq, who was much more receptive.

"Don't worry, Terry. I'll make sure to look after you," Tariq said.

"Come back soon. Please."

Uaithiel nodded as they disappeared into the sky.

Terry looked back only briefly before opening the skein of water and taking a large gulp. She looked at the two men sitting across from her by the fire, disappointed that they wouldn't be helping her to find her brother. She wanted to think them selfish, they had each other and didn't think they needed anyone else. It had been that way with her and Yukaio for a brief period before Uaithiel had found them. Thoughts of her brother fighting the Umbra raced through her mind, his glaive swinging through the air as if he had done it a million times before. Who knew, maybe he had. Terry's eyes fell to the axe-knife hanging at Malik's side. *A gift from the Gods*, she thought to herself. *A wasted gift.*

"It's called a bhuj," Malik said, catching Terry's glance. "The handle is like an axe, but the curved knife at the end makes it a more versatile weapon."

"It's very nice," Terry said stiffly. "It almost reminds me of the weapon that my brother carries."

"Does your brother also have a bhuj?" Tariq asked.

"No, he has a glaive," she answered. "But it was a gift from the Gods, just like your bhuj."

"Why do you think it's from the Gods?" Malik asked.

"That's what Uaithiel said, that all of the Guardians have gifts from the Gods," Terry looked him directly in the eyes. "And not just their fighting skills or the power that flows through their veins, but physical weapons too. Weapons that can hurt and destroy the Umbra and protect the innocent."

"You think me selfish and cowardly for not joining, don't you?" he returned her stare. "All I can remember is my brother, and I won't lose him on some fool's mission."

"You don't know that's what it is, you wouldn't even let Uaithiel finish explaining everything."

"I didn't need to hear it to know that I'm not interested," Malik said. "My brother and I have always taken care of each other, and we will continue to do so."

"Maybe you should get some rest," Tariq interjected quickly before Terry could respond.

She looked from Tariq to Malik, still angry at their decision despite all they had done for her in the past day.

"Just one more question for you, Malik," she said. He nodded for her to continue. "You said you and Tariq were out scouting a path when the fire broke out and you found me. Why were you scouting in the middle of the night?"

Both men just looked at each other. Neither of them had been able to sleep the night before, and as they sat around their campsite, they decided to make the best use of their time. Crossing the river at night had been a risk, but they'd done it to see what lay on the other side, if there were any option better than the village that lay to the west. But the fire had stopped them in their tracks and forced them to turn back. But somehow, they had gotten turned around when they heard Terry calling out for help and decided to save her.

"I can't answer that," Malik eventually said.

"Why?"

"Because I don't know," he admitted. "I don't know why we decided to go out there."

Terry, although unsatisfied by the answer, turned to lay on the ground by the fire. She snuck one final glance at Malik as she rolled over. At least her question had gotten him to contemplate what led him to her, even if he still hadn't decided to go with them to find the rest of the Guardians. Closing her eyes, Terry imagined Uaithiel flying overhead. She hoped that they were watching over them, especially Malik. Even more so, she hoped that they were using that special gift to sense the other Guardians and that soon she would be back with her brother. With the sound of the campfire cackling behind her, Terry struggled to fall asleep, lying there well into the night. Finally, when exhaustion overtook her, thoughts of her brother faded as she drifted into a dreamless sleep.

Chapter Ten

It wasn't the shaking that awoke Sethos - it was the scream. Rising up, he looked at his sister, she had heard it too. Only moments later the earth beneath them began to tremble. Debris from the roof of their hut fell to the ground around them. Iisha sprang up and ran to her siblings, still wiping the sleep from their eyes. Another shake had Sethos also up and running towards his family, pulling them outside the shaking hut.

A large groan and a crack sounded through the air. Sethos emerged just in time to see the large oak tree reach up as if it were alive and pull its roots from the ground. Darkness swirled around, blacker than a normal night, the moon and stars veiled.

"What's happening," Kalida asked, stepping forwards.

Sethos quickly reached for his little sister, pulling her back towards him. He glanced around the village, nearly everyone was outside staring at the wonder happening so near to their homes. He saw Tsuna and her two young sons staring, fear written across all their faces. Her husband had an arm wrapped around her shoulder, holding her close to him. Sethos tightened his grip on Kalida with one arm, the other reaching for Iisha's hand. She held it firm, her eyes fixed on the tree.

The earth around them continued to shake as the roots pulled up out of the ground and began thrashing about. And before long, the darkness around the tree dissipated, the waving and thrashing of branches and roots turned to a dance of victory. The roots burrowed down back into the earth, but not as deep as they had been. No, most of the roots now stood above the earth, as if frozen in an eternal dance of victory.

Sethos stared as the tree again froze into the earth. The night wind dissipated as quickly as the darkness had, stars again shining in the sky beyond. Leaves and branches rustled despite the growing calm.

"There's someone in there," Mitesh whispered.

Without a second thought, Sethos swung the now-half full quiver over his shoulders and scooped up one of the bows from inside the doorway. Tossing Kalida into his twin's arms, he ran towards the tree, an arrow already nocked in the bow by the time he arrived. He slowed as he approached the dancing roots, unsure if they would start moving again. He looked up into the branches, keeping his arrow aimed and ready to fly. The *crack* of a branch sounded as a large object fell through and landed on the ground with a *thud.* Sethos jumped back to avoid being hit and then stepped forward to examine the object. It was a weapon of some kind, a long stick with a curved blade at the end.

"Sorry about that," a voice called from above. "I lost my grip."

"Who are you?" Sethos demanded, aiming his arrow high above him.

"Don't shoot! My name is Yukaio," he said. "My friends and I are going to come down now."

"How did you get in there?" Sethos asked.

"That is a very long and a very complicated story," a female voice said from behind the first.

"Let us come down, we will try to explain."

Sethos lowered his weapon and stepped away from the tree. He turned back towards the village, everyone still staring at the scene unfolding in front of them. Looking back at the tree, he saw two males and a female moving from branch to branch. The first male that spoke, Yukaio, moved with ease as if the tree were an extension of his own body. He leapt from the lowest branch and landed on one of the roots now curved above the ground. Sliding down to the earth, he strode over towards Sethos.

"I'm sorry if we woke you," he said, noticing the audience in the distance.

"What was that?" Sethos asked.

He surveyed the boy standing before him. Boy, definitely not man. Yukaio looked to be barely older than the younger twins. His features were young, but his eyes looked older, as if they had seen too much already. Sethos stood at least a foot taller than the boy, towering over him. Yet he didn't balk or stammer. Yukaio held as firm as the earth beneath them.

"That was the darkness," Yukaio explained. "It was created by creatures called the Umbra."

Two soft thuds from behind Yukaio drew his attention away from the tall man standing before him. Sagira and Tiergan landed on the ground, the latter falling to his knees at the sudden impact of the solid earth. Sagira reached out a hand to her brother, helping him back to his feet.

"These are friends of mine," Yukaio gestured towards them. "Sagira, and her brother, Tiergan."

"I'm Sethos," he said, removing the arrow from his bow and returning it to the quiver on his back. He reached out a calloused hand, which Yukaio shook firmly.

"Is that your family?" Yukaio asked, looking

behind Sethos.

Sethos let go of the boy's hand and turned around. Iisha strode up beside him, the young twins not too far behind.

"This is my sister, Iisha," he said. "And those are our younger siblings, Mitesh and Kalida."

Mitesh ambled up between his sisters and stared at the group of newcomers. The brother and sister that had just fallen from the tree now stood beside their friend. He surveyed them, their dark skin causing them to blend in with the night. Between them, their friend, Yukaio, stood out. His skin was lighter but still very tanned. Mitesh noticed his muscled arms and hands, one of which wrapped around the polearm of a glaive, the weapon almost taller than him. Yukaio noticed the boy's attention on him and met his gaze, smiling. Mitesh blushed before quickly looking away.

"Where did that . . . thing come from?" Iisha asked.

"It took us several days ago, from our campsite," Sagira answered. "I'm not sure where it was taking us, though."

"What happened to it?" Kalida asked, looking at the roots, thinking about how much more fun it would be to climb it now.

"I'm still trying to work that out," Yukaio said. "We'd been trying to escape for days, had almost given up. But something . . ."

"Something what?" Sethos asked.

"You're probably going to think this sounds crazy," Yukaio admitted. "But something called out to us, this tree or something. It called our names and told us we could fight back."

Sethos stared and the boy, unblinking. He wondered how much truth there was to his story, and how much he was leaving out. Surely there had to be more to it than what they'd admitted. But getting them to tell the rest of the story, would it be worth it? He looked at his sister, her face emotionless. Sethos suppressed a smirk, he was proud of how well his sister could appear timeless.

"Do you think . . ." Iisha started, but Sethos cut her off with a subtle wave of his hand.

"Your story is very interesting," he said.

"Sethos," Iisha whispered in his ear. "What if this has to do with what we buried?"

"What did you bury?" Tiergan asked as all eyes looked to him.

Sethos narrowed his eyes, staring at the dark-skinned boy.

"I have exceptionally good hearing," Tiergan said. "Apparently."

Iisha and Sethos exchanged a look, trying to decide what to do. Sethos shook his head.

"It's caused nothing but trouble," he said. "It's left well enough alone."

"Left alone?" his sister asked. "The tree leapt from the ground and attacked a cloud of darkness. I don't think leaving it alone is much of an option now."

Sethos sighed. He looked back towards the village. Many of the others had gone back inside their huts. Though her husband had taken their boys back inside, Tsuna still stood outside the hut. Through the darkness, Sethos could barely make out the expression on her face, but he knew what would be going through her mind. Fear, anger, worry. She had wanted to get her boys out before something bad had happened, and tonight only solidified that thought in her mind. Sethos wondered how many others were now thinking of leaving tomorrow - how many of them had gone back inside not to go back to sleep, but to pack their belongings and move on.

"Kalida, Mitesh, you two should go back to bed," Sethos said.

"I'm not tired anymore," Kalida said.

"Yeah, me neither!" Mitesh added.

"You should listen to your brother," Iisha said.

"Oh, come on," Kalida pleaded. "It's not like we're little children."

"You are kind of little," Tiergan interjected. "You've got to be at least half my age."

Kalida stomped her foot. "Am not! I'm fourteen!"

He stepped up towards the younger twins. Though not as tall as the older twins, he still towered over the younger pair.

"You know," he continued. "I'm feeling kind of tired."

Tiergan looked at his sister and nodded. He didn't want to be left out, but he knew Sagira would tell him everything later. And he realized that if the young twins stayed there, they might not get any information at all. He knew that Sagira understood his comment when Sagira looked to Iisha with a pointed glance.

"There's lots of space in the village," Iisha offered. "Maybe Mitesh and Kalida could help you find somewhere to sleep for a bit."

Iisha indicated to her siblings. Mitesh opened his mouth to protest, but a stern look from Sethos made him close it again. The young twins turned to walk back to the village, Tiergan now in tow.

"Tell your brother thank you for us," Iisha said to Sagira once the others were out of earshot.

"I will," Sagira promised. "Can you tell us what it was you buried now?"

Sethos looked to Iisha for confirmation before he strode to the side of the tree. He walked between the upturned roots, the earth around them soft. Bending down by the base of the largest root, he began to dig. Dirt packed underneath his fingernails as he silently moved the earth. Eventually, he reached down into the hole he had created, now nearly a foot deep, and pulled up a dark, dirt-covered cloth.

"We buried these because they only brought trouble," Sethos said.

"We couldn't bear to get rid of them, not completely," Iisha added. "But we had hoped that by burying them it would keep away the trouble."

"What kind of trouble did they bring?" Sagira asked.

"Darkness," Sethos said. He looked up at the tree as if he could still see the cloud of darkness swirling around it, battling it.

Yukaio looked to Sagira, wordlessly wondering if maybe Tiergan's theory had been right. He watched as Sethos bent down before all of them and placed the cloth on the ground. Taking a deep breath, he pulled back the cover and revealed two small orbs. One was a bright golden, as if it contained the light of a thousand suns - the other pale and silver, like the moon shining above them.

"You're Guardians," Yukaio blurted out.

"We're what?" Iisha asked.

"Guardians, like us," Yukaio said. He reached into his pocket and pulled out his orb, the brown as firm as the earth around them.

Iisha and Sethos stepped closer to see the orb in his hand. As they did, Sagira showed them hers, the deep purple as dark as night. Iisha reached out a hand, and Sagira handed her the orb. Iisha rolled it around in her fingers, looking it over. She glanced at the two orbs sitting on the dirty cloth in front of them, comparing them. It was identical in every way, except for the colour. But the feel of it, Iisha recognized that feel. She handed it back to Sagira, who put it back in her pocket.

"Where did you get those?" Iisha asked.

"I've had it for as long as I can remember," Sagira answered.

"As long as you can remember . . ." Iisha repeated.

Yukaio looked at the female twin, noticed how her gaze drifted away from the group.

"You've had yours for as long as you can remember as well, right?" Yukaio asked.

Iisha nodded.

"And let me guess, that means about a month or so now?" Yukaio said.

"What?" Iisha said, her attention snapping back to the young boy.

"What makes you say that?" Sethos asked.

"Because that's about how far back our memories go, too," Sagira said.

"Give us some time and we can explain everything," Yukaio said.

The twins led them back towards the village as the sun started to rise behind them.

Chapter Eleven

Sethos stared up at the sun as he laid on the grass, his knees bent and his head resting on one arm. It had been a long night, and it was hard to believe that the tree that everyone was now calling the dancing tree was the same one that his siblings had climbed only yesterday. It felt like it was ages ago. He had been laying on the grass since shortly after sunrise, right after Yukaio and Sagira had finished telling their tale about the Guardians. Or as much as they could, they'd admitted that they didn't know everything, not yet.

Sethos and Iisha had listened, often exchanging curious glances towards one another. On the one hand, it did actually explain a lot about their lives in the past few weeks. On the other hand, how could they be part of these Guardians? It seemed so preposterous. So Sethos had walked out, claiming he needed some fresh air and some time to think.

Just as he had found a spot on the grass, he could hear mumbling from nearby huts. Tsuna and her boys weren't the only ones leaving. Sethos counted three separate families with packed bags heading away from the village. That left only about seven people in the village, not counting his family, or the new arrivals. He didn't blame any of the people for leaving. If it hadn't been for all that he'd seen before finding this former haven, he might have considered leaving too. But Iisha was happy, finally being able to sleep in the same place night after night. Mitesh and Kalida were happy, too. Of course, all it took for them to be happy was to be able to spend their days together, playing and climbing as many trees as they could find. He had considered teaching Mitesh how to hunt with the bow, maybe try and instill some responsibility in him. It would likely be a waste of time, he realized, and that he'd be better off training Kalida. *Perhaps I'll teach her how to hunt, she has the reflexes for it*, Sethos thought, remembering how she snatched Mitesh from the air when he was falling through the tree.

He placed a hand on his pocket, the golden orb that had been buried under the tree now back in its home. It felt right to have it back. Yukaio had explained how it was a part of his soul, how it tied him to his magical powers. What those powers were, however, he didn't know. Sethos certainly hadn't felt any magic flowing through him, neither had Iisha, he realized, as she reacted the same way he did to the news. He wondered what kind of power it would be, if his would be, like everything else, the opposite of Iisha's. Shaking his head, he put the thought out of his mind. He didn't need magic, he had other skills. The one thing he knew he was good at was archery. He could strike a rabbit in the eye from over a hundred feet away.

The sounds of approaching footsteps made Sethos look back to see who it was. Mitesh plopped down on the grass beside his big brother.

"What are you doing?" Mitesh asked.

"I'm thinking."

"You look like you were sleeping."

"Well, I wasn't."

"You're grumpy. Are you sure I didn't just wake you up?"

"What do you want?" Sethos poked his brother in the side.

"To come and bug you," he said with a playful smile.

"Well, that's nothing new."

Mitesh laid down on the grass beside Sethos, mimicking his position. He rolled his head to the side and looked at his big brother. His dark hair was tangled with grass, and a few grass stains were forming around the edges of his tunic.

"So, Kalida and I heard some of what the strangers were saying," Mitesh said.

"You two were eavesdropping?" Sethos asked.

"Well, no, not exactly. We just weren't asleep when you came back inside," Mitesh admitted. "It isn't our fault you started talking to them with us in the room."

Sethos sighed. He hadn't even considered he should have checked to see if they were asleep before talking about everything. The newcomer's brother was in the hut next to theirs, supposedly. He wondered if that boy was awake the whole time too.

"Are you going to do it?"

"Do what?"

"Go with them, go be Guardians."

Sethos shook his head. "Doubtful."

"Why not?"

"It's a very complicated situation, I'm not sure how much we can trust what they're saying," Sethos explained. "We don't know them or where they came from . . ."

"We don't know where we came from," Mitesh interrupted.

"We don't know anything about them," Sethos continued. "The story they tell is almost too preposterous for it to be made up. Which is precisely why I think there's something they're not telling us. It would be too dangerous for us to just go off and fight some unknown battle. Besides, we have you and Kalida to look after."

"We aren't little kids anymore, Sethos," Mitesh said. "We can handle ourselves."

"I know you can," Sethos smiled. "But I still don't think it's a good idea."

Mitesh rolled over, looking up at the sky.

"Why don't you go get Iisha for me?" Sethos asked. "I need to ask her something."

"No need," Mitesh said, sitting up. "She's already on her way over."

Sethos craned his head to see his sister approaching. The sunlight glimmered on her skin, her eyes reflecting the light.

"Can you give us a chance to talk alone?" Sethos asked.

Mitesh rolled his eyes as he got up and ran past Iisha back to the hut. Sethos sat up in the grass, brushing the loose bits of grass from his hair. Iisha knelt beside him.

"So, what do you think?" she asked.

"I don't think it's a good idea."

"I agree," Iisha said. "And I think that's why we need to do it."

"What?"

"I know it's going to be dangerous . . ."

"Dangerous is an understatement if last night is any indication."

"If last night is any indication, this darkness is going to follow us whether we join them or not," Iisha said. "Going with them just feels . . . right."

"We don't even know if we can trust them or not," Sethos argued.

"But you want to, don't you?" Iisha asked. "Doesn't it feel like some part inside of you wants to believe that what they're saying is true."

"Maybe . . . I don't know," Sethos said. "I don't understand what I'm feeling."

"Just because you don't understand it, it doesn't mean that you need to be afraid of it," Iisha placed a hand on her brother's shoulder, her soft smile warming her face.

"What about Mitesh and Kalida?" Sethos asked. "Do we take them with us? Do we leave them behind? I don't know which would be worse."

"Sagira's brother is fifteen, and Yukaio has a sister that's only thirteen," Iisha said. "They've joined their siblings on this journey."

"And Yukaio's sister is missing," Sethos argued.

"Technically, Yukaio is the one that is missing," Iisha said.

Sethos looked away from his sister. The dancing tree, with its roots above the ground, stood there watching them. Judging them. What had compelled him to bury their orbs beneath that tree? Would the same thing have happened if they had buried them under a different tree, or a different type of plant? Or if they hadn't buried them at all.

"There are too many unknowns," Sethos said.

"We know three things," Iisha said as Sethos turned to face her again. "One, we're together and we love each other. Two, we make a good team, we can hold our own."

"And what's the third?"

"We have a chance to make a difference in this world."

«‹‹○›»»

By the time noon came around, Sethos and Iisha had packed up much of their home. There wasn't much for them to take with them - beyond the clothes on their backs and a few weapons, they had very few possessions. They'd picked up a few things from other families that had left and couldn't take everything with them. It made Iisha sad to have to leave behind the things that would remind her of this place.

Iisha rolled the bedroll as tightly as she could, securing it to Mitesh's sack. Mitesh and Kalida were, for once, helping as much as they could. Once they had decided to leave, Sethos had agreed to go hunting once more and took Yukaio with him. The two men had returned an hour later with a basket full of food. Sethos had tracked them to where there was a bunny hole, and Yukaio had used his earth powers to coax them out. Between the two of them, they had caught five rabbits that were now being skinned and cooked by the young twins. Yukaio had offered to help Mitesh with the skinning, but he had just blushed and said he could handle it.

By the time Iisha had finished packing up their hut and went outside, she found the meat cooked and laid out to dry. There was enough food there to last them at least a few days, even with nearly doubling the size of their group. Iisha turned at the sound of Sagira's approaching footsteps, her arms full of root vegetables.

"They're easy to find if you know what you're looking for," she said as she placed them down beside the drying meat.

"This should be enough food to last us nearly a week," Iisha said.

"Yes, and Tiergan said that he could see some apple trees further down the path," Sagira said. "He climbed one of the trees while I was picking the roots to see if he could see anything about where we're going."

"That's good, we can pick some when we get there," Iisha said. "I'll be sure to leave enough room in the sacks for some apples."

"Are you sure you want to do this?" Sethos asked his sister.

"Save room for some apples? Of course, I'm sure," Iisha grinned.

Sethos rolled his eyes. "You know what I mean."

"Yes, I do," Iisha nodded. "And yes, I am sure."

As the boys added the last of the supplies to the packs, Iisha picked up one of the quivers of arrows. Quickly counting, she noticed it was nearly full. And so was the second quiver still on the ground.

"When did you finish carving the arrows?" Iisha asked.

"What are you talking about?" Sethos said. "I haven't . . ."

He paused, noticing the two full quivers. Taking out one of the arrows, he examined it.

"This isn't my work," he said, turning the arrow in his hands. "None of these are."

"Then, where did they come from?" asked Iisha.

"I don't know," Sethos admitted. He scrunched his forehead, remembering some of the stories Yukaio had told. "Hey Yukaio, what did you say about those weapons of yours?"

"You mean my glaive?" he asked. "I was told that it was a gift from the Gods, that it could cut down the Umbra and the other agents of the darkness. Why?"

"Last night our quivers were half empty, now today they're full, and these carvings were not made by me," Sethos showed him one of the arrows. "Could these be gifts from the Gods too?"

"It's possible," Yukaio said.

"If they are, then why didn't they replenish like this before?" Iisha asked.

"You had the meaminas buried," Sagira said. "Your orbs."

"Yes, that makes sense," Yukaio added. "The meaminas are what connect us to our powers and to each other. Maybe they connect us to the Gods too?"

"So, with it buried, it blocked it's power?" Iisha asked.

Yukaio shrugged.

Sethos placed the arrow back in the quiver and handed it back to his sister. "Makes just as much sense as anything else."

Iisha swung the quiver over her shoulder, securing it tightly, and attaching the bow so it wouldn't fall off. She said goodbye to the few people remaining in the village and again thanked them for everything they had done. The group gathered their belongings and set off.

"Are you sure this is the right way to go?" Yukaio asked.

"Not really," Sethos said. "But last night, the darkness looked like it was coming from this direction, so hopefully going this way will lead us back to your sister."

"Are you worried about her?" Kalida asked Yukaio.

"Yes and no," Yukaio said. "The first memory I have is of waking up and seeing her. She was injured, and it was a difficult first few days. I love her more than anything, and I want her to be ok. But I also know that she is strong, both in mind and spirit. She's the one that convinced me I should train with Uaithiel. And if they're still together, I know Uaithiel will look after her too."

"I can't wait to meet her," Kalida said.

"I think you'll like her," Yukaio smiled at the young girl. "We just have to find her first."

Chapter Twelve

Terry sat across from Tariq, the campfire burning between them. He passed her another helping of the fish Malik had caught in the river that morning. It was a long night with the fire blazing in the distance, but by morning the billowing smoke had started to dissipate. None of them had gone back across the river to assess the damage; there wasn't anything they would be able to do about it anyway. Terry ate her fish silently, waiting for Uaithiel to come back. They hadn't said how long they would be gone scouting, but she had expected them to be back by sunrise so they could continue to look for Yukaio and the other Guardian that he had hopefully found.

She looked up at the sky to see if she could them flying overhead. The sky was clear, barely even a cloud in sight.

"We need to move out soon," Malik said.

"Uaithiel isn't back yet, brother," Tariq replied.

"I need to wait for them to get back," Terry said.

"Then stay and wait for them," Malik said, gathering his supplies.

"We can't just leave her," Tariq stood to face his brother. "We promised . . ."

"One night. We promised one night we would look after her," Malik said. "It's been that, and then some."

Malik stepped around his brother and stopped

right in front of Terry, kneeling down to where she sat.

"I am sorry," Malik said. "You can come with us if you want, but we aren't going to be looking for any other Guardians or anything. Or you can stay here and wait for the angel to return."

"I can't just give up on my brother," Terry said.

"What makes you certain he's even still alive?" Malik asked. "How do you know that Uaithiel hasn't been hurt or killed too? Or maybe they just abandoned you."

"No, they haven't."

Malik raised an eyebrow. "You answered that awfully quickly."

"I know my brother, he wouldn't give up on me, so I'm not going to give up on him," Terry said. "And you shouldn't underestimate Uaithiel."

"I hate to agree with my brother on this, but you would have died in that fire the other night if it weren't for us," Tariq said. "Uaithiel would never have saved you in time."

Terry shook her head. "They were doing the best they could."

She couldn't believe what the two of them were saying. Granted, they had only met Uaithiel very briefly and didn't have the benefit of being trained with them. But Malik was supposed to be a Guardian! He was supposed to protect the realm, not just one person. But she held firm to her beliefs, Uaithiel wouldn't abandon her, they wouldn't do that. They promised Yukaio they would protect her.

"Please," Terry said. "Just wait a little bit longer."

"I'm so sorry, Terry. Truly, I am," Malik said. "I know you don't believe it, but it's true. I wish there was more we could do to help you, but there isn't. We'll stay for one more hour, enough time to pack up the campsite. If Uaithiel isn't back by then, my offer stands - you can come with us if you want."

She shook her head. "I won't abandon my brother."

Malik nodded. He understood how she felt, he felt the same way about his own brother. He watched as Tariq moved about the campsite, packing their belongings. It was already past noon, and they hadn't moved at all. The sense of urgency inside Malik grew with every passing minute. He wanted to be gone from this place as soon as possible. Although he didn't particularly care about Terry, he could tell that Tariq had grown fond of the girl. He treated her like the sister that they never had. While Malik would have preferred to keep it just the two of them, he made the offer to let Terry join them for his brother. Even though she would slow them down, he knew Tariq would have a hard time leaving her behind.

"This is your last chance to join us," Malik said as he stomped on the last of the embers in the fire pit.

"Thank you, but I have to wait for Uaithiel," Terry said.

"Are you going to go searching for them or just wait here?" Tariq asked.

"I'll wait here a bit longer," she said. "If they don't show up, I'll move on."

"We won't water out the firepit, in case you need it tonight," Malik said. "The embers should light again fairly easily if you need."

"I appreciate that," Terry said.

She stood up and extended a hand to Malik. He looked at her and then down at her outstretched hand. Slowly he shook it. His grip was firm but gentle. She turned to Tariq and extended her hand. He smiled as he shook it for a moment, then reached down to hug her as well. Terry wrapped her arms around him, squeezing tightly.

"Please, stay safe," he told her.

"You too," she said.

Terry stood in the clearing and watched the two men walk away. Tariq turned around to wave once more, and she waved back at him. In some ways, Tariq reminded her of her own older brother. A brother that she had no idea where he was, or if he was ok, or if . . .

"No," she said to herself, stopping her train of thought.

She sat down and picked up a long stick to poke the empty fire pit.

"Come on Uaithiel, where are you?" she asked no one.

«««○»»»

Despite the power of their wings, the fact that Uaithiel had been flying all night and now most of the day meant they were starting to get tired. They could feel all of them, the Guardians. They were so spread out, finding all of them would take a long time. Too long. They needed a miracle. Especially if other Guardians reacted the way Malik did. Although Uaithiel remembered how stubborn Malik could be, it was a surprise that he outright refused to join the Guardians again. Even Tariq couldn't change his mind this time.

Perching on the top of an overgrown oak, Uaithiel was finally able to rest their wings. Closing their eyes, they did another quick summary of the Guardians. The nearest one he could sense was Malik, only a couple hundred feet away now. Then there were two moving south and quite quickly. Two more nearby, but perhaps not close enough to be in their path. Even if they did cross paths, without knowing they're Guardians, it wouldn't do them any good. There were another two out in the east. And the last three, they were all on their own, spread out over the continent. Two were in the far north. Although they were so close to each other, they were far enough away that it was unlikely they would cross paths. The last was further west. If Malik did indeed continue that direction, it was possible they might meet up at some point.

Of the three pairs of Guardians that Uaithiel could sense, they had no idea which was Yukaio and the other Guardian that he had found. There had only been one other Guardian, which narrowed down the possibilities of who it was. Uaithiel didn't dare guess. Each of the Guardians is important, they reminded themself, Yukaio teaming up with any of them would be a good thing.

"Two pairs in the south and one in the east," Uaithiel said. "Two chances are better than one."

Of course, Malik was the closest, but he had already given his answer. Uaithiel didn't have time to change his mind, not now. That would have to wait until later. Lifting off from the tree, the angel turned southward. They paused a moment and looked back to where they had left Terry. *Despite everything, Malik is a good man*, Uaithiel thought. *He'll take good care of her.*

«« « ○ » »»

Terry sat at the campsite, poking the fire for what felt like hours.

"They won't abandon me," she told herself again.

It had become a sort of mantra, repeating it every few minutes. Each time she said it, she believed it a little bit less. Yet she kept repeating it to herself. As the sun went down and she relit the fire, the mantra became a lullaby she sang to herself as she went to sleep. It was the first night she had been truly alone since waking up nearly a month ago. Even the nights Uaithiel had gone scouting, she knew the angel was just overhead. But tonight, it was different, she didn't know where they were - or if they were coming back. As sleep washed over her, she thought of her brother.

"I won't abandon him."

Terry awoke with the rising sun. The fire had burned down to embers at some point in the night, but the darkness had left her alone. It had no interest in her, a lone human in the woods. She forced herself to get up and put out the last few embers. Tariq had left her enough food for a couple of small meals, half of which she ate while deciding what to do. Uaithiel had said they would be gone one night - it had now been two. She couldn't rely on the angel to come back for her.

"I won't abandon him," she repeated to herself as she stood up and started walking south.

Chapter Thirteen

The darkness swirled around the peak of the mountain, blocking out the light of the sun. No light ever reached here, day or night, not for the last ten thousand years. The evergreens lining the mountainside were dusted with snow and ice, an eternal winter. The blackness stretched for miles around, and where there were once mighty oaks and maples, only stumps remained. The crest of the mountain was barren - no life could exist there, not anymore. Deep inside the mountain, a gaping cavern stretched upwards. Level after level of cold, jagged rock jutting out from the walls.

Clanging echoed through the walls as pickaxes and hammers pounded against the stone, crushing it into dust. The dust that would one day strengthen the army of Umbra. Ever burning candles lined the walls, the shadows cast from the miners near indistinguishable from the Umbra that swirled around them, watching, waiting.

Amatheon looked over the servants of the darkness as they toiled away, never seeing the sun. He admired the carts of Umbra dust as they were rolled past him to the refinery. It pleased him to know how well his plans were going. He was not the general of darkness for nothing. Strolling through the cavern, he moved away from the miners and into a smaller chamber. There was no door for him to close, but privacy wasn't an issue, there weren't any who were stupid enough to try and follow him in there.

He stopped before a large altar at the centre of the room, a single candle burned on the table. Amatheon knelt before the altar and bowed his head. His long, black hair draped over his shoulders, and his wings were cloaked in shadows, concealing them.

"O Lord of the dark abyss, I summon thee. Bless me with your presence, for I am your servant eternal," Amatheon said.

His voice echoed throughout the small chamber. An eerie wind passed over him, the lone candle flame flickering. On the other side of the altar, darkness swirled, so dark it could have been a void in the mountain. A deep, dark voice floated out of the void, speaking an ancient language. Amatheon kept his head bowed as he listened silently.

"No, my master, not yet," he said.

The voice spoke again.

"I will not fail you, my lord," Amatheon bowed his head to the ground before rising as the darkness dissipated.

Standing tall, he squared his shoulders and set his face to a look of pure determination. Turning from the altar, he walked back into the main chamber. The miners and servants scurried by, attempting to avoid the demons glare as he passed them. He halted near a small group of Cambion servants, most swinging axes into the stone. One stood a short distance away, scratching notes into a ledger.

"You, half-breed," Amatheon called.

The Cambion turned to face him and quickly approached, bowing low as he did.

"Erathus, my lord," he said. "At your service."

"How much of the dust have you prepared?" Amatheon asked, his voice cold and distant.

"As of now, we have ten kilograms ready to go, and we will have another two kilograms by the end of the week," Erathus said.

"How long will it take to convert the amount you already have into fully functioning Umbra?"

"We can have three legions ready by tomorrow night, and another two the day after that."

"I want all five by tomorrow night."

"That isn't possible, my lord," Erathus said, voice shaking. "It takes time . . ."

"I didn't ask you if it was possible," Amatheon looked down at the male. "I don't care what needs to be done for this to be ready in time. You will have it done, or you will face the wrath of the darkness. Is that understood?"

"Yes, my lord," Erathus bowed. "I'll see to it personally."

Amatheon watched as he scurried off, shouting orders at those around him to work faster. Amatheon smirked as the clanging and pounding echoing throughout the mountain increased. Turning his head upwards, he willed the shadows concealing his wings to dissipate. Stretching them wide, he rose off the ground with a few powerful flaps and shot straight upwards. None of the servants dared look away from their work as he soared up and up and up. The opening of the mountain was narrow, barely wide enough for him to get through. He tucked his wings in tight as he passed through so as to not scrape them on the jagged rocks.

Rising above the mountain, Amatheon soared through the darkness until he was above it. He looked down, admiring the blackness draped like a blanket over the mountain and surrounding forests. Nothing could pass through unless the darkness willed it. Though he wasn't the darkness itself, he was its trusted general, and he had free rein. The servants inside were a different story. One small corner of him felt a tiny pang of pity for them, never seeing the light, often ripped from their families far too young and sent to the cavern. But he also knew that they should be proud, they had a chance to serve the darkness and live not in hell but in Madeira, a world full of opportunities.

Screams erupted from beneath the blanket of darkness. Shrill screeches pierced the air around him for miles. The Umbra were being born. The ash mined in the darkness of the Contenebris Mountain, refined and infused with the essence of the darkness, gave life to the Umbra. Even more so than the demons and half-breeds that served the darkness, the Umbra were the ultimate warriors. They didn't feel fear or pain, they didn't experience hunger or fatigue. Very little could destroy them. Although the Guardians did have weapons that could fight against them, for now, the Guardians had no memories of their past. Amatheon smiled, remembering how well he had succeeded in his mission.

Light and darkness flashed by, days and nights passing in the blink of an eye as he fought an eternal battle. The angel, Uaithiel, countering his every move with sheer determination. Amatheon's power flashed, sending the angel flying back before they swung around and charged forward, sending a beam of light into his wings. Amatheon faltered for a moment but shook off the pain. This was one battle that he could not afford to lose, for if he did, one way or another, it would cost him his life.

"Where have you hidden them?" Amatheon asked the angel.

"You will never find them," Uaithiel said.

"Don't be so certain of that," he replied. "I will not

stop until I am victorious."

"You will never win!"

They battled on and on as days, months, years passed. Centuries passed, millennia transpired, and their battle was forgotten by time. Amatheon, ever holding his own against the angel, growing weary of their battle, cheated. Summoning the darkness, he blanketed Madeira. Uaithiel watched in horror as the darkness spread across the land, the various citizens horror-stricken as the light faded from their lands. In the south, the darkness recoiled, a surging of light pushing back. Amatheon knew he had found what he was looking for at long last.

He raced the angel back to the mortal realm, knowing his victory was close at hand. The still shining waters of a lake glistened not from the sun above, but from the light within, beneath the surface. Summoning them with his magic, ten perfectly spherical orbs emerged from the water. Amatheon stretched out a hand to grab his victory.

"Arrghhh!" he shouted as Uaithiel ran a sword through his spine.

Whirling on the angel, Amatheon attacked and missed, momentarily blinded by pain. Uaithiel moved between him and the orbs, ready to continue their battle.

"You will not take them," Uaithiel promised.

"Maybe not," Amatheon said. "But maybe it's time for them to wake up."

"No," Uaithiel whispered.

Amatheon raised his hands in front of him, dark lightning striking the angel's wings sending them hurtling down, down, down to the ground below. Turning his attention to the orbs, he again raised his hands, black lightning surging. They struck the light of the orbs and exploded. Both angel and demon were knocked back. An efflux of power pulsed across the land, pushing the darkness back, the sun shining once more.

Uaithiel reached up their hands, a white light racing for the orbs, encircling them. Amatheon summoned the darkness, entwining with the light around the orbs. Locked in a battle for the souls of the Guardians, both angel and demon called upon every last bit of power they possessed. As Uaithiel focussed on protecting the souls, Amatheon struck. Black lightning cracked across the ground, knocking Uaithiel down. The light around the Guardians' souls began to fade, the darkness permeating every inch of them.

"Good luck finding them again," Amatheon taunted as he willed the darkness to disperse. The souls flew out of the darkness, spreading across the lands.

"I will find them again," Uaithiel promised. "And we will defeat you."

"That might be difficult for them to do without their memories," Amatheon said.

The demon pushed off the ground, soaring through the air, leaving the angel alone by the side of the lake, watching as the trails of light from the Guardians' souls faded. Amatheon watched as the angel took off, starting what they both knew would be a very long search.

The shrieks from beneath the cover of darkness around the mountain pulled Amatheon back into the present. He hadn't lost in the battle with that angel, but he hadn't necessarily won either. Who the victor would be was still to be seen. The Guardians needed to be destroyed before they could remember who they were, how powerful they had become. He knew that Uaithiel had found some of them, the angel had inadvertently led him right to the Guardian of lightning. *A man after my own blackened heart,* Amatheon thought.

The Umbra would be ready soon for battle. But there was more that needed to be prepared, and Amatheon had promised that it would be prepared. Steadying his determination, he again dove into the darkness.

Chapter Fourteen

Kalida had never had so much fun in her life as she did picking apples. She ambled her way up the first tree she saw that had the plump, delicious-looking fruits. Her brothers asked her to toss some down, so she dutifully obliged. Pelting her family with apples was just as much fun as she imagined it would be.

"I'm so sorry," Iisha said to Sagira amid dodging incoming fruit.

"Don't worry about it," she replied, catching an apple mid-air and taking a bite.

Before long, the rest of their bags were near bursting with the fruit Kalida had picked. And when she was done, rather than climbing down, she decided to jump down. Sethos scolded her for being so reckless as she landed on the ground. She merely waved him off and took one of the applies Mitesh offered her and began to chomp away.

"Hey," Yukaio said, standing behind Mitesh.

The young boy whirled around to see Yukaio looking down at him, also eating an apple.

"It's Mitesh, right?" he asked.

Mitesh nodded, quickly taking an extra-large bite of his apple, giving him an excuse to not talk for a moment.

"Your brother said you're quite good at climbing trees too," Yukaio said. "I was wondering if you could help me scout from the treetops later."

"Really?" Mitesh asked.

"Sure, why not?"

"I . . . I mean . . . I'm not one of you guys," Mitesh stammered. "You know, a Guardian."

"You don't need to be a Guardian to be special," Yukaio said. "Or strong, or smart . . ."

"Or able to climb trees?" Mitesh said.

"Or to climb trees," Yukaio repeated, smiling.

Mitesh smiled as he turned away, his face as red as the half-eaten apple in his hands.

The group strode through the forest, casually conversing until the sun started to set. As it began to dip behind the trees, Yukaio motioned for Mitesh to join him up the nearest tree. The young twin jumped for the first branch, his fingers falling a few inches short. Yukaio reached out a hand towards the tree and closed his fingers, pulling his hand down slightly. The branch lowered as if being pulled down. Mitesh jumped again, his fingers now wrapped around the branch as Yukaio opened his hand, the branch returning to where it had previously. Mitesh reached down a hand to Yukaio, who jumped and grabbed onto it, letting the boy help haul him up onto the branch.

Mitesh looked at the forest spread out before them from the highest branches of the tree. "Oh, wow."

Yukaio climbed up beside him, placing a hand on his shoulder to steady himself as he stood on the top branch. Mitesh looked up at him, admiring his skills.

"Do you recognize anything?" Mitesh asked.

"No, I don't," Yukaio said, turning to look in every direction. "It all looks the same to me, unfortunately."

"I'm sure we'll find your sister soon," Mitesh said.

"Yes, I'm sure we will, too," Yukaio said.

"So . . . what exactly are we supposed to be looking for up here?" Mitesh asked.

"Anything that could pose a threat or anything that might be beneficial to a campsite," Yukaio said. "Here."

Yukaio reached down to help Mitesh stand up beside him. Mitesh waved his arm, trying to keep his balance. Yukaio kept a firm grip on his shoulder, making sure he wouldn't fall.

"Look over there," Yukaio said, pointing to an area not too far off. "See those fallen logs and the parting in the bushes?"

"Uh-huh," Mitesh said.

"That means that there's probably some kind of large animal that makes a nest near there," Yukaio explained. "And over there, where the trees are really dense? That would be a bad spot to start a fire, the extra foliage would run the risk of a large forest fire starting."

Mitesh listened intently as Yukaio explained how to spot the different types of hazards and how to find a good campsite. After several minutes, they had decided on a site just a bit further down their current path. Making their way down through the tree, the rest of the group waited for them at the bottom.

"It's about time," Sagira said impatiently. "The sun is almost down. We need to get the fire going."

"Just up there," Mitesh said, pointing down the path. "There's a good spot for a fire pit, not too far away."

«««○»»»

The wind howled at the screams emerging from beneath the mountain. Day and night were no different, for the darkness penetrated every moment. Amatheon hovered high above the ground, mighty wings keeping him aloft. He watched below as the dust spread over the barren forest floor began to glimmer. The ash, as black as the abyss itself, shimmered, reflecting the darkness above. Slowly, smoke began to rise as black flames carpeted the ground. The smoke began to take shape, turning to shadow. One after another, the Umbra rose up from the ground and took their places in front of Amatheon.

Nothing grew in these fields. It had once been a lush forest, but the creation of the Umbra sucked all the life from around them. The trees had been cut down, the stumps burned. Anything that remained shrivelled and withered away the first time the dust was spread, as if thousands of years had passed in a matter of moments.

Amatheon grinned as he surveyed the growing force of Umbra. Row after row after row they lined up, his perfect army. In less than a few hours the rest of his forces would rise up, ready to strike. Deep down, he hoped that they would be successful, that they would be able to stop Uaithiel from rallying the Guardians against them. Hiding any doubt, he set his face into a look of pure determination. Raising his arms, the battalions of Umbra before him howled in response. Their war cry sounded for miles as the ground shook.

«««○»»»

The sun had fully set by the time the group made it to the campsite and got started on the fire.

"Anyone have any powers that can make this go any faster?" Tiergan asked, repeatedly striking the flint.

"Sorry, no," Yukaio said.

"I've got air, but it isn't controlled enough to help with the fire, sorry," Sagira said.

"What about you two?" Tiergan asked.

"Honestly, I'm still not sure what our powers are," Iisha said.

"You want me to hunt something, I can shoot it from a hundred feet away, but that's about it," Sethos said.

The whistling of the wind was suddenly accompanied by howling and shrieking. The light of the moon and stars faded a bit as Tiergan tried to work faster. Iisha pulled Kalida and Mitesh in close to her, keeping an arm around each of them. She looked to Sethos, who nocked an arrow, watching for any of the Umbra to appear. Yukaio and Sagira readied their weapons to strike.

"There," Kalida whispered, pointing into some nearby trees. "I saw something in the bushes."

"Umbra?" Yukaio asked.

"I don't think so," she said. "Its eyes were glowing."

"Umbra don't have eyes," Sagira said. "At least, not ones that glow."

Kalida took a small step forward, Iisha's arm still around her shoulders. She shook her head and stepped back into her sister's side.

"It's gone now."

Sethos looked at his young sister as he stepped in front of her, arrow ready in front of him. The leaves rustled again, and Sethos paused. Snapping twigs sounded as leaves fell to the ground. A hearty grunt came from within. As Sethos inched another step, a small figure rolled out of the bush. His plump figure stretched and stood up before Sethos. The Guardian looked down at the creature, barely a foot or two tall.

"What is it?" Tiergan asked.

"I don't know," Yukaio shook his head. "I've never seen anything like him before."

"You could just ask me," it sneered.

"I'm sorry," Sagira said, stepping forward and kneeling down to the creature's level. "I'm Sagira, who are you?"

"Winwer the gnome," he sketched a mocking bow, a wicked grin spreading across his face. "At your service."

Before Sagira could respond, the too-familiar shrieking of the Umbra filled the sky above them. She turned to look up, stepping back to join the rest of the group. The gnome's grin widened, its lips parting to reveal a row of razor-sharp teeth. A second shriek sounded, and Winwer rushed forward, biting Sethos in the ankle.

"Oww," he screamed, kicking his leg up.

Winwer fell to the ground, shaking his head before getting up. Raising an arm, he echoed the shrieks in the sky and ran forwards. The bushes behind him shook as dozens of gnomes tumbled out, falling into line behind Winwer. Sethos let loose an arrow, but as it soared through the air, Winwer froze, suddenly turning to stone. The arrow cracked as it rebounded off the stone's arm and landed on the ground. Winwer's razor-sharp smile came back to life as he stepped over the fallen arrow.

"Please tell me someone else has an idea," Sethos said as he retreated.

Yukaio stepped forward, angling the blade of his glaive towards the ground. One of the gnomes rushed forwards, pausing before reaching the Guardian. Yukaio swung the glaive, hitting the gnome as he too turned to solid stone. The blade bounced off. Turning back to flesh, the gnome snickered.

"Our weapons won't work on them," he said.

"I think I proved that with the arrow," Sethos said.

"Fighting each other isn't going to help," Sagira stood between the two men. "We need a plan."

The earth beneath them shook as a roaring wind passed over. Above them, a wave of darkness rushed past. Countless Umbra moved as one.

"No, we can't give up," Mitesh wormed his way out of his sister's arms and ran forwards. He raised a hand, ready to strike the nearest gnome.

"Stop!" Iisha shouted.

Mitesh froze mid-attack. Iisha reached for him, moving past the rest of their group, also frozen in place. As she reached her little brother, she looked around. For a moment, the world had gone silent, the gnomes had ceased their sneering, and the shrieking of the Umbra had stopped. The silence was chilling. Iisha looked down at the small creatures, none of them were moving, as if they had turned back to stone despite still looking flesh. As she wrapped her arms around her brother and pulled him back, the sounds of the world pierced her ears. Sethos pushed his sister and brother back behind him once more.

"What just happened?" Iisha asked.

"What do you mean?" responded Sagira.

"Everything froze," Iisha said.

"I wish it would freeze," Sethos said as he stepped in front of her.

Iisha narrowed her gaze at her twin; had he not realized what just happened? Or was she the only one who had experienced whatever that was? Sethos was slowly nudging the group further away from the advancing gnomes.

"I don't think fighting is a good idea," Yukaio said.

"Then what do you suggest?" Sethos said.

"We run."

As the group turned, darkness filled the forest around them. Not even an ember sparked in the firepit for them to use. None of them could see what lay in wait in the darkness now the path. Sethos drew an arrow from his quiver - it might not do any good against the gnomes, but he knew they worked against the darkness.

"I'm going to fire down the path," Sethos said. "As soon as I do, run. Follow the path."

"Uh, Sethos?" Kalida said quietly. "Why is your arrow glowing?"

Sethos looked down at the arrow he held nocked in his bow. It emanated a light as pure and bright as the sun. He marvelled at the light as it grew around them. Above them, the Umbra balked, gaps growing in the sheet of darkness. Despite the single light, more and more Umbra circled the forest.

"Get ready to run," Sethos said.

He raised the bow in front of him and released the arrow down the path.

Chapter Fifteen

"The sky keeps getting darker," Tariq said to his brother. "It like the stars are hiding."

"They aren't hiding," Malik said.

He looked up to his older brother as he ran a stone along the blade of his bhuj. The sparks were drowned out by the glowing of the fire pit. Malik was reluctant to stop for the night, he wanted to keep going. They had passed a small village earlier in the day. The people there warned them about the darkness that hunted in the night, not realizing that they already knew all about it. But the villagers had also told the brothers about what lay on the path ahead. A deep ravine cut across the land, too wide to jump, and too steep to climb down and back up on the other side. Not to mention it was too deep to see what was at the bottom. But there were a series of rope bridges that had been constructed at some point, one every few miles. No one could agree on how old the bridges were, some said they were thousands of years old and made by the Gods themselves. But they all did agree that the bridges were still as sturdy as the day they had been built.

Malik had decided that was where they would aim, towards the nearest crossing point. He had wanted to cross over as soon as possible, leave this dreaded forest and everything they experienced behind them. But Tariq was tired, he needed to stop and rest for the night. Malik eventually conceded to his brother and started a fire for them. He watched Tariq, trying to understand his preoccupation with the sky. It was nighttime, of course it was dark, every night was. Malik looked up, the stars blinking distantly. Perhaps they did look a bit dimmer than before.

"You should get some sleep," Malik suggested. "That way, we can head out at first light and hopefully make it across the ravine by midday."

"You seem eager to get across," Tariq said. "What are you expecting to find?"

"It's not what I'm hoping to find," Malik explained. "It's what I'm hoping to leave behind."

Tariq understood what his little brother meant. Even though he had turned down Uaithiel's request, it still hung over him. He knew Malik would never admit it, but even leaving Terry behind had been difficult for him, for both of them. But looking after one person was one thing, to be asked to fight and defend an entire world was something else entirely. While Tariq believed that if it were him, he would have made a different decision, he didn't fault his brother for his choice. It was his decision to make, and whatever the consequences of that decision, he would stand by his brother.

Tariq watched as Malik laid his weapon beside him on the ground and curl up near the fire. He knew it wasn't for the warmth; the night air that kissed their skin was already warm. Tariq lay on the other side of the fire, making sure there were at least a couple of branches nearby to grab and use as torches if they should need them in the night. As sleep began to wash over the brothers, a shrill cry pierced the air.

Malik jumped to his feet, weapon ready as Tariq grabbed the branches that he had prepared only moments before, lighting the ends. He tossed one of the branches to his brother, who caught it in his free hand. Lighting two for himself, he moved to stand back-to-back with his brother. They scanned the forest and the sky for any sign of the Umbra. Malik swore under his breath and nudged his brother in the side, motioning him to look up. Like a blanket being draped over the world, the Umbra raced towards them. The darkness blocked out the fading light of the stars as it descended towards their camp.

"We need to make a run for it," Tariq said. "There's too many of them."

"To where? The ravine?" Malik asked.

"Anywhere that isn't here!"

Malik took off at a brisk pace, his brother mere steps behind him. As they moved, the wave of Umbra shifted direction, following them. Looking over his shoulder, Malik tried to count how many Umbra there were. But wave upon wave blocked out the light, and they became indistinguishable from one another in the darkness. The brothers screeched to a halt as a wall of darkness formed in front of them. One by one, the umbra emerged from the wall of darkness and attacked. Malik and Tariq stuck back, waving their torches to hold back the Umbra.

Jumping in front of his brother, Malik blocked an attack with his bhuj, knocking the Umbra back before destroying it with the flame. Slowly he worked his way through the line of Umbra before him, dodging attacks and striking back. In minutes, the ground was littered with smoking ash. Malik barely dared look away from his opponent for a second to glance back at his brother. Tariq was holding his own, though his strength was fading fast.

A wave of power rippled through the air as a light shot through the Umbra, reducing them to ash. The men turned to see Uaithiel descending from the sky, striking down several Umbra, all fighting against Malik.

"Thank you," Malik said, nodding to the angel.

"This is not a battle you can win," they said.

"What do we do?" Tariq asked from across the field.

"I will do my best to clear a path," Uaithiel urged them. "You must run."

Tariq moved towards his brother, fighting his way through the Umbra as best he could. They watched as Uaithiel prepared to unleash their power. Light blasted through the Umbra as if they were nothing, smoking ash on the ground the only remnants, and a clear path now visible. As Umbra moved to fill the gaps, Uaithiel prepared to strike again. The angel barely heard Tariq scream as a wave of darkness crashed around them. Uaithiel was knocked to the ground as a swarm of Umbra surrounded them, blocking their light.

«««○»»»

Howling and shrieking filled the air as the Umbra regrouped. Several dozen now surrounded the angel, holding them to the ground, while many others attacked the Guardian and his brother. Malik felt as if he had been fighting for hours, arms growing heavy as he continued to slash and block, attack and dodge, jump and strike. He could hear Tariq's grunts as he brandished the flames. Sweat dripped from his brow as he waved his arms around. The precise strikes he had managed earlier now escaped him as he barely dodged another blow from the Umbra. Unable to balance himself quickly enough after dodging, the next blow struck him. Tariq slammed back into a tree, the impact reverberating through him. His fingers strained to remain clasped around the base of the torches.

"We need a miracle," he said quietly, recovering himself.

A scream from in the trees caught his attention. But it wasn't a scream of fear or terror - it was a battle cry. Bushes shook and parted as Terry emerged, her own torches in hand, and surveyed the scene around her. She quickly smiled at Tariq and moved to attack the first of the Umbra before they could fully register that she was there and that she was a threat to them. Her movements as wild as the torch flames, she made her way across the battlefield to Tariq. With a hard blow, she ran the flame through the two Umbra moving on her, turning them to ash with a shriek.

"Are you ok?" she asked Tariq.

"I'm fine," Tariq said. He pushed himself away from the tree behind him, standing beside Terry. The flames cast shadows that danced on her face, a mask of fury and determination.

"Malik?" she asked.

"He's holding his own," Tariq said. "But Uaithiel needs help."

Tariq could have sworn that Terry's expression had turned colder than ice for a moment before she started moving forward. She moved through the Umbra as if it were a dance. Turning and jumping, dodging and striking, Tariq couldn't help but admire her skill. He imagined how she would fight if she had a weapon like Malik's that could take down the Umbra instantly.

Terry reached the cocoon of shadows that encircled the angel. With all of her might, she slashed through the Umbra with the flames. Shrieks and howls filled the air as many dissipated into ash, the rest dispersing back into the battle. Uaithiel stood, their light glowing around them once more. The angel looked down at Terry, their eyes locked with hers. Neither of them blinked, a battle of wills silently taking place.

"Do something," Terry said.

"Go," Uaithiel shouted as they again used their power to clear a path.

Tariq ran past Uaithiel, grabbing Terry's arm as he did, pulling her along with him, breaking the gaze she had held with the angel. Malik followed behind. He hadn't noticed when Terry had shown up, but was glad she did, for his brother's sake. Malik was slower as he continued to fight the Umbra, hoping to buy Tariq and Terry a few more minutes. He looked up at the angel, doing their best to keep the path clear.

"What do we do now?" Terry cried.

She looked down off the precipice as she stood at the edge of a ravine. The gap in the earth ran longer and deeper than she could see, especially in the dim light. She looked back at Tariq, who stood at her side.

"Over there," he said, indicating a rickety rope bridge a hundred feet away. "We can cross there."

Terry silently ran towards the rope bridge. She sized up the contraption before her. Three ropes ran from one side to another in the shape of a vee. Every few feet, smaller ropes attached the two upper guides to the single rope on the bottom. She would have to hold onto both sides to be able to keep her balance. Looking at the torches in her hands, she got an idea. She flipped one torch, and drew her arm back, preparing to hurtle it through the air like an arrow. The flaming torch fell short of the other side, falling into the ravine, its light quickly fading. Taking the second torch in her hand, Terry again drew back her arm. She summoned all her strength and shot the torch into the air. Spiralling through the air, it made it to the other side, piercing the ground, and standing as a beacon to summon her over.

Tariq indicated for her to cross first. She had no time to let her fear get the best of her. This wasn't like the river, she couldn't take her time. Here they were counting on her to get across as quickly as possible. Tariq looked back at his brother as Terry began her crossing.

"Malik!" he shouted.

"I'm coming," he called back. "Go!"

Tariq turned to follow Terry onto the bridge. It trembled with the weight of both of them. Their legs shook, nearly buckling as they made their way across. Terry set her face in determination as she lifted one foot in front of the other. The rope was slick in the warm night air, and more than once she lost her footing, gripping the guide ropes for dear life. Eventually, she made her way to the other side and pulled herself onto the solid land. She ran to grab the torch and turned to watch as Tariq also finished making the crossing.

"Malik!" Tariq shouted.

His brother turned at the call, distracting him from the Umbra that attacked. Malik flew through the air, crashing to the ground near the side of the ravine. Rolling on the ground, he stopped himself a few feet away from the edge of the precipice. He looked up in horror at the scene that unveiled before him. Tariq's call had attracted the Umbra, now realizing they were alone and near unprotected, only one torch between the two of them. Neither of Tariq's throws had been enough to clear the gap.

Umbra swarmed around Tariq, tossing him to the ground. Terry waved her torch, destroying one of the Umbra. Before the ashes had even hit the ground, two more were there to take its place. Despite her strength, she wasn't fast enough to stop the attack that came from behind. She gasped as the wind was knocked from her lungs, falling to her knees. The torch rolled away from her hand. As she moved to reach for it, another Umbra appeared before her, striking a blow to her chest, sending her flying. She landed against a tree, her head thudding against the trunk. Terry didn't hear Tariq screaming her name as she fell to the ground, unconscious.

The Umbra turned on Tariq. He looked to the torch - his only hope to defeat them. He dove for it, rolling close to the edge of the bridge. His fingers brushed the edge of the branch as a strike from the Umbra knocked him off balance. His hand slid across the ground, knocking the torch further away from him. Tariq watched as it rolled off the edge of the earth and fell into oblivion.

"Uaithiel!" Malik shouted. "Help him."

Tariq rose to his feet as he eyed the Umbra circling him. Malik's shouts were as distant as the fallen torches. From the corner of his eye, he saw Malik struggling to get to his feet, pushing the Umbra out of the way as he tried to make it to the bridge. As Malik neared the edge, a dagger flew through the air. It skimmed along the edge of the Umbra before implanting in the side of the rockface, severing the main walking rope at one end. The ropes groaned as the weight increased on the guide ropes, pulling on their holds. Malik looked at the rope in horror as it dangled in mid-air.

Tariq screamed as an Umbra knocked the wind

out of him. Doubled over, clutching his stomach, Tariq struggled to catch his breath. A shadowed hand reached for his throat, lifting him off the ground. His fingers clawed at the shadow, but it was like trying to catch mist. Gasping, he kicked his feet, hoping to hit something, anything solid. But it was to no avail.

"Tariq!" Malik screamed. A light hand appeared and held him back as he lunged for one of the ropes. Malik squirmed in Uaithiel's grip, trying to get free, trying to get to his brother.

The shallow gasps from Tariq's throat stopped, and silence filled the air. His hands fell to his side, limp, as his feet stopped kicking. Malik froze, looking at his brother's dark eyes, the life wholly gone. He could have sworn that he heard the Umbra laugh as it tossed his brother's body to the ground, his limbs sprawled around him, unmoving.

Then Malik exploded.

Chapter Sixteen

Sagira rested against a tree, bent over her knees, her breath panting. Somehow, they had escaped. Outrunning the gnomes had been easier than they expected. With their short stubby legs, they weren't very fast, and it seemed to her that the only magic they had was their ability to turn into stone for a few seconds at a time. If they had tried to stay and fight, it would have been near impossible – running was the right decision. But the sheet of Umbra overhead had given them pause, literally. The group had let Sethos shoot his glowing arrows ahead while they stayed behind, hidden in bushes. The Umbra had passed by them.

The group hadn't questioned their luck while running, and certainly not now as they paused to catch their breath. Between the gaps in the trees, they could see the swelling darkness in the near distance. Yukaio stared at the darkness, silent and unmoving.

"What is it?" Mitesh asked.

"I'm just wondering what's drawing their attention," Yukaio said, not taking his eyes from where they stared.

Sethos gasped for air. "You're really going to question our luck?"

As if in answer, the sky boomed with thunder as bursts of lightning erupted from the clouds. The group stared in awe at the growing storm. There hadn't been any signs of rain in days. Even if there had been, what befell before them was no ordinary storm. Dozens upon dozens of bursts of lightning shot down from the sky over the circling Umbra. Piercing shrieks filled the air, as if signing against the thunderous booming.

"We should find out what that is," Sagira said. "It might be your sister."

"My sister doesn't have any powers like that," Yukaio said, shaking his head.

"No, but you said she's with an angel. Maybe Uaithiel has those kinds of powers," Sagira suggested.

Yukaio looked at her, eyes wide. His fingers tightened around his glaive as he looked at the rest of the group.

"No," said Sethos flatly.

"What?"

"We have no idea what is going on over there, other than there are a lot of Umbra," Sethos explained. "I'm not taking Mitesh and Kalida anywhere near that."

"We can handle ourselves," Mitesh said. His twin nodded beside him.

"No," Sethos repeated.

"Then we'll stay here," Tiergan said. The group turned to him. "I'll stay here with the twins, I'll watch them while the rest of you go."

"Are you sure, Tiergan?" Sagira asked.

"Yes," he nodded. "If there's a chance that Yukaio's sister is there, you have to do it. If it were you looking for me, Sagira, I know you would do it in a heartbeat."

"Thank you," Yukaio said.

"We'll be fine here," Kalida told her older siblings.

Reluctantly Sethos agreed as he and Iisha joined the other Guardians. Tiergan sat down beside the tree near the young twins and motioned for them to join him. He smiled at Sagira as she turned to walk with the others.

"Wait," Tiergan whispered as he felt Mitesh squirming beside him.

"For what?" he asked.

"Just wait. Not yet."

"We're not going to just stay here, are we?" Kalida asked.

"Not a chance."

«««○»»»

The four Guardians approached the storm still raging against the darkness. As they moved closer, they could see the individual Umbra. Scurrying about, attempting to dodge the lightning, many being struck and immediately cut down. Ashes floated in the air, covering the whole scene in a dusty haze. They raised their weapons as the Umbra marked their presence. Fighting through the darkness, the flashes of lightning briefly illuminating the scene around them, Yukaio spotted a figure on the ground. He worked his way through the battlefield.

"Terry!" he screamed.

Yukaio ran towards his sister lying on the ground, still and silent. The lightning struck around him as he ran, completely ignoring everything except the sight of his sister. He tossed his glaive aside as he wrapped his arms around her, pulling her into his lap as he knelt on the grass. Placing his fingers in front of her face, he held his own breath until he could feel hers against the tips of his fingers. Letting out a sigh of relief, he hugged her close to his chest. The motion caused her to stir. Blinking rapidly, she opened her eyes and saw her brother's face staring down at her.

Terry's arms sprang up around his shoulders, hugging him. "Yukaio," she said. "You're ok."

"So are you."

Across the field, the twins moved through the darkness, trying to find the center of the storm. Sagira lingered behind them, covering any attacks coming at them from behind. Her axe found its mark each time she struck, taking down one Umbra after another. The twins paused when they saw him - a man glowing in yellow light, a permanent thunderbolt emanating from him. Between them lay a deep precipice with no way across, remnants of what appeared to have been a rope bridge dangled off the edges of the rock face. Above the man hovered a being of pure light. Sagira turned as the light drifted towards them. Though she had never seen the angel herself, from the way Yukaio had described them, there was no doubt in her mind that this was Uaithiel.

"Guardians," the angel said, landing before them. "How . . ."

Uaithiel's voice trailed off as they noticed Yukaio in the distance, clinging to his sister.

"Thank you for coming, I assume that if you're here together, then Yukaio has explained at least the basics of what you are," said Uaithiel. "We need to end this battle. Now."

"Looks like he's doing a pretty good job of that already," Sethos indicated towards the man in the lightning.

"Malik's strength is waning," they explained. "We need the sun."

"How?" Iisha asked.

"Have you discovered what your powers are yet?" Uaithiel asked, to which both twins shook their heads. "That will make this slightly more difficult, but not impossible."

"What do we do?" Iisha asked.

"Sagira, we need you to keep the Umbra occupied for a moment," Uaithiel explained. "Please, I need you all to trust me."

Sagira nodded and turned away from the others, preparing to distract any Umbra that got too close. Uaithiel turned to the twins once more.

"Iisha, you are blessed by the Goddess of time," Uaithiel explained. "Ironically, I will be able to explain better when we have more time. And Sethos, you are blessed by the God of light. What we need to do will require almost all the strength that you have, this will drain you and push you to your limits."

"No easing into this then, eh?" Sethos asked.

"I'm afraid not," Uaithiel said.

The angel set about quickly explaining how to tap into their powers, draw them out. Iisha would need to reach out far beyond herself, to the world around her, and help the sun rise faster. Sethos, once his sister drew out the sun, would enhance it. He would become like the sun itself, radiating the light from his very soul. Uaithiel backed away from the twins, lightning continuing to crash around them.

Iisha closed her eyes and reached out her hands. She could feel it - time itself. It was like a series of woven threads interconnecting everything around her. With her mind, her soul, she pulled on the threads. Using all her strength, she pulled until she felt them give, and the first rays of the morning sun peaked over the mountain hours before it should have. Sethos watched the sun emerge, raising his hands to it. The light from the sun pulsed, beaming not only from the glowing orb in the sky but from himself as well. The remaining Umbra fell to ash, completely coating the ground around them. The grass suffocated beneath the smoking layer above it.

"Malik," Uaithiel said, floating over to the other Guardian.

At the sound of the angel's voice, Malik lowered his hands, fingertips still sparking with electricity. He looked up at Uaithiel, dried tears marring his face, his eyes filled with rage. The sun's light bounced off his yellow-green eyes, setting them ablaze.

"Tariq," his voice was barely a hoarse whisper, his throat sore from screaming.

"I'm so sorry," Uaithiel said.

Malik fell to his knees, new tears flowing from his eyes as he punched the ground, black dust flying in all directions. His breath quickened, his chest rising and falling as he sucked in a deep breath and let out a scream. The cry sounded through the air, calling for a brother that was no longer there. Malik didn't even look up as Uaithiel took off.

The rest of the Guardians gathered at the edge of the ravine, watching Malik's sorrow. Iisha was slumped on the ground, her breath catching in heavy clumps in her chest. Sethos knelt beside her, also panting, as he rested a hand on her shoulder.

Tiergan and the twins had shown up near the end of the battle just as the sun rose. The younger twins silently watched their siblings, awe-stricken. Tiergan assessed his sister's wounds. She had a few bruises up her arm and a small cut on her hand from where it had scraped against a tree. Though she knew she was fine, she let him fuss over her.

Terry clung to her brother, trying not to scream. She had seen Tariq's body when she stood up and had immediately run for him, trying to shake him awake. Yukaio pulled her away and held her close. Uaithiel landed beside Yukaio and looked down at the young Guardian. Terry saw them land out of the corner of her eye and quickly looked away. Tears streamed between her closed eyes, soaking her brother's shirt.

"Yukaio, I need you to use your powers now, to reform the bridge that was destroyed," Uaithiel said.

"How?" he asked, looking at the frayed ropes.

"What about roots?" Sagira said quietly in his ear.

Yukaio looked up at the angel who nodded in confirmation. Hugging his sister tight once more before passing her into Sagira's waiting arms, he stepped up to the edge. The earth began to rumble as tree roots began to rise up from the ground. Weaving and tanging as they stretched across the ravine, they braided themselves around each other before securing themselves firmly on the other side.

Malik looked up from where he knelt on the ground. The first sight he saw was Terry, pushing away from Sagira, waiting for him at the end of the newly formed bridge. Standing at the edge of the bridge, Malik put one tentative foot on it. When it held firm, he practically ran across, past the gathered group and once more collapsed to his knees beside his brother's body.

He placed a hand over Tariq's eyes, closing them gently. Malik brushed his brother's hair out of his face and straightened his shirt. Beneath the collar, he could see black marks scaring his neck as if the shadow that choked the life out of him had branded him as well. A soft hand squeezed Malik's shoulder as tears fell to the ground beside him. Terry knelt down beside her friend and placed her other hand on Tariq's still chest.

"I'm so sorry," she said. "I wasn't able to help him."

"I wasn't able to help either of you," Malik looked at Terry. A bruise was starting to form on the side of her temple, no doubt from her fight with the Umbra. She placed a hand on his shoulder.

"I don't think he would blame you," she said.

"He should," Malik said. "It's my fault."

"He loved you more than anything."

"I know. But I failed him."

Chapter Seventeen

Iisha stared at the sun in the sky as she sat on the grass. Uaithiel knelt beside her.

"So, what now?" Iisha asked. "I mean about the day. I sped it up, so what happens now?"

"It continues as normal," the angel said. "The power that you exhibited this morning was extraordinary. All of you were."

"But how does it work?" Iisha asked. "The passing time has changed."

"It's quite complicated, but I will try to explain," Uaithiel said.

They reached down to scoop up some of the dust into a pile. Then, waving a finger through it, they drew a stick figure and a large circle around it.

"That's you, and that bubble is your power," they started. "You expanded it from beyond yourself to the rest of the battlefield, holding it still as your sped up everything outside of that bubble. The beings outside of it would have experienced time as normal, even though for the rest of you hours passed in seconds."

"So, did I actually speed up time then, or did I slow it down?" she asked.

"That is indeed the question," Uaithiel said, standing up. "It's all a matter of perception."

Iisha watched the angel walk away as she contemplated the well of power that resided within her. She thought back to the previous night, it seemed so long ago, and the gnomes. When Mitesh was in danger, she panicked. In that panic she had frozen time, she now realized. She looked at her twin, now talking to the angel. Her twin's power, light, she realized was just as strong. It had come to them when they needed it to light their way. And he had again called upon it to save them today. She didn't know how her brother wasn't completely exhausted after everything that had happened.

"The other Guardians," Iisha said, calling after the angel. "Are they just as powerful?"

"Oh yes," Uaithiel said. "All of your powers were gifted by the Gods. That is why it is imperative that we find them sooner rather than later."

Sethos watched as the angel spoke to his sister. He could tell how exhausted she was, he was as well. But some part of him inside knew that he had to appear to be ok. He glanced over at Yukaio and Terry, her head resting in her brother's lap as she slept. He could still see the trails left by the tears as they rolled down her face. Yukaio laid a gentle hand on his sister's shoulder, comforting her as best he could. Malik knelt by his brother, his head bowed in sorrow. Sethos could only imagine what he was feeling. He looked at his younger siblings, once again up a tree, and wondered what he would do if he ever lost one of them. It was unimaginable in his mind.

The campsite was silent, too silent for Sethos to feel comfortable. He walked over to his twin and sat down beside her. She smiled at his approach and leaned her head on his shoulder as he wrapped an arm around her side.

"I've been thinking," he said in a low voice. "Maybe this isn't such a good idea after all."

"What isn't a good idea?"

"This, being Guardians. It's too dangerous."

"We knew that when we agreed to help Yukaio and Sagira."

"I don't mean for us," he looked at his sister. "What if Mitesh or Kalida get caught up in all of this? What if they get hurt, or worse, end up like Tariq?"

"I would be lying if I said I wasn't thinking the same thing," Iisha admitted. "But they were the ones that urged us to agree."

"That was before any of us saw battle," Sethos said. "We need to think about our own family first."

"Do you honestly think the twins will let us walk away?" Iisha asked. "They've become quite close with the others, especially Mitesh."

"It would be for their own good."

Iisha raised her eyebrows at her brother. He chuckled and shook his head to get the hair out of his face as he turned back to her.

"Ok, maybe that wouldn't go over too well," he said. "But we are older than them, what we say goes."

"Oh yes, because that works so well with them," Iisha said, her words laden with sarcasm.

Iisha looked up as footsteps approached. Mitesh and Kalida plopped down beside the older twins, offering their siblings some food.

"What are we talking about?" she asked.

Iisha and Sethos looked at each other, both taking large bites of food to delay answering. Eventually, Sethos swallowed his food and answered.

"Actually, we were thinking about possibly leaving," he said.

"What? Why?" Mitesh exclaimed.

"This is too dangerous, especially for the two of you," Sethos said.

"And you agree with this too, Iisha?" Mitesh asked.

"I've been considering it," she said. "But I'm not sure."

"We should stay," Kalida said. "It's your duty."

"Our duty is to keep the two of you safe," Sethos said.

"And staying in a large group would be better than being on our own," Mitesh said. "We can all look after each other."

"If we lost either of you, it would be devastating," Sethos said.

"That's probably how Malik is feeling now," Kalida said, looking over at him. "He's just lost his brother. We can't abandon him now."

"We don't even know him," Sethos argued.

"But that doesn't mean that we shouldn't help him," Kalida said. "We can do a greater amount of good if we stay together than if we split apart."

"We should stay," Mitesh agreed.

Sethos looked between the young twins. "When did you two grow up so much?"

Mitesh shrugged. "I don't know, maybe when Iisha sped up time?"

Iisha couldn't resist a smile.

"I guess we're staying then?" Sethos asked, looking at his own twin.

"Maybe you should go help Malik," she said. "I know everyone is exhausted, but we should probably move on from here."

Sethos nodded. Iisha was right, as usual. Everyone was exhausted, but there was still so much to be done before they could leave this place. Sethos rose to his feet and walked over to Malik.

"We should bury him," Sethos said gently. Malik turned to face him, glaring.

"I'm not ready," he said.

"I know, but we need to keep moving," Sethos said. "Let us help you."

"It's my fault," Malik said quietly.

"What is?" Sethos said.

"This, all of this," Malik explained. "I told Uaithiel I didn't want to be a part of the team, I thought Tariq and I were better off on our own."

"I understand how you feel."

"But now, I'm all alone."

"No, you're not alone."

Malik looked up at him.

Sethos held out a hand. "Let us help you."

Malik reached out, grasping his hand as he nodded.

Sethos rose and returned to the rest of the group, organizing them. Yukaio shifted the earth beneath them, creating a grave for Tariq, while the others wrapped the body in a sheet. Malik was still as he watched everyone work. Words failed him, and so he stayed silent as they gathered around the grave.

"Do you want to say anything?" Sagira asked.

"Tariq . . ." Malik said as he stepped forwards. "He . . . He was . . ."

Malik shook his head. He had so much to say about his brother, but he couldn't find the words for any of it. They must have had an entire life together, but only the last few weeks were in his mind. Guilt washed over him.

"Do you mind if I say something?" Terry asked.

Malik looked at her and nodded. Out of everyone there, other than Uaithiel, Terry was the only one who had known his brother.

"I only knew Tariq briefly," she started. "But he was a good person. He saved me from a forest fire, helped me cross a river, and was a good friend. He was strong and fiercely loyal, he fought until the end. He's gone, but we won't forget him."

"Thank you," Malik said quietly.

Sagira summoned the wind around them and

gently lifted Tariq's body before lowering it into the grave. Dirt filled in the rest of the hole around him. Malik watched as his brother's body disappeared from sight.

"What Sethos said earlier is true, Malik," Uaithiel said. "You are not alone. Although you have lost a brother, you are still a Guardian. I know none of you are able to remember yet, but you have been like family to each other throughout the war."

"I hope we can be one again," Sagira said.

"I hope so as well," Uaithiel said. "But first, we must find the rest of the Guardians. There are still five of them out there in the world."

"Where do we start?" asked Iisha.

"First, you all need to train, to be able to trust each other in battle," Uaithiel said. "It will come with practice and hard work. But you also need a leader."

"Isn't that your role?" Yukaio asked. Terry tensed at his side, avoiding eye contact with the angel.

"No, Yukaio, it isn't," the angel explained. "My role is a protectorate - a watcher of the Guardians. It is my job to look after you, train you, make sure you are able to fight this war. But my role is not to lead you."

"Then whose role is it?" Yukaio asked.

"For now, Malik, it is your role."

"What?" Malik said, suddenly looking up. He glanced at the rest of the group, all eyes were on him.

"The hierarchy of the Guardians was determined by the Gods long before any of you were even born," Uaithiel said. "In the absence of the group's true leader, Kai, the role will fall to you, Malik. Will you accept it?"

Malik looked from the angel down to the earth, where soft dirt raised above the ground. *What would Tariq do?* Malik wondered. His brother was strong, his brother would have been a good leader for this group. But his brother was gone, he reminded himself. Perhaps doing this would honour his memory. Turning, he walked away from the group.

He would start being a leader tomorrow.

Chapter Eighteen

Malik felt every rock and twig dig into his back as he lay on the ground. Tears still streamed down his cheeks as they puddled on the ground beside him. Though every other breath caught in his throat, he didn't bother to try and steady them. Looking across the campfire, he stared at the empty space where his brother should have been. He could have been if only . . .

Malik shook his head. It was his fault, and it didn't matter what anyone else said. He had been the one to make the decision to go off alone with Tariq. Even if his brother had agreed, it didn't help to fill the gaping hole left in Malik's chest. Watching him be lowered into the earth had shattered him, and he didn't know how he would recover from it, let alone find a way to lead the other Guardians. With thoughts still swimming in his mind, eventually, sleep washed over him, the tears slowly drying in the night air.

Malik looked around him, through the darkness the world was fluid and misty. *I must be dreaming*, he thought to himself. He took a step through the world, watching as the forest passed by. He recognized the forest, it was the one he had been in the day before. The last day he had spent with his brother.

"Hello, Malik," a sinister voice said from behind. Malik whirled to see a tall, dark, winged figure standing there. His long black hair was tied back, revealing a greyed, chiselled face as cold and unmoving as if it had actually been carved from stone. He clasped his hands in front of him, staring at Malik.

"Who are you?" Malik asked.

"I must admit I'm a bit surprised that Uaithiel hasn't told you about me," he said. "Allow me to introduce myself. I am Amatheon."

Malik backed away a step. Though the angel hadn't used his name, they had warned Malik about the demon now standing in front of him, about the powers that he had and how he commanded the army of Umbra.

"This is only a dream," Malik said. "None of this is real."

"Not quite," Amatheon said. He tilted his head as a mischievous grin spread across his face. "While it's true that you aren't awake, this is very much real."

"How?" Malik asked.

"It's unimportant, but perhaps one day, I will explain it to you," Amatheon said. "For now, there are more important things to discuss."

"I have nothing to discuss with you," Malik spat. "So, fly off or disappear or whatever it is that you do."

"I am very sorry about the loss of your brother," Amatheon said. "In the end, it was quite unnecessary, he needn't have died."

"He died because of you!" Malik shouted, rage building inside of him.

"You don't truly believe that, now do you?" Amatheon said. "I can see your thoughts, you know."

Malik paused. He stared at the demon standing before him. Amatheon stood still as stone as he watched the Guardian shake his head and take a step back. The demon moved forward, keeping the distance between them the same.

"But of course," Amatheon continued. "As your rage is misplaced, so is your guilt."

"What the hell are you talking about?"

"Don't you remember what happened during the battle?" Amatheon asked.

"You killed my brother! Your Umbra murdered him!"

"Your brother was your best friend, wasn't he? Why didn't you save him? Why didn't you go to him, fight with him?"

"I tried," Malik said. He gasped for air as the grief roiled in his chest again. "I tried. I couldn't get to him."

"I think you need to watch it again," Amatheon said.

Malik watched, helpless, as the demon raised his hands and the scene around them shifted. The mist cleared to reveal the ravine where they had previously battled. The grass swayed gently, not yet covered in ash. Malik looked up to see the Umbra from the battle raging all around him. He saw himself fighting, each movement as fluid and as strong as he remembered.

"Watch closely," the demon said as he stood behind Malik.

Malik wanted to scream, and he wanted to cry. He didn't want to watch this, he didn't want to see his brother die again. Once had been enough to shatter him inside. He didn't know what watching it again would do.

"Please, stop," he begged. "Stop this."

"Watch," was all Amatheon said.

Malik tried to pull his eyes away from the scene unfolding in front of him, but whether by his own will or some force of the demon's, he couldn't help but watch. His attention fell to Tariq as he called out for help. Malik watched as his previous self scrambled for the bridge to get across the ravine. But before he reached the bridge, the ropes loosened, falling from the far edge. He looked at the other end of the bridge as a dagger embedded in the rock face where the ropes had been attached. His brothers dying screams filled the air before the *thud* of his body hitting the ground reverberated through Malik.

"I couldn't get to him," Malik fell to the ground. "I couldn't . . ."

"Pay attention," Amatheon said.

The scene reset. Malik looked back at the demon as Tariq's screamed once again filled the air. An ice-cold hand gripped his arm, pulling him back to his feet. He opened his mouth to protest but closed it as the demon indicated for him to turn around and watch. From the corner of his eye, he saw himself from the battle breaking free of the Umbra's grasp and moving towards the bridge. Behind that, a bright light caught his eye. Uaithiel hovered above the battlefield, watching. Only watching and not fighting, even as they held a dagger in their hand. Malik stared as he recognized the weapon.

"No!" he screamed, but to no avail.

Uaithiel raised an arm, aiming the dagger as they threw it. The blade gleamed in the moonlight as it spun through the air with deadly precision. Malik watched as the dagger flew past all the Umbra and cut through the ropes of the bridge before meeting the rocks.

Malik again dropped to his knees as he watched the ropes slacken once more. Looking up, he stared at the angel. Uaithiel hovered there, watching. They didn't spare a look down to the Malik that was still crawling towards the frayed bridge. Their eyes were focused on the Umbra that circled around Tariq, slamming into him, squeezing the life out of him.

"Please, stop," Malik said, turning to Amatheon. "Please don't make me watch this, not again."

"You've seen what you needed to see," Amatheon said.

With a wave of his hands, the scene ended. The Umbra vanished into nothingness. The forest cleared away, and again Malik was alone in the mist-filled world with the demon. Malik stared at the ground, his breath heavy as he tried to comprehend what had just happened.

"So, you see now that your brother's death was not entirely your fault. Nor was it mine," Amatheon said. "That angel has manipulated you."

"What?" Malik looked up at the demon.

"The angel does not have your best interests in heart. They only have their mission and will complete it regardless of who gets hurt or killed along the way. It isn't the first time they have gone too far," the demon said. "I, on the other hand, wouldn't kill someone's brother to force him into a war."

Malik shook his head. Uaithiel had orchestrated his brother's death. It couldn't be possible – Uaithiel was a protector, they had said as much earlier that evening.

"Why?" Malik asked. He looked up at the demon before him. "Why?"

"Perhaps that is something you should ask them," Amatheon said. "And when the angel's answer is unsatisfactory for you, feel free to seek me out again."

Amatheon faded into the mist as the last of his words lingered.

Malik awoke with a start. The first rays of daylight stung his eyes as he rubbed them, still laden with fatigue even as he sat up. He looked around the campsite to find everyone else awake. Sagira, upon noticing he was awake, offered him some food. He ignored her, ignored everything going on around him, the voice of the demon still echoing inside his head. He sprang to his feet, a singular purpose in mind.

"Where is Uaithiel?" he asked.

"I'm over here," the angel said.

Malik turned around. The angel stood near the edge of the clearing, their wings flapping slightly as if they had just landed. The morning sun illuminated their face as their violet eyes sparkled in the light. The angel's wings draped around them, near glowing with the sun.

"You," Malik said, stomping towards the angel. "It was your fault!"

"I'm not sure what you're talking about, Malik," said Uaithiel.

"You know damn well what I'm talking about," Malik said. "You threw that dagger. You threw it on purpose!"

"What are you talking about?" Yukaio asked.

The rest of the group had turned to face Malik as he stared down the angel, the shouting pulled their attention from their morning tasks. Malik huffed as he looked from one to the next.

"When we were fighting at the ravine, Tariq and Terry and I, the bridge snapped," Malik said. "It's because Uaithiel threw a dagger that cut the ropes."

"Malik, you're upset. You must be mistaken," Yukaio said. "Uaithiel is our protector, they wouldn't do that."

"No, they would," Terry stepped up. She walked straight up to the angel and, standing beside Malik, stared them down. "Uaithiel only cares about the Guardians, not the rest of us. We aren't special enough to be important."

"Terry, you're upset, I know, but you have it wrong . . ."

"You abandoned me!" she shouted.

"What?" Yukaio said, looking from the angel to his sister.

"Uaithiel and I travelled for a while to find you, Yukaio," his sister explained. "But the first chance they got, they left me behind. Uaithiel asked Malik and Tariq to stay with me for one night while they scouted ahead. Malik kept his promise, they stayed with me for the night, but even though they departed, Uaithiel never came back. I waited for a day and a half."

"You said you would look after her," Yukaio said.

"I said I would do my best to . . ." the angel started.

"You call abandoning her your best?" Yukaio screamed.

"Of course, it isn't," Terry cut in. "They said as much last night. Their job is to make sure the rest of you are able and willing to fight in this war. Malik," Terry turned to face him, "if Tariq was still here, would you have agreed to lead the Guardians?"

"No," Malik said under his breath. "I didn't want anything to do with this."

"You are all taking this out of context," Uaithiel said. "My actions . . ."

"So, you did do it then?" Sagira stepped forward. "You abandoned Terry, and you stopped Malik from getting to his brother?"

"Yes," Uaithiel said. They looked from one Guardian to the next, each wore a similar expression.

"So why should we trust you then?" Sethos asked.

"Because you don't know the full story, I had no choice in my actions," Uaithiel said.

"Oh, go on then, try and explain," Yukaio said, crossing his arms over his chest.

"This war has been going on since long before any of you were born," Uaithiel started. "Long before there were the Guardians, it was the celestial host that fought the war - my siblings and me. We were the foot soldiers of the Gods, the only thing standing between the darkness and humanity. I took my job seriously, as did the rest of my kind. But my actions . . . at times they were extreme."

"Like killing an innocent person?" Terry said. "Or abandoning someone you swore to protect?"

"Worse," Uaithiel said. "Although I saved many lives, I also made many mistakes. But I don't regret my actions, I can't. When word had reached the council of Gods about what I had done, I was recalled from the war. I was forced to sit and watch my siblings fight and fall while I waited for the Gods to determine my fate. But by then, they had decided to form the Guardians, all of you. They knew that your lives would be difficult and fraught with danger, even before you were called to fight in the war. They knew that you would need someone to watch over you. That job was given to me to be my punishment."

"Some kind of punishment," Malik said sarcastically.

"You don't understand," Uaithiel continued. "When they named me protectorate of the Guardians, it bound my powers. I only have a fraction of what I once did, and what little I have left can only be used to defend Guardians. I am helpless to protect the many other inhabitants of this world. I am forbidden from intervening to save them from the darkness or any other threat. The only ones I can protect are you, the Guardians."

"You might have explained that bit before I left my sister with you," Yukaio said.

"I am sorry, Yukaio," Uaithiel said. "You're right, I should have explained sooner."

"Yes, you should have," Terry turned and walked away, followed by her brother.

One by one, the rest of the group turned and followed Terry and Yukaio back to the campsite until only Malik remained by Uaithiel. He stared at the angel.

"That still doesn't explain why you stopped me from saving my brother," Malik said.

"Part of the conditions of my punishment is to make sure that all of you are able to fight in this war," Uaithiel said. "With your brother around, you wouldn't have agreed to fight. To protect the Guardian of lightning, it was necessary."

Malik silently turned and followed the others away from the angel.

Chapter Nineteen

Amatheon soared through the air, passing through the barrier of darkness around the Contenebris mountain. He landed without a sound before the entrance and strode through. The familiar sounds of the mountains - the clanging of metal against rock, the orders being shouted, and the many, many screams - welcomed him. Holding his head high, he didn't pause or even look down as overseers called for his attention. He strode through the open chamber into the small alcove.

The candle on the altar flickered in an eerie wind as Amatheon knelt before it.

"O lord of darkness, I summon thee. Bless me with your presence, for I am your servant eternal," Amatheon said.

He kept his head bowed as the darkness swirled before him. Amatheon listened as an ancient voice spoke. He sucked in a deep breath, squaring his shoulders.

"No, my lord," he said. "The Guardians still live. But I . . ."

The voice resumed, cutting him off. Amatheon obediently fell silent as he listened to the ancient voice.

"I have infiltrated one of the Guardian's minds," he said quickly as the ancient voice paused. "It will take some time, but I have already begun to sow the seeds of doubt. He and the others are questioning the angel's guidance."

The voice resumed. Amatheon listened, absorbing each word spoken.

"What?" Amatheon said, looking up suddenly.

The darkness seemed to intensify before him. Amatheon wordlessly watched as the darkness swirled and reached for the altar. The flame disappeared in the darkness, sucking out the only light in the room. The demon continued to kneel before the altar, waiting, until the darkness finally drew back, the light of the flame once again emerging. In the low light, Amatheon's gaze was drawn to a small object on the table. A smooth black box sat there, an otherworldly presence emanating from it. The demon reached out and took the box into his hands, an icy coldness seeping into him as he held it close to his chest.

"I understand, my lord," Amatheon said, bowing his head once more, his long black hair falling around his face. "It shall be done."

«‹«○»›»

The Guardians and their sibling sat around a table inside a small cabin. They had spent the past few days in mostly silence as they journeyed. Eventually, they had come across an abandoned cabin. Though small, it had enough room for all of them. They had agreed that they would claim it unless the owners returned and wanted it back. None of them had spoken to Uaithiel in days, and they didn't bother to track if the angel flew after them or not as they journeyed through the forest.

There hadn't been any sign of the Umbra or the demon that commanded them since the night Tariq had died. Despite the calm, they were all still on high alert. Only once they explored every inch of the cabin had they gotten any rest. Finally, having been able to sleep in beds, most of them sharing due to the small space, and get some real rest, they had gathered. The nine of them crowded around the table in what was likely the kitchen, though no food remained.

"I suppose we need to discuss what we're going to do now," Malik started. "Are there any suggestions?"

"Are we going to fight in this war?" Iisha asked.

"It's what we were meant to do," Sagira said as she looked at the others. "Despite everything, I don't think that has changed."

"No, it hasn't," Yukaio agreed. "But how are we going to go about it is what we need to decide."

"We're not trusting that angel," Malik said, his voice firm.

"I agree," Yukaio nodded.

"We need the rest of the Guardians, I think," Sagira said.

"How do we find them?" Sethos asked. "We have no idea who they are or where they could be."

"They . . ." Terry started as everyone turned to her. "They . . . um, Uaithiel would know how to find them."

"Don't say their name," Malik snapped.

"Watch it," Yukaio said.

"Yukaio, don't," Terry said. "I'm sorry, Malik. I don't like it either, but I don't think that there is another way. They can sense the presence of all of the Guardians."

"So, they probably know where we are right now, then?" Sethos asked.

"Most likely," Terry said.

"Wonderful," he replied. "Any way we can change that?"

Terry shook her head. "Not that I know of."

"Terry, you spent the most time with them," said

Sethos. "Did the angel say anything else about the rest of the Guardians?"

"Not really, only that all of you need to be together if you want to have any chance of winning this war," she said. "I hate to say it, but we might need to ask for their help."

"I'm not going anywhere near them," Malik said.

"Neither am I," Yukaio agreed.

"I'll do it," Sagira offered. "I don't want to either, but someone has to get the information."

"Thank you, Sagira," Malik said.

"What should I ask?" she asked.

"We need to know who the rest of the Guardians are, and where to go to find them," Sethos said. "Once we know that, we should be ok on our own."

Malik paused. He had heard those words before, he had spoken those words before. He looked up at Sethos, who returned his stare. Silently Malik reconsidered his opinion. Fighting alone had gotten his brother killed. *You're not alone*, a voice sounded in his mind. The rest of the Guardians had told him that numerous times over the last few days. As he looked at each of them in the eyes, he nodded.

"We can do this," he said. "Together."

«« « ○ » »»

Sagira stood alone in a small clearing. The rest of the Guardians had decided to stay behind. Although her brother had wanted to go with her, she felt it was better to go alone. Reaching up into the air around her, she called upon the wind. The treetops blew around, leaves ripped from their branches, falling around her. She tried to feel for the angel, tried to call Uaithiel to her.

"Sagira," a voice said from above eventually.

163

She looked up to see Uaithiel descending towards the ground in front of her. Their wings tucked in close to their side as they stepped forwards.

"I hope that you are all well," they said.

"Tell me about the other Guardians," she said by way of greeting.

"I can take you, all of you, to them," Uaithiel offered.

"No," Sagira shook her head. "Just tell me about them. And where they are."

"As you wish," Uaithiel said, bowing his head. "But I cannot give you exact details. I can sense where Guardians are, but I can't sense which Guardian it is, my abilities are not that specific."

"Anything you can tell us is helpful," Sagira said. "Which one is closest?"

Uaithiel waved a hand in the air, and a map appeared in front of them. They knelt down, placing the map on the ground and unrolling it for Sagira to see. With a second wave of a hand, a small jar of ink appeared beside the map.

"This is where we are now," Uaithiel pointed to the map. They dipped a finger into the ink and made a small mark, and then another slightly west. "There is one Guardian to the west of here. It's the direction you've all been travelling in the last few days, so it isn't much further. That is the closest one."

"Any guesses who it is?" Sagira asked.

"It might be Ciara, or possibly Elbridith," the angel said. "Hopefully, it's the former."

"Why?"

"Let's just say that Elbridith has a rather . . . strong personality," Uaithiel said. "Although, come to think of it, that one in the west might also be Bhurak, although it's less likely."

"So, you really do have no clue then," she said.

"There are two in the east," Uaithiel continued, ignoring her comment. "They're together and have been for some time. If I were to guess, I would say that's Kai and Saora, they're siblings and both Guardians."

Uaithiel reached into the ink and made two small dots on the map right beside each other.

"They've moved around a bit, but they've mostly been in the same area," they said. "It shouldn't be too hard to find them or to convince them to join."

"Kai . . . that's the one you said is the true leader, right?" Sagira asked. Uaithiel nodded in confirmation. "And the last two?"

"They're both in the north, one in the mountains, here," Uaithiel said, drawing another mark. "That one is most likely Bhurak. Those mountains can get quite cold, especially at night. You will need to take precautions there."

"Is Bhurak's power to do with the cold?"

"It's ice."

"Makes sense," she said. "And the last one?"

"A bit further north, not too far from the other one," Uaithiel drew one final mark on the map. "They're just outside the mountain range, so it doesn't get as cold in that region, but it is quite close to the Contenebris mountain. You will need to be cautious there."

"What's that?"

"The demon's base of power," Uaithiel said. "You must avoid it at all costs. The darkness there is pervasive, nothing can grow in it, save for evil."

"Thank you," Sagira said, rolling up the map. She stood and turned to go.

"I can help all of you. It is my job after all," Uaithiel said.

"You've already done quite enough, thanks," Sagira said.

She turned and walked away from the angel, ignoring the rest of what they said. Glancing down at the map in her hand, she hoped that she had gotten enough information. She knew the Guardians' names and where to find each of them.

»«»«○»»»

Gathered around the table once more, the Guardians poured over the map. Five small dots, and one larger one indicating their current position, shone in dark ink.

"The one to the east is definitely the closest," Yukaio said.

Sagira had filled in the others on everything Uaithiel had told her. The names of the Guardians, the bits of information about where they were, and the guesses as to who each one was. The group nodded at Yukaio's comment.

"Should we split up?" Sethos asked. "Half of us go west, half go east, and then meet back here?"

"That would make sense," his sister agreed. "It will take a long time to go west and then backtrack and go east."

"We should stay together," Malik said.

"We can always meet up here before heading north for the last two," Sethos said.

"We stay together," Malik said firmly. He stared at Sethos. Though Sethos was older, and taller, Malik didn't back down. The rest of the Guardians had agreed that, for now, at least, they would continue to follow Malik as the leader of their small group.

"Ok," he said.

"When do we head out?" Yukaio asked. "We've had a couple of quiet days; it's been good for everyone."

"Day after tomorrow," Malik said. "Take some time to gather our food stores and supplies. We don't know what we're going to find, we need to be prepared for anything."

The group agreed and dispersed. Malik remained at the table, staring at the map. As he looked at the continent, the weight of his decision bared down on his shoulders. He kept his face as neutral as possible until everyone else was out of the room. There wasn't any space for doubt, not yet. He looked at the two dots in the east - likely Kai and his sister. The true leader of the group. Malik felt it might almost be a relief to be able to pass on the burden of command once they found them.

He rolled up the map and tucked it into a pocket as he set off to prepare for their journey to find the rest of the Guardians.

Part Two

Chapter Twenty

Malik tossed and turned on the hard ground as he tried to fall asleep. Yet as he stared up at the sky above, sleep continued to elude him. He knew that he was safe with the others. They had agreed to stay together and worked out a rotation of who would stand watch while everyone else slept at night. Despite that, he still couldn't sleep. Finally, sitting up, he looked around to see who was on watch.

Iisha sat by the fire, arms wrapped around her knees, pulling them in close to her chest. Even in the dim light of the flickering campfire, he could see how beautiful she was. Her full lips pressed together, her face a mask of concentration as her sparkling eyes darted from one side to the other, looking for any signs of danger. The ground rustled beneath Malik as he stood, causing Iisha to look in his direction.

"I can take over the watch now if you want," he said, sitting beside her.

"I've barely been up an hour," she said. "You haven't slept much, have you?"

"I don't think I slept at all tonight, actually."

Malik rubbed his eyes. He wished he could sleep, but since it was going to be elusive, he figured he should at least make himself useful and let Iisha get some sleep. She watched him, noticing the growing bags under his eyes.

"It isn't just tonight, though, is it?" Iisha said. "You

haven't slept much in a few days. Is everything ok?"

"Not even remotely," he said before realizing that maybe he should have lied and said yes.

"Is there anything I can do to help?"

"No, not really," Malik said. "Look, I'm awake anyway. Why don't you get some sleep? I'll take over the watch."

"I can sit up with you if you want," she offered. "You don't have to be alone."

"Thank you, but at least one of us should get some sleep."

"Alright, but if you need anything, don't hesitate . . ."

"Don't hesitate to wake you," Malik cut her off. "I know."

"Actually, I was going to say, don't hesitate to wake Sethos," Iisha laughed. "His watch is supposed to be next."

Malik forced a smile. He watched as Iisha moved over closer to the fire and take over the spot he had been laying in earlier. She was asleep almost as soon as her head hit the ground. Her breath softened as pleasant dreams washed over her. Malik turned away, surveying the forest for any signs of danger. But the night was quiet, even the wind was silent overhead, barely rustling the leaves as it passed by.

In the darkness, Malik felt alone. Though the rest of the Guardians slept nearby, it didn't change anything. He had felt alone since the day they buried his brother. Tariq was the one person he had been able to talk to about everything. Malik desperately wished his brother was there, especially now. Especially since everything that had happened that now kept him awake at night. While that first night he had seen Amatheon in his dreams had been the most jarring, it wasn't the only time he had seen him. It seemed that every time Malik closed his eyes to sleep, the demon appeared. The nightmare was relentless.

And Malik was exhausted.

But he sat up, staring into the distance. He knew that if he didn't sleep, the demon couldn't reach him. He made excuse after excuse for why he didn't sleep, from not being tired to claiming he had a lot of thinking to do. But the one thing he never said was the truth - that he was haunted by Amatheon. Malik didn't know what it meant that the demon was able to get inside of his mind so easily. None of the others had said anything about seeing him, none of them seemed haunted by a secret. So, he kept it to himself, a secret he wouldn't tell the others, not yet, not until he knew what it meant.

He watched as the moon drifted through the sky, and darkness eventually gave way to light.

«««○»»»

Malik held the map before him, hands shaking with fatigue as he navigated their way through the forest. He tried to steady his hands to keep the others from noticing. Shooting a quick glance over his shoulder, he saw Iisha staring at him. She knew, she had to know. She was awake last night when he got up. He hadn't woken Sethos until the sun was fully up, taking the rest of the night's watch himself.

It had been days since they left the cabin, and though they hadn't encountered any Umbra, the silence left each of them wary. Each had a theory as to why they hadn't seen any Umbra, yet very few put the group at ease. Something was growing in the distance; they could feel it.

The group paused while Malik consulted a local villager about their direction, making sure they were still going the right way. Also, to make sure that they wouldn't come across any surprises.

"We should be getting close," Malik said. "There are some open plains ahead, and beyond that is where . . ."

He paused. Malik didn't want to say the angel's name.

"That's where we should be able to find the Guardian," Iisha finished for him.

Clouds passed overhead as they entered the clearing. The afternoon sun was blocked out as raindrops began to pound the ground around them. *Of course, it rains once we're out of the trees*, Malik thought to himself. He considered suggesting they go back and take cover until the storm passes, but no one else seemed to be bothered by the rain. The young twins were running ahead, splashing in mud pits that formed along the path. Yukaio looked as happy as ever, the rain nourishing some deep part of his soul. He noticed Sethos was the only other one who seemed to be disturbed by the rain.

"Do you think we should take cover?" Malik asked.

"I would be tempted to say yes, but I doubt anyone else would listen," Sethos replied. "Even if you are supposed to be the leader."

"Maybe it's for the best we continue anyway, we don't know how long this storm will last," Malik said.

"I agree," Sethos said. "Can I see the map again?"

Malik passed over the parchment, Sethos unrolled it, using his body to shield it from the rain. He mentally marked where they were and how far the village was.

"At this pace, we should be able to reach it before nightfall," Sethos said.

"We keep going then," Malik said. "And hopefully find some shelter for the night."

Sethos rolled up the map and passed it back to Malik. Above them, thunder clapped through the sky. Silently Malik counted the time between the bursts of lightning and the thunder that followed. The time was decreasing and rapidly.

"The center of the storm is getting closer," he announced. "We need to pick up the pace."

"Can any of you stop it?" Tiergan asked, looking from one to another.

"None of us has control over the rain. Besides, even if we did, using our powers is too taxing," Iisha said.

Kalida jumped in a puddle in Tiergan's path as she smiled. "Don't worry, Tiergan, I don't think you're going to melt."

They had spent the past few days practicing using their abilities in small amounts. Though each of them was gaining more and more control over them, each time they used their power, it was exhausting. Malik had deemed that as important as practice was, conserving their energy was also just as important. If they ended up in another battle, they needed to not only be ready to fight but to have enough energy to be able to do so. Practicing would be done one at a time so that they didn't all tire themselves out at the same time.

As the lightning flashed around them, the group picked up their pace, the edge of the plains were in sight. Smoke rose from a burnt-out fire pit. Behind it, a series of log cabins were scattered across the field. The door of the nearest opened as they approached. A tall man strode out. His dark hair was plastered to the side of his pale face, as rain dripped down from the ends. His hazel eyes surveyed the approaching group. A flash of lightning drew his attention upwards, and the sky around them boomed.

"Come inside, quickly," he said by way of greeting. "It isn't safe to be out here in this storm."

Malik and Sethos exchanged brief glances before ushering everyone else inside.

"Thank you," Sethos said as he entered the cabin.

The man smiled and closed the door behind him. The cabin was mostly one large room, a table and chairs adorned one end, and a pair of small cots the other. Along the far wall, logs smoked in the fireplace, water dripping from the chimney above it.

"I'm sorry it's not very warm," he said. "But at least it's dry."

"We appreciate your hospitality," Sagira said.

"Why were you out in that weather?" he asked, sitting on one of the chairs.

"We're looking for someone," Malik said. "But it's been a long journey, perhaps we can tell the story later."

Sethos glanced at Malik approvingly. He had no desire to tell this stranger anything more than needed at this point. The stranger watched as the group got comfortable, most sitting on the floor near the extinguished fireplace, the last dregs of heat dissipating through the narrow chimney.

"We don't really have anything to pay you back for your hospitality," Sethos said.

"I didn't ask for anything in return," he smiled. "Just glad to be able to help someone. You can call me Seran."

"Sethos," he replied. "This is Malik, and these are our friends."

Seran smiled at each of them in turn and offered them some freshly cooked food. The group eagerly ate the warm food without hesitation, devouring it in minutes. Malik nodded in thanks as he sat beside Sethos to eat. Seran placed the now-empty basket down on the table and returned to his seat to gaze out the window. Malik studied his face. His skin looked pale against the dark storm outside. His eyes stared off into the distance as if watching or waiting for something.

"We shouldn't linger here too long," Malik said quietly. "We need to keep moving."

"I agree, but we should until the storm passes," Sethos said. "Or at least until morning."

"We don't know how long this storm could last," Malik said. "And I'm getting a bad feeling about this."

"Me too," Sethos said, stealing a glance towards their host. "But it's only going to get worse before it gets better. And it's almost nightfall, we did say we needed shelter for the night."

Thunder shook the cabin as blinding lightning flashed through the windows. Kalida grabbed her twin's hand, her eyes frightful at the growing storm. Sethos watched as his brother held Kalida close, reassuring her it was going to be ok. They didn't have much choice to wait until the storm passed, but Sethos couldn't shake the feeling that something wasn't quite right.

"What are you waiting for?" Sagira asked.

"What?" Seran said.

"You look like you're waiting for something," she explained.

"My sister," he responded. "She went out to get more firewood before the storm started, and she hasn't been back yet."

"Maybe she found shelter somewhere," Yukaio suggested. "She might be waiting for the storm to pass, too."

"I hope so," he said as he turned to face the window once more.

Silence fell throughout the cabin as the

Guardian's exhaustion took hold. Without a word, Seran jumped up from his seat by the window and rushed to the door. Rain splattered against the floor as a cloaked figure carrying a small pile of soaked logs rushed in. The door slammed shut as a gust of wind blew around the house. The drenched figure used her free hand to pull back her hood, a puddle forming beneath her as she undid the fastener on her cloak and let it fall to the floor.

"I've been so worried about you, Ciara," Seran said, embracing his sister.

"I told you I would be fine," she replied, looking around the room. "I see we have some company."

"Ciara?" Malik asked.

"Yes?" she replied.

Malik turned to Sethos, silent with shock. Uaithiel hadn't mentioned that Ciara had a brother, but then again, Malik realized, for whatever reason, they didn't care about non-Guardians. Sethos nodded to Malik in encouragement. He stood and strode over to the siblings, still standing in the puddle by the door.

"My name is Malik," he introduced himself, holding out a hand.

"Nice to meet you," she shook his hand.

"Your brother was kind enough to give us refuge from the storm," he said.

"Yes, he's quite good like that," Ciara studied the group gathered in the small living room. "Though I see he didn't keep the fire going for you."

"Too much rain down the chimney," her brother said. "I couldn't keep it going. But perhaps . . ."

His sentence trailed off, the words dying on his tongue as he looked around the room. Nearly everyone was staring at him and his sister. He looked to her, unsure if he should explain. She placed a reassuring hand on his shoulder, and he sighed, grateful that she was there. Ciara stepped past Malik and the rest of the group. She knelt beside the fireplace, rearranging the logs and adding the new ones.

"They're drenched," Mitesh said.

"That's not a problem," Ciara said, smiling at him.

Mitesh watched as she worked. Once she was satisfied that the logs were in place, she placed her hand in the fireplace, her palm low to the ground at the base of the logs. Closing her eyes, she focused her energy. The fire in her veins swept through her until it finally emerged. Flames tickled the ends of her fingers, leaving glowing embers to dance in the fireplace as she withdrew her hand. Mitesh and Kalida, grateful for the warmth, moved closer to the fire.

"Thank you."

"You're welcome," Ciara replied.

She stood and turned to face the rest of the group. The warmth from the now roaring fire spread around them like a blanket. Shivers passed through the group as the cold faded from their bones. Ciara watched for reactions, fear or suspicion, but found none.

"Ok, not that I'm complaining," she started. "But none of you look surprised at what I just did."

"Because we're not," Sethos said.

Heaving himself up from the ground, he turned to face her. Holding out one hand, he closed his fist, and a moment later opened it. A small ball of light now gleamed above his palm. He looked from the light to Ciara as a joyous smile spread across her face.

"I'm not alone," her voice was barely more than a whisper.

"There's quite a few of us, actually," Sethos said.

Ciara looked at him and forced a smile. She

looked over towards the firepit, small flames rippled at her fingertips as she watched the flames dance on the other side of the room.

"Ciara?" her brother said softly.

Ciara shook her head, the flames at her fingers suddenly extinguishing. She nodded towards the others before taking a seat at the table. Pulling a piece of fruit from her pocket, she bit into it, juices running down the side of her mouth.

"Do you know how we got these powers?" Ciara asked after a long moment of silence.

"Well . . ." Sethos started.

"It's a long story," Malik cut in, looking at Sethos with a stern glance. "And a lot to take in. Perhaps you should rest for a bit before we discuss it. We all need some rest."

Ciara silently nodded. She wasn't going to push for information. Taking another mouthful gave her an excuse not to join in with the conversations springing up throughout the room. Her gaze lingered on the young twins sitting by the fire. She watched as Mitesh laughed at something his sister said. He fell to the ground in a fit of giggles, and Ciara couldn't help but smile herself.

"What is it?" Seran said quietly as he took a seat beside his sister.

"Not here," Ciara said, looking around the room once more. "Not now."

Seran furrowed his brows at his sister's reluctance. She gave him a knowing glance, telling him not to ask anymore, at least not there. The siblings watched as their guests began to curl up to sleep for the night. The rain pounded against the roof all night, the sound echoing through Ciara's mind. She listened as the conversations grew silent and faint snoring replaced the sound of voices.

"Now?" Seran asked as quiet as he could, the

pounding rain masking his voice.

"I met someone . . . interesting," Ciara said.

"Do I need to be concerned?" he asked.

"Not yet," she shook her head.

"What else . . ."

The sound of one of the men groaning in his sleep started Seran. He looked to Ciara, who shook her head. This conversation would have to wait until another time, until they were alone again. The siblings bid each other good night before making their way past the Guardians to their cots to sleep. They didn't have any formal sleeping quarters, and even if they did, with the number of guests they had in their home, it likely would have still been crowded. Ciara looked at her brother as they laid down, but he had fallen asleep as soon as his head hit the pillow.

«« « ○ »»»

The morning sun peaked through the rain-drenched trees, shining through the mud-splattered windows. Sethos and Malik sat across the table from Ciara, explaining as much as they could about their powers. They told her about the meamina that is the source of her power as she rotated the red orb between her fingers. She balked at the thoughts of being Gods-blessed with powers but continued to listen obediently. As Sethos got to the part about Uaithiel, he paused.

"What is it?" Ciara asked.

"This part is . . . difficult," Sethos said. He looked at Malik, who braced his arms on the side of the table, a solemn expression on his face, his lips pursed tightly.

"Why?" she asked.

"Each of us encountered, at one point or another,

an angel," he said.

"An angel?" Ciara exclaimed. "They exist?"

"Apparently," Sethos said.

"Unfortunately," Malik grumbled in a low voice.

"Yes," Sethos continued. "But unfortunately, our experiences weren't the best. The angel, Uaithiel, said that they were here to help us navigate our powers and our destiny. But there was a lot that they didn't tell us. Actually, I think they tried to keep the information from us on purpose."

"What happened?"

"They betrayed us," Malik said. "Uaithiel killed my brother."

Ciara's eyes widened in shock. She looked from Malik to Sethos, the latter nodded in confirmation. "I'm sorry," she said.

"Uaithiel abandoned Yukaio's sister and left her on her own, Malik and his brother saved her," Sethos explained. "But then when they were attacked, instead of helping, Uaithiel stopped Malik from getting to his brother, and he . . ."

"He died," Malik said flatly.

"I'm so sorry about your brother," Ciara said.

She stared at her hands folded on the table, fidgeting with her fingers. She didn't know what else to say. They were right about how much information it was to take in at once.

"So, we left them behind," Sethos continued. "We know where we need to go, what we need to do. We can do it without the angel."

"Are you sure?" Ciara asked. "It sounds like there's a lot you still don't know, maybe Uaithiel could fill in some of that information for you. Maybe they could help us get back the rest of our memories."

"No, I don't think so," Sethos shook his head. "If they could do that, they would have helped us with our memories already."

"Unless they want us to forget everything that happened before," Malik said.

"I can't imagine how hard it is to lose your brother," she looked at him sympathetically. "I don't know what I would ever do if I lost Seran. But are you sure going this alone is a good idea?"

"We found you without Uaithiel, didn't we?" Sethos asked.

"It was quite by accident though, wasn't it?" Ciara said.

Malik shrugged.

"I'm sure we can find the rest of the Guardians too," Sethos continued.

"Finding each other is one thing, but what about fighting?" she asked. "You said that they helped each of you develop your powers."

"We've helped each other develop our powers, and we will continue to do so," Malik said.

His eyes focused on Ciara. There was no light left in them that morning, even the sunlight reflecting through the windows didn't brighten his dark gaze. She nodded in agreement.

"Where to next?"

"East," Sethos said. "There are two more Guardians that way, and last we heard they were together."

"When do we leave?" Ciara asked.

"The sooner, the better."

Chapter Twenty-One

Clouds veiled the moon, covering the land in shadow as Amatheon soared through the air. He flew swiftly and silently above treetops and fields. Tucked under his arm, he held the small box presented to him by the darkness. Amatheon tightened his grip on it as a gust of wind blew against him. Pounding his wings harder, he flew against the current. The world below was silent during the chilly night. The greens and browns of the earth eventually gave way to a large lake, still and silent, reflecting the crescent of the moon peeking out from behind the clouds.

Amatheon landed softly on the ground and strode to the edge of the lake, holding the box in front of him. Kneeling down near the shoreline, he nestled the box into a soft tuft of grass and opened the lid. Inside, on a soft cushion of deep blue velvet, lay a golden arrowhead. The base of the arrowhead was attached to a small shaft that resembled a twisted golden rope. Gently Amatheon picked up the object, holding the weight in his hands as he stretched out his arms and rose to his feet.

Stepping around the small box, he entered the lake. Water began to swirl around him as his dark robes swayed in the cold water. His wings shuddered as the water soaked through the feathers as if a weight were pulling them down. He didn't balk at the freezing temperature as he continued until the water reached his torso. Raising his arms above his head, the arrow glistened in the moonlight. He looked up as he spoke.

Daughter of the waters, master of the tides
Awaken now from your slumber deep
Find inside where your power resides
What was lost now found is yours to keep

I call upon thee, queen of the seas
Darkest soul from the depths
Once again feel the breeze
Arise and serve, Zeneviva

Amatheon placed the arrow on the water before him, and as he removed his hands, it floated. The wind picked up around him, and the waters began to swirl. He backed away, watching the sight before him. The arrowhead sat atop a growing whirlpool reaching down to the depths of the lake. With a thunderous roar, the lake exploded into a geyser, sending water high into the sky. Amatheon shielded his face with his arms as he peeked out from underneath.

In a moment, the water settled back down to the lake as smooth as if nothing had happened. Above the former whirlpool, a glowing figure hovered. Her taupe skin, with undertones of green hues as dark as algae, reflected on the water. In her hands, she held a long trident, its black staff attached to a solid golden rope that parted into three points. While the outside points were sharp, the middle point ended in a stump. Amatheon watched as the figure floated down, landing on the water. Her feet made barely a ripple as she stood tall and proud in front of the golden arrowhead still floating on the water.

"Why have you summoned me?" she asked.

"Zeneviva, I come on behalf of the darkness, to ask you to join us in concurring this world."

"I recognize your face," she narrowed her gaze at Amatheon as he stood waist-deep in the water. "You failed before 7000 years ago, and many of us were vanquished as a result. Why do you think this time will be different?"

"Because I shall have you at my side," he said. "I brought you a gift if you will accept it and me."

Zeneviva grinned. Amatheon made to move forwards to grab the arrowhead. She held up her palm, and he paused, watching as she then turned her hands with her palms facing upwards. The arrowhead slowly rose before her, rotating, so it pointed upwards. Zeneviva watched as it joined with her trident in a blinding flash of light.

"This is not a gift that is yours to give, it is mine by birthright," she said.

"Then name your price," Amatheon held his arms open wide.

"The one who defied me and stole my throne," Zeneviva said. "I want her head."

"Help us, serve the darkness, and she is yours," Amatheon said, bowing his head.

"Serve?" she growled. The water trembled, sending ripples out across the lake. "I am a daughter of kings and Gods; I bow before no man."

"The darkness is no man," Amatheon said. "It is the force that guides us and the strength that lives inside of us. It is greater than you or I could ever hope to become."

"Speak for yourself, demon," Zeneviva said. "I am the granddaughter of Atlas, great-granddaughter of Poseidon, and heir to the lost realm of Atlantis. I was born of a queen of the seas and a fallen angel. You are nothing compared to me."

"Yes, I've heard that you were sired by Leviathon," Amatheon said. "You possess their powers?"

"Of course, I do, I am of the Nephilim," she grinned. "How dare you think to question me!"

Also grinning, Amatheon bowed before Zeneviva.

«««○»»»

Uaithiel stood at the far end of the lake, watching the interaction between Amatheon and Zeneviva unfold. The angel had been too late to stop the demon from summoning her, and Uaithiel knew that with two of them together, any fight would likely be over before it even began. They stepped forward, pausing as a twig snapped beneath their foot. Uaithiel stood frozen for a minute before breathing a sigh of relief that they continued to go unnoticed. Carefully they moved closer.

They watched as Amatheon exited the lake, shaking the excess water from his wings. He offered a hand to Zeneviva, who ignored him as she walked along the top of the water until she reached dry land. Tentatively she put one foot on the solid ground, making a face at the feel of the dirt between her bare toes, before placing the other foot on the ground as well.

"It has been far too long since I walked on land," she said.

"Of course, you prefer the water," Amatheon said.

"My dominion is over all of the seas and oceans in this realm," Zeneviva said. "This lake is small compared to vast greatness beyond the continent. It has been my prison for far too long now."

"I am only more than happy to take you away

from it, then," Amatheon sketched a bow. "There is no time to waste, the Guardians grow more powerful every day."

"There is time enough," she said. "We needn't rush things, give our forces time to grow. That was how you lost last time - by striking too soon."

"You weren't present at the battle seven thousand years ago; you have no idea what happened."

"No, because the hastiness of your master left me exposed and without support! I will not allow that to happen this time," she stared at Amatheon. "If you want my help, then you will do this my way."

"The darkness . . ."

"The darkness can sod off for all I care."

"How dare you speak that way!"

"I shall speak however I want to, and if you don't like it, well then, you can fight this war all on your own," she grinned. "Is that what you want, demon?"

"The darkness will force you to obey."

"We shall see about that."

"You don't understand," he said. "The chosen host is poised to return."

In the faint light, Uaithiel could see that Amatheon's expression was grim. Zeneviva huffed at the suggestion made by the demon. Amatheon gave a wordless gesture for Zeneviva to follow him. As she began to fall into step behind him, she paused. Closing her eyes for a moment and reopening them, her grin was wider than before.

"What are you doing now?" Amatheon demanded.

"You always were careless," she said.

"What are you talking about?"

"You failed to mention that we had an audience."

Zeneviva turned towards the treeline where Uaithiel stood, frozen. In a swift motion, she whirled her trident around her head and slammed the end of the staff into the ground. Ropes of water from the lake shot towards the angel. Uaithiel made to draw their sword, but the water encircled them before they could move. Wrapping around their arms and legs, the water dragged them forward, across the top of the lake, and held them before Zeneviva.

"And who do we have here?" she asked. Uaithiel pressed their lips tight, refusing to speak.

"Their name is Uaithiel," Amatheon said.

"The protectorate?" Zeneviva said, smiling. "At last, we meet."

"You should kill them now, while you have the chance," Amatheon urged. "Without them, the Guardians will be lost."

"I have a better idea."

With a wave of her trident, the waters shoved Uaithiel to the ground, forcing them to their knees. They looked up with a defiant gaze, refusing to be broken down. Zeneviva walked towards the kneeling angel and paused right in front of them. She placed a hand under their chin and lifted it towards her.

"You are going to help us find the Guardians and destroy them," she said.

"Never," Uaithiel spat.

Zeneviva let go of the angel's face and raised her arms in the air. Behind Uaithiel, an ancient roar sounded. A breath caught in their throat as they recognized that sound. Zeneviva spoke an ancient language, commanding the creature in the water. Uaithiel felt its hot breath down their back.

"Whatever you're planning, it won't work," Uaithiel said. "I will stop you."

"Not if you can't remember any of this," Zeneviva replied.

Lowering her trident, she placed the tip of it

against Uaithiel's chest as she finished speaking the ancient ritual. A wave of nausea came over Uaithiel, and it was only the binds holding them in place that kept them from swaying. The angel blinked rapidly, trying to stay conscious, focusing on the sea queen. As the creature in the lake huffed another breath, and hot, moist air encompassed Uaithiel, their eyes closed, and their head fell forward.

Watching from the side, Amatheon took in the sight of his opponent, weakened and defenceless. He wanted to strike, to kill the angel now, but to do so would mean breaking the newly formed alliance with Zeneviva. Amatheon glanced towards her, watching as she completed her spell.

"Are you sure that it will work?" he asked as she stepped away from the angel.

"Of course, it will work," she said. "Uaithiel will have no memory of this encounter. They will wake up in a few hours, alone, and think that they passed out sometime in the night from exhaustion."

"And how will that help lead us to the Guardians?" the demon demanded.

"The spell I cast will let me track them no matter where in Madeira they go," Zeneviva answered. "Without knowing it, Uaithiel will lead us right to the Guardians when they least expect it."

She raised her arms, and the binds of water released Uaithiel. They slumped to the ground, unconscious. Smirking, Zeneviva turned towards her new ally.

"Come, Amatheon, we have much to prepare."

The two figures disappeared into the night.

Chapter Twenty-Two

Mitesh splashed through a muddy puddle, covering Kalida and Terry with mud from head to toe. The girls tackled him into the ground, the still-wet grass soaking the trio. The sounds of Sethos yelling at them echoed in the clearing as Iisha tried and failed to hold him back. Yukaio and Sagira helped Malik divide up their resources into equal packs.

Ciara watched the mismatched group, surveying her new companions. She smiled slightly as she leaned against the doorframe, Seran grumbling beside her.

"If we're packing up the entire house, it would have been nice to have a bit more notice," Seran said.

"You don't have to come," she said.

"You really think I'd let you leave me behind?" he asked.

"Well, you're clearly upset about having to pack everything, even though I told you we don't need *everything*," Ciara said.

She glared at him as he tried to shove a large bowl into his rucksack. She peered beneath the bowl to see almost every kitchen utensil they had shoved in haphazardly. Ciara shook her head.

"You don't need to bring everything," she repeated.

"The way I understand it, this isn't just a holiday,

Ciara," he stood to face her, tossing the bowl on the ground. "This is going to be a long journey, and who knows what we will face along the way. We need to be prepared."

"Be prepared?" Ciara asked, bending to reach into the sack she pulled out a single item. "An eggbeater? Is this for if we get attacked by giant eggs?"

"You never know when I might want to make a nice breakfast," he swiped the utensil back from his sister.

She raised an eyebrow, and her brother heaved a sigh before throwing it to the ground. The eggbeater clattered in the discarded bowl.

"I know you don't understand most of what is going on, but for now, I need you to trust me," Ciara said quietly, placing a hand on her brothers' shoulder.

"Of course, I trust you, it's the rest of this that I'm not so sure about," he surveyed the group. "I know you're keeping something to yourself."

Ciara leaned back against the doorframe and closed her eyes. She placed a hand in her pocket, curling her fingers around the small red orb, her meamina. Her mind drifted back to the previous day.

The rain drizzled through the treetops. Lightning flashed through the dark clouds above, thunder booming all around. Ciara sat on a log, wetness soaking through to her skin. Her strawberry blonde hair was pasted to the sides of her face with rain, reddish hues glistening as she stared at the small fire before her. Reaching out her arms, she rested her elbows on her knees, holding her hands as close to the fire as she could, she rubbed them together, attempting to steal any last remnants of warmth. It did little to soften the biting cold that nipped at her skin.

She watched as the fire danced before her, rain evaporating in its heat. The smoke sizzled in the air around her. She had meant to only go out quickly to gather more firewood, but now she sat here, alone, burning most of the wood that she meant to take home. She looked up at the sky, her reddish-brown eyes analyzing the storm clouds. It would likely still be hours before it began to clear. As she turned back to the fire, a bright light in the distance caught her attention.

She sprang to her feet and stepped forwards. The light didn't flash like lightning. And it was getting closer to her. She watched the light grow as it neared. Backing up towards the fire, she moved to stand with the flames between her and whatever it was that now approached. The light was near blinding in the darkness of the storm. She placed a hand in front of her eyes to shield them as she squinted, trying to make out what it was.

From the light, she could see a figure, tall and fair, with long white hair. Large, white, feathered wings emerged from either side. It had a soft face that smiled at her.

"What are you?" Ciara asked, her voice rasp from being out in the cold for so long.

"My name is Uaithiel, and I am an angel," they said. "And I have been looking for you for quite some time, Ciara."

"How do you know my name?" she demanded.

"I know a great deal of things about you, Ciara," Uaithiel said. "You don't need to be afraid. Please, have a seat and let me explain."

Ciara looked at the angel standing before her. They returned the look, unblinking. Ciara nodded and sat back down on the log. She looked at the fire which had nearly gone out in the rain. Reaching out a hand, she willed the fire to grow. Her brows furrowed as she focussed, sending all her energy to the tips of her fingers. Flames danced higher and higher, warmth once again reaching out to her.

"You can do a lot more than just that, you know," Uaithiel said. "With practice, of course."

"How?"

"You are one of several Guardians that have been gifted by the Gods," they explained. "Your fire, your magic, is inextricably linked to your soul."

Ciara reached a hand into her pocket and pulled out a small, red orb. She held it out for Uaithiel to see, and they nodded in return. Looking at the orb, she felt something stir inside of her. A warmth emanated from the orb as she held it in her hand. Closing her palm, she put it back in her pocket and shook her head.

"No, I don't believe it," she said.

"And what makes you not believe it?" Uaithiel asked.

"It doesn't make any sense, I . . ."

"Yes?"

"I can't remember anything," Ciara said. "I woke up over a month ago beside my brother in the middle of nowhere, and that's the first thing I can remember."

"I'm afraid that is partly my fault," they said. "It was my job to protect the Guardians, but I failed, and as a result, you all were . . . injured in a way."

"Are these other Guardians missing their memories too?"

"Yes, they are."

"Can you help me get them back?"

"I may be able to guide you through a meditation that can help you restore some of them," Uaithiel said. "But now is not the time for that."

"Why not?"

"Because there is an urgent matter that I need to

discuss with you. Time is of the essence here."

"Would my memories help with this urgent matter?" Ciara asked.

"I don't believe it would make a difference. Besides, the point is moot, we don't have the time to waste," the angel said.

Ciara stared at the angel as she listened to the brief history of the Guardians. Her heart raced in her chest as she comprehended what she heard. Being told that she was a crucial part of a war that she didn't even know was going on . . . It was a lot to accept. She stared at her hands and bounced her leg in anticipation as Uaithiel finished speaking. Shaking her head, she stood up and faced the angel.

"That's a lot to spring on someone at once," she said.

"I'm sorry," Uaithiel said. "But it is important for you to know what is happening because I need your help."

"So, I'm the first one you've found then since we all woke up?" she asked.

"Not exactly," they said. "It's a bit of a complicated situation right now."

"What do you mean?"

"In the past month, I have brought together half of the Guardians, and together they have thwarted several attacks by the forces of darkness," the angel explained.

"So, where are they now?" Ciara asked.

"They chose to part ways with me after a . . . misunderstanding."

"What kind of misunderstanding?" Ciara narrowed her gaze at the angel.

"There is much that you, and they, don't know yet, and don't understand," Uaithiel said. "It is crucial that you understand my role as the protector of the Guardians. It is my gift and my punishment."

"What happened?"

"One of the Guardians, Malik, lost his brother some time ago in battle, and he blames me."

"Was it your fault?" Ciara asked.

"That depends on your perspective."

Ciara stared at the angel.

"I made a decision that I knew would impact not only Malik, but also the rest of the world. If his brother were still here, Malik wouldn't be with the other Guardians - but they need him just as much as he needs them. The world needs all of them."

"So, anyone that stops the Guardians from being together you would kill?"

"I will not harm your brother, I give you my word."

"How do I know I can trust your word? I don't even know you," Ciara said.

"All I can give you is my word that this is the truth," Uaithiel said. "Your role among the Guardians is crucial, and without your help, this mission will surely fail. But despite that, I would not harm your brother to convince you that this is the right thing to do."

"Answer one question for me, and then I'll listen and consider your request," Ciara said.

"Very well," the angel nodded.

"Why you?" she asked.

"What?" Uaithiel said.

"Why were you picked to be the one that we should follow?"

Uaithiel looked away from her. The rain continued to fall all around them. Slowly, they began to tell the story of the war before the Guardians. Uaithiel explained how they fought alongside the other angels but made choices that led them to be punished by the Gods.

"And do the others know this too?" Ciara asked.

"Yes, they know most of that," Uaithiel said. "But there is one thing that they do not know that I didn't tell them."

"And what's that?"

"In addition to being bound to the Guardians, to watch over and protect them, and only them, I also fell from heaven."

"What?"

"My powers are diminished not only because I'm bound to the Guardians, but also because my grace was ripped from me as I was kicked out of heaven," Uaithiel said.

"And when we win this war, will you get it back?" Ciara asked.

"It is punishment for my actions, but no matter what I do, I will never be able to atone for what has been done," Uaithiel shook their head. "I have nothing to gain from this, the Gods made sure of that. They made sure that my reasons for guiding and protecting the Guardians are pure and unselfish. Of course, I'm still struggling with that."

Ciara sat back, pulling her arms in close to her chest. She considered all that she had been told. Looking into the angel's eyes, she debated whether she believed they were telling the truth. Their face was solemn, as if a weight was carried over them. Eventually, Ciara nodded.

"Alright," she said. "What do you need me to do?"

"The Guardians need to be reunited and fast," the angel explained. "Your job will be to lead them on that path, but also to help convince them that they are better off with my guidance."

"Are we, though?"

"Yes, you are," Uaithiel said flatly. "There is much that you all still need to learn about your pasts, your powers, and about each other."

"And this war that we're supposed to be fighting?"

"Yes, that as well," they nodded. "But you mustn't tell the others that you have met me, that it is I that has put you on this mission. They may not trust you otherwise."

"So, I should do what you've done and lie to them?" Ciara raised an eyebrow.

"No, not so much lying as just avoiding certain truths," Uaithiel said. "This path is dangerous and will be full of sacrifice. But you were chosen for a reason, you all were."

"And if I can't do this? If I can't convince them to trust you again?"

"Then the Guardians stand almost no chance of being victorious."

"What do I do?" she asked.

"The rest of the Guardians have made their way to your village, and they are taking shelter with one of the residents there."

"Which one?"

"I wasn't close enough to see exactly, but I believe it's the easternmost cabin."

"Skinny guy? Tall, dark, and handsome?" Ciara said.

"Yes."

"Oh good, that's my brother," Ciara smiled.

"I doubt they know that," Uaithiel said. "Fate is already weaving the threads that tie you all together. Go to them, find a way to let them know that you are a Guardian without revealing this encounter. Trust them."

"What about my brother?" Ciara said.

"You may tell him about this if you wish," Uaithiel said. "I will not ask you to keep secrets from your kin, but you must ensure that none of the others become aware of this."

"I understand," she nodded.

"Once they believe they have convinced you to join them, they will want to move on to find the next Guardians," they continued. "There are two in the east, and two in the north. They will likely head east first before going north. I will meet you near the northern mountains when the time comes. But in the meantime, there is another matter that I must take care of."

"You're leaving?"

"Yes, for a while."

"How will you find us again?"

"You don't need to worry about that, Ciara," Uaithiel said. "My powers are tied to those of the Guardians, I can sense your presence no matter where you are. My ability is not strong enough to determine which presence is which Guardian, unfortunately, but sensing seven or eight of you together will be quite obvious."

"What if I can't do this?" she asked again.

"Why do you doubt yourself?" asked the angel. "Your powers are strong, you are strong."

"I can make and control fire, that's it," Ciara said. "I don't really have any other skills."

"Your gifts will come to you when the time is right," Uaithiel said. "You just need to have faith."

"Faith in what? The Gods?"

"No, much more important than the Gods," they said. "You need to have faith in yourself."

Ciara looked down at her feet as she moved her foot back and forth in the mud. She could feel the heat from the fire reaching out to her as if to remind her of her own strength.

"When you woke up, other than the orb, was there anything there with you?" Uaithiel asked.

"My brother."

"Other than him, too."

"Just this," Ciara reached behind the log and

picked up a solid black mace. The chain clinked as the weight of the ball hung from it.

"That was a gift from the Gods," Uaithiel said. "It will always find its way back to its true owner, no matter what."

"The other day, Seran and I were attacked by those . . . what did you call them, Umbra," she said. "This was the only thing that could fight them off."

"Keep it close, and it will keep you safe on this perilous journey."

Ciara closed her eyes. Opening them, she looked at the face of her brother.

Seran stared at his sister. He lifted a foot and kicked the side of his bag, utensils spilling out onto the ground. Ignoring the clatter, he looked up at her as she returned his stare. He just shrugged.

"You can't say any of that to anyone else," Ciara said.

"But they should know," Seran said.

"They can't, at least not yet."

Ciara looked at the group around them. None of them had heard what she said to her brother. None of them knew that she had met Uaithiel and had her own mission alongside theirs. Bending down, she helped her brother finish packing his sack, making sure they only took the essentials. Throwing a bag over her shoulders, Ciara joined the rest of the Guardians.

"You sure you know where we're going?" she asked.

"Sagira has our map," Sethos said. "She got us here just fine, she'll get us to where we need to go."

"Can I see the map? I know this area a bit better than you do probably," Ciara said.

Sagira pulled the map out of her pocket and unrolled it on top of one of the bags – the ground still too wet to risk laying out flat. Ciara studied the markings that indicated where they were and where the rest of the Guardians most likely were residing. The drawings were crude but easy enough to understand.

"If we can, we should avoid that lake," Ciara pointed to the map. "I've heard bad things about it, there are creatures that dwell there that are quite dangerous."

"Well, if they're anything like the gnomes we encountered a while back, I vote we stay away," Sagira said.

"Gnomes?" Ciara asked.

"Devilish little things with sharp teeth," Sethos said. "And the moment you try to attack them, they turn to stone, so it's basically impossible to hurt them."

"The creatures that I've heard of in the lake aren't like that, fortunately," Ciara explained. "I've heard that they're some type of sprite. They can be mischievous and curse travellers passing by."

"I vote we avoid the area," Iisha said, dragging her younger siblings behind her. Mitesh and Kalida plopped to the ground, mud slushing around them.

"It'll add at least a day to our journey, but it might be worth it," Yukaio said. "Is everyone ready to go?"

Yukaio looked at Mitesh, who gave him a sheepish smile in return. The corner of Yukaio's mouth twitched as he suppressed the urge to smile back. The sight of the young boy with mud dripping from his hair was funny, but he didn't dare risk the wrath of the older twins by encouraging him to play in the mud even more.

Mitesh pawed at his hair, pulling out bits of dirt and grass, wiping it on the ground. It did nothing to help the layer of mud now coating his hands. Rubbing them together only smeared the mud even more, so he wiped his hands on the side of his pants, much to the dismay of Iisha. Yukaio couldn't help laughing this time as he watched her scold Mitesh for being careless.

Sagira marked an X over the lake on the map before rolling it back up and returning it to her pocket. She looked over the pile of supplies they had and did a mental tally. With the growing size of their group, they needed to have enough food and resources. She played the route over in her mind; the first bit was easy, essentially backtracking for a couple days and then continuing further east.

Picking up her bag, Sagira smiled at Ciara, clapping her on the shoulder. Ciara returned the smile before turning back to face her home. Her smile faded as she wondered if it was the last time she would see the small cabin she and her brother had made their home. Seran appeared beside her and took her hand in his, giving it a reassuring squeeze. She nodded at her brother as they turned to follow the rest of the group down the mud-soaked trail.

Chapter Twenty-Three

The darkness loomed all around as a young man walked past a series of stone pillars. The once colourful stonework was now faded and crumbling. He stepped over a large chunk that had fallen from the ceiling, likely years ago, the dust having now settled on it as a permanent coating. The torch in his hand flickered as the dull flame barely illuminated a few feet in front of him. Despite the darkness, his steps were sure as he walked down the path he'd taken many times before. He paused as a rumbling sounded around him. As the earth beneath his feet shook, he looked up to the ceiling. In the distance, cracking and then a loud thud sounded as another piece of the ancient city fell to the ground. Although it shook vigorously, the pillars held firm. He breathed a sigh of relief and continued onwards.

"Saora?" he called out into the darkness.

Footsteps approached from his left, and he turned to find his sister standing there, smiling at him.

"What are you doing over there?" he asked.

"Part of the ceiling came down in the last quake," she said. "I thought it was best to move."

"What about . . ." he started.

"Don't worry, Kai, I got all of our stuff out."

"Thank you, Saora."

She held out a small bag for her brother. He took

it in his free hand and passed her the torch.

"Any idea's where we should settle now?"

Saora pointed off into the distance. "The western section still seems to be the strongest."

"I thought that was south?"

"No, it's west."

"How do you know?" Kai asked.

"It's just a feeling," she shrugged.

Saora gave her brother a grin as she shook her head. Grabbing him by the arm, she began to walk down the corridor leading to the western part of the ancient city.

"Any luck today?" she asked.

"No, just more of the same," he said. "One crumbling pillar after another."

"I was thinking . . ." she started, but paused, looking at her brother.

"What is it?" he said, returning her look.

"I just wonder if it wouldn't be better if we left this place."

Kai stopped walking and turned to his sister, unlinking his arm from hers.

"I know you're comfortable here, I am too, but it's literally falling down around us," Saora continued. "This is the third time in two weeks that we've had to move our campsite because of falling debris. Maybe the city is telling us it's time to go."

"I don't think so," Kai shook his head. "When we were staying above ground, we got attacked by those . . . things, practically every other night. Down here, we haven't been bothered by them, not even once."

"No, we've just had to avoid falling rocks, giant scorpions, and the occasional gargoyle," she crossed her arms.

"I'd take scorpions and gargoyles over those shadows any day or night," Kai said.

Saora rolled her eyes at her brother.

"I miss the sun," she said. "It's cold and dark down here. And I know the darkness makes you feel right at home, but it might be time to face the light."

"Just a few more days, please," Kai said. "Maybe the western part of the city will be safer. We've got enough food for three more days. Once we get low, if we haven't found the answers we're looking for here, we'll leave."

"Promise?"

Kai smiled as they continued walking. "Of course, I promise."

"Oh, you didn't ask if I had found anything today."

"I didn't know you went looking," he admitted.

"Well, not intentionally. But when the ceiling started to come down, and I left, I took the narrow path, the one we were going to look at together," she said. "There wasn't much, the glyphs on the stones were just as faded there as everywhere else, but there was this."

She reached into her bag and pulled out a dusty tome, passing it to her brother. Kai brushed some of the dust off the cover. The leather had been dyed a deep teal that had started to fade over time. He leafed through some of the pages, choking on the dust that filled the air.

"I didn't have a chance to start reading it yet," she said. "But it might have some answers about this place and about us."

"I hope so," Kai said.

Kai threw out an arm in front of his sister as he stopped walking. The faint sound of scuttling claws scraping against the stone began to grow louder. Saora quietly placed the torch on the ground and drew a pair of sais from her belt. The triple points of the weapons gleamed in the firelight as she moved into a defensive stance. Beside her, Kai unsheathed his sword.

"You were saying about preferring scorpions?" Saora grumbled.

Kai didn't respond, there was no point in trying to argue with his sister. He narrowed his eyes, looking around the dark hall, trying to determine where the scorpions were coming from. The sound of their pincers echoed off the walls, filling the air around them.

"There," he whispered, nudging his sister's side.

Saora turned to look where Kai indicated. She envied her brother's ability to see in the dark as the faint glow of the flame wasn't enough for her to see the approaching threat yet. She stepped forward, angling her sais to strike the moment her prey got close enough.

"How many?" she asked.

"I see five, all pretty big," he said.

Kai followed his sister as she moved forwards to the edge of the light. The scraping of claws quickened as they approached, sensing the two people in their territory. A shrieking hiss announced their arrival as the first leapt towards the pair. Kai stepped forwards quickly, swinging his sword in front of him, his hands grasping it tightly to keep from shaking. The blade swiped clean through the first scorpion, both halves falling to the ground, unmoving. Kai didn't have time to wipe the black blood off his blade before the next struck.

Saora, now close enough to see them, stepped out from behind her brother and swung her sai. One of the scorpions jumped back and then lurched forwards, striking with its tail. Saora blocked the attack with one swing of her sai and then skewered it with the other. It shuddered before falling limp. Pulling her weapon out, black blood sprayed her.

She wiped a bit out of her eye just in time to see one of the creatures leap through the air towards her. She tucked down and rolled out of the way, immediately springing back up to her feet to attack. Back to back, she stood with her brother before they both moved to strike.

Kai breathed a sigh as the last of the scorpions around them stopped moving. He listened carefully for anymore, but only silence greeted him. He nodded to Saora to indicate that they were safe now. She bent over one of the gigantic scorpions and suck it with her sai, picking it up.

"You know, if you want to stay down here longer, you could always eat this for nourishment," she held it out towards her brother. The black blood dripped from the creature, coating the area around its hard shell where her sai had pierced it. Kai made a face and backed away.

"That's gross," he said. "And you're gross too, just for even suggesting it."

Saora rolled her eyes as she used her foot to slide the scorpion off the blade. She wiped both of her weapons against the soft material of her pants. The once blue material was now almost entirely black with dust and scorpion blood. Saora watched her brother as he cleaned his sword and re-sheath it at his side.

"Maybe west isn't such a good idea after all," she said.

"It could have been just a fluke," Kai said.

"Since when has that ever been our luck?" she laughed.

Saora picked up the torch and continued down the pathway. The large hall began to narrow into a smaller passageway, before breaking off into two different directions.

"Left, or right?" Kai asked his sister.

"Left," she said.

"Are you sure?"

She turned to walk down the left hallway. "Not even a little bit."

Kai rolled his eyes as he followed his sister. They walked silently as he continued to peruse the tome that Saora had found earlier. He mumbled slightly as he slowly moved his finger along a line of text. He was so immersed in the book that he failed to notice the debris on the ground ahead of him. He let out a scream as his leg collided with a large column that had tipped over. He fell to the ground, the tome flying through the air, landing a few feet away. Saora stared at her brother as he sat on the ground holding his leg, rubbing the spot that he bumped. She shook her head with a sigh and picked up the tome, fixing the pages that had bent as it landed on the ground.

"I think I'll hold onto this until we get to where we're going," she said, placing it back in her bag.

"That definitely wasn't there a minute ago," Kai argued.

"How would you know? You weren't paying attention to anything other than that book," she said. "You're lucky all you hurt was your leg. And probably your ego."

"Well, my ego would be hurt if it was my fault, but it wasn't."

"So that column just rolled into your path then?"

"Yes."

"Then why didn't I trip over it too?"

"I don't know what kind of tricks you get up to," Kai shrugged.

Kai made his way to his feet, hopping a few times before putting pressure on his injured leg. After a few limping steps, he declared that he was fine. Saora rolled her eyes at his dramatics and continued down the hallway. After what Kai swore was an eternity, they came to another hall. The massive columns rose high above them into the darkness. The stones were greyed with age. Saora wiped her hand across one of the walls, clearing thousands of years of dust. Beneath it, marble peaked through. She looked around the hall. There were no glyphs or murals on any of the surfaces, it was all marble. Dark veins ran through the stone, all leading towards the center of the room. A large fountain lay in the center of the hall, while narrow streams of light peaked through the cracks in the ceiling, bathing the fountain in light.

Saora approached the fountain as if drawn to it by some ethereal force. She looked up at the cracks in the ceiling where earth and sun broke through. Though the cracks reached all the way to the earth above the ceiling, the debris that had fallen to the floor was nowhere near as large as what was in the rest of the underground city. Saora knelt down beside the fountain and wiped off small bits of dirt and dust.

Upon a pillar in the center of the fountain sat a marble sculpture of the most magnificent creature that she had ever seen. It resembled a swan but with much larger wings that feathered out around it, as delicate as if they had been carved from moonlight. The creature's long tails flowed around the entirety of the fountain as if wrapping it in stars.

"What is it?" Kai asked his sister as he knelt beside her.

"I don't know," she said. "But it's gorgeous."

"Maybe there's something about it in that tome you found," Kai said.

Saora passed it to him without taking her eyes off the sculpture. The creature was so lifelike she felt it could come alive at any moment and fly away.

"I bet it was even more gorgeous when the fountain worked," she said.

"We could find out," Kai said.

She looked at her brother. He raised his eyebrows and nodded his head towards the fountain. Saora looked back at the fountain and stood up, reaching her hands out towards it. Closing her eyes, she summoned the lifeforce within her, and felt the power flow towards her outstretched hands. As she opened her mind, she watched water appear and swell up before her. The tricking turned into a heavy stream that filled the fountain to the brim. The sounds of rippling water surrounded them as she watched the fountain. Water shot forth from the peak of the pillar, showering the bird before falling back down into the pool. Water droplets landed on the swirling tails and ran down them, clearing away the ages of dust. Saora gasped at the sight. The light reflected off the water, giving the creature the appearance that it was glowing.

"It's called a lumanix," Kai said. "A twin to the phoenix, as one is fire and the other is water. It's just a legend, they aren't actually real."

"That's a shame," Saora said. "I would like to have seen one."

"Its dominion is of the right . . .no, I mean night," Kai said slowly, still perusing the book, his fingers hovering over the lines of text. "They can fly for ear . . . ea . . . years, yeah, years, without resting before diving into the water to be reborn."

"Incredible," Saora said, finally pulling herself away from the statue, the water still caressing the mythical bird. "How did you find that out so fast."

"Luck," Kai shrugged.

"Really?"

"No, it was the pictures. Here."

She turned and leaned back against the edge of

the fountain and took the book from her brother. The drawings on the page, though clearly the same bird, did not do the sculpture justice. While the marble statue behind them was full of life, bathed in magnificence, the picture on the page lacked any reality. Clearly, the artist didn't have the same imagination as the sculptor, Saora thought. Most of the page was taken up by the drawing, and there was little information actually written about the bird. Saora sighed and turned the page, finding description after description of various mythical creatures. Eventually, she came to a picture of the grand hall they had first entered weeks ago.

"Here we go," she said, leaning towards her brother. Kai looked over her shoulder at the page. "This city was built in the year 6289 of the fourth age, and it took almost 200 years for it to be completed."

"What year is it now?" Kai asked.

"No clue," Saora continued to flip through the book.

"The book doesn't say?"

"Yes, Kai, because the book itself is magic and knows what today's date is," Saora rolled her eyes. "That's not how books work."

"I know how books work, Saora."

"Oh, really?"

"Shut up."

Kai nudged his sister in the arm before getting up to continue exploring. He walked past the towering columns, the sound of the trickling water in the fountain growing more and more distant as he went. Reaching the far wall, Kai ran his finger along the marble slabs. They had held up remarkably well despite the condition of the rest of the city.

"There's some smaller chambers over here," Kai called back to his sister as he examined one of the doorways. "I'm going to check them out."

He didn't wait for Saora's response before stepping through into the darkness. It was as if the light of the main hall couldn't permeate the threshold into the smaller chamber. Narrowing his eyes, Kai looked through the gloom. Near the far wall was a pair of altars, each covered with the remnants of cloth. Kai reached out to touch it but pulled his hand back for fear that it would disintegrate completely at his touch. Two large murals covered the wall behind the altars, each was of a crowned, faceless figure, one male and the other female. Behind each figure, multiple silhouettes flanked either side of them, fading back into the distance.

Kai moved from chamber to chamber. But beyond the first one, he found them all empty. Occasionally, he noticed spots on the floor where large furniture once was, but the thick layer of dust indicated that they had been taken away long ago. After what seemed like hours, he returned to the fountain to find Saora still perched against the side of it, reading.

"How can you still be reading that?" Kai asked.

"Unlike you, Kai, I can sit still for longer than five minutes," she said without looking up.

"Well, sorry, I like to keep busy."

"I am busy, I'm learning."

"Anything interesting?"

"Apparently, this place was built as a place of worship for some demi-Gods."

"What's a demi-God?"

"It isn't really clear about that, but apparently they're quite powerful."

"That might explain the altars I found."

"Altars?"

"Yeah, in one of those chambers off to the side,"

Kai pointed towards the far wall. "The first one had a pair of altars and murals of some faceless figures, probably those demi-Gods."

"So, then, we must be in the temple of the acropolis," Saora said.

"Weren't those normally built on hills?" he asked.

"I guess so, but considering this entire city is underground, this does appear to be the closest part to the surface, so I guess that counts as a hill," Saora said.

"Alright then," Kai said. "Anything that might explain why we can't remember anything?"

"No, nothing," Saora started. "And nothing about our powers, either."

"That's too bad," Kai sat down beside his sister. "Wait, you're not just saying that so we can leave, are you?"

"I'll admit this part of the city isn't so bad, it feels . . . right."

"I agree."

As Saora closed the tome, the room began to shake. She covered her eyes as dirt fell from the ceiling. Despite the shaking, the ceiling held firm, only tufts of grass fell around her and her brother.

"Not again," Kai said.

"This feels different," Saora replied.

The sound of a large crack filled the air. The siblings looked up in time to see a large, circular crack form in the ceiling nearby. The deep fissures spidered out from the main point. Kai and Saora watched in horror as the ceiling shattered around them.

Chapter Twenty~Four

Mitesh dragged his feet across the ground as he swung his arms beside him, sighing loudly.

"Will you cut it out, Mitesh?" Sethos pleaded with his younger brother.

"We've been walking forever," he moaned.

Sethos gave Iisha a pleading look. She merely shook her head and walked away.

"It hasn't been that long," Sethos said.

"No, it's definitely been that long," Kalida agreed with her twin. "We've checked three separate villages today alone, can't we stop for a bit?"

"It might be a good idea to update the map," Sagira said. "Malik, what do you think?"

Malik paused as he turned to face the rest of the group. He had led them through the forest for the last week and a half. They had stayed south of the lake as Ciara suggested, adding a couple days to their journey. But after more than a week, they had arrived at where the map was marked. The last three days had been spent searching the area. After visiting over a dozen towns and villages in the area, they still had no leads on the Guardians' locations. No one had thought to ask Uaithiel what they looked like, so they couldn't give a very good description of who they were looking for beyond their names. The last town they had visited that day said the last time anyone had seen either Kai or

Saora was over a couple of weeks ago, and that they had probably moved on.

Tensions were running high as exhaustion took hold. Hearing that they might be further from their goal than they had hoped was crushing, and with their enthusiasm extinguished, everyone felt a bit more irritable. Malik looked over at his friends. He could tell many of them were tired, he was too; bags had permanently formed under his eyes the past few days. They all turned to face him, waiting for his decision. Despite being their friend - and he had become close enough to them to consider them friends - he was also their leader, too. The decision would be up to him on what they would do next.

"Let's make camp, go over the map, and pick up in the morning," Malik said.

His voice was firm despite being unsure if he was making the right call or not. The group breathed a collective sigh as they put down their bags and began to make camp. He watched as everyone moved into their usual roles. Their time together had gotten them into a routine that worked well – everyone had a job to do. But today there was little conversation, Malik noticed, as he gathered rocks to encircle their firepit. Arms full of rocks, he looked up to see Iisha approaching.

"Can I talk to you?" she asked.

"Of course," he nodded.

"You need to sleep tonight," she said. "You think no one notices, but they do."

"I'm fine," he said.

"No, you aren't," Iisha said. "You grow more irritated every day. And the bags under your eyes are starting to make you look a bit like a raccoon. Let someone else take watch tonight, you know we've all been practicing our powers as much as possible."

"It isn't that," Malik said. "I trust all of you, truly."

"Then why won't you go to sleep?"

"Because . . . Because . . ." Malik stammered. He looked up at Iisha, whose soft glance was reassuring. "Every time I close my eyes, I still see . . . him. That demon."

"Oh," Iisha said. "I thought it was just the one dream you had."

"No," Malik admitted. "And they aren't dreams. They're different. I can feel him inside of my mind, and when I sleep, I can hear him, I can't shut him out."

"Is there anything I can do to help?" Iisha asked.

"No, not unless you can somehow shield my mind from him at night," Malik laughed.

"Maybe . . ." Iisha said. "Maybe I can, sort of. I have an idea."

"Really?"

"Meet me later after everyone else goes to sleep, I have something I want to try," she said.

Malik nodded as he placed the rocks around the firepit. Part of him doubted that anything would work, but as exhaustion weighed down his bones, he was willing to give it a try.

«««○»»»

Ciara sat by the crackling fire, arms wrapped around her knees. Each day the weight of her secret grew within her chest. She didn't like lying to the others - no matter what Uaithiel called it, she knew it was definitely lying. Ciara reached out a hand towards the fire, the flames dancing a bit higher, spreading the warmth around her. She looked at Seran, already asleep under a thin blanket. She didn't like lying to him either. Though she had told him most of what the angel had said, there was one part she hadn't.

"You have the power to be able to do this," the angel reassured her as she stepped away from the fire, letting the rain extinguish it for her.

"I just hope you're right," she said.

"You were chosen for a reason, a very special reason," Uaithiel said. "And I am sorry that your fate has to be such, but you should know what lies ahead for you."

Ciara listened as the angel spoke. Her arms slackened at her side as she took in their words, the mace slipped through her fingers and clattered on the ground. She closed her eyes and bowed her head.

"Why me?" she asked quietly.

"Because the Gods know that you are strong enough to do it," they said. "They know that when the time comes, they will be able to trust you."

"How will I know when the time is right?" Ciara asked.

"You will know," was all the angel said before departing.

The sounds of her brother rolling over made Ciara look up. She pulled her knees in a bit closer. Footsteps approached her, and Sagira sat down beside her. Silver bracelets clinked together as she reached out for the fire to warm her hands.

"It's nice having someone who can make a fire," Sagira said.

"Glad I'm useful," Ciara said.

"I didn't mean it that way," Sagira responded. "You know the first night I met Yukaio, I accidentally snuffed out our fire with my powers, and we ended up getting attacked by Umbra because of it."

"Seriously?" Ciara turned to face her.

"Yup," she nodded. "Although it's been a while

since we've seen any Umbra, not that I'm complaining, of course."

"Probably means something bad is coming," Ciara said.

"You're probably right," Sagira agreed, smiling at her. "Are you all right?"

"Sure, why?" Ciara shrugged.

"I know I don't know you very well, but you seem to kind of keep to yourself," Sagira said. "I just want to make sure that everyone is making you feel welcome, especially the guys. They can be a bit . . ."

"Intense?" she finished Sagira's sentence.

"Exactly," Sagira nodded. "Are you ok?"

"It's a lot to take in," Ciara said. "Gods, powers, Guardians, demons, war. I'm still trying to figure out how to make sense of it all."

"Well, if you need anything, don't be afraid to ask," Sagira smiled again. "I'm going to turn in for the night, and you should do the same too. Sethos and Tiergan have first watch tonight."

"Thanks," Ciara said as Sagira laid down by the fire and closed her eyes.

Ciara sat staring at the flames for another hour before the desire for sleep finally washed over her, and she faded into dreams.

«««○»»»

Malik watched as the group settled in for the night. Once he was sure that no one would notice him, he got up and walked into the trees. A moment later, footsteps approached behind him. He turned to find Iisha standing nearby, the moonlight shining on her long, black hair. She raised a hand to push the hair over her shoulder as she motioned for Malik to sit down with her. He watched as she sat down, barely swaying the grass as she got comfortable. Malik awkwardly tried to cross his legs before giving up and just pulling his knees into his chest.

"So, what's this idea that you have?" he asked.

"You said that you can't sleep because as soon as you do, he appears in your mind," Iisha started. "But what if he didn't have time to do it?"

"I don't understand what you mean," Malik said.

"What if you slept for a whole night, but it was actually only a few minutes," she explained. "I've been working on making a time bubble, speeding up time in just a small area. I tested it with some plants a few days ago. There was a flower about to bloom, and I sped up time around it, watched it bloom and eventually die. It should have taken a couple days, but it only took less than an hour."

"So, you want to do this around me? Create a time bubble?"

"Yes, I think it can work."

"But at what cost?" Malik asked. "The amount of energy you need to do that, to create a bubble big enough for a person, it's going to take a lot out of you."

"Well, maybe you'll let me out of taking watch later tonight as reparation," Iisha smiled. "As long as I get a good night's sleep, I'll be fine."

"I don't know, it sounds risky," Malik said.

"For you or for me?" Iisha crossed her arms.

"Both."

"If you're too scared to take the risk, then . . ."

"I'm not scared," Malik said, his voice firm. "But we need to consider all the ramifications."

"Like you eventually passing out from not sleeping?"

"Fair point. But still . . ."

"Malik, I know myself and my powers better than you do. I can do this," she said. "Let me help you."

"Very well," Malik nodded. "Do you want to try it now?"

"Yes, lay down."

Malik uncurled his legs and stretched them out. He could feel every rock and branch underneath him as he lay on the ground. He spared a quick glance to the campsite where they had cleared the ground, and the others were sleeping comfortably. Shifting his torso back and forth, he tried to make himself more comfortable. Iisha waited, patiently watching as he got ready to go to sleep. She slid towards him, propping herself up on her knees beside him and rested her hands on her lap.

"When you wake up, you're probably going to be a bit disoriented, so try not to panic," she said. "Just try to relax."

Malik nodded as he lay his head on the ground and closed his eyes. Iisha raised her hands above Malik, a soft light emanating from them. Staring at the light, she shifted her body so it wouldn't be seen by anyone who might still be awake. Closing her eyes, Iisha felt the power flow around her, and she willed it towards Malik. A moment later, a bubble of soft light encompassed him. Her breath began to grow heavy as she held the time field. After several long minutes, the light started to flicker, and Iisha felt her power waning. Lowering her hands, she dropped the field and stared at Malik.

Iisha placed a gentle hand on his shoulder and shook him just enough to wake him. Malik's eyes blinked a few times, and he moaned as he forced his body back to wakefulness. Fully opening his eyes, Malik sprung to a sitting position and looked around. It was still dark, and Iisha was still beside him. She rested her hand on his shoulder and gave him a soft smile.

"How do you feel?" she asked.

"I . . . I feel . . ." Malik stammered. "I feel really good, actually."

"Really?"

"Yes, I feel like I slept for days."

"I'm glad to hear it, you do look a bit more refreshed," Iisha said.

"Thank you, Iisha," he replied. "Truly, thank you."

Iisha nodded as she yawned.

"Now, you need to get some rest," Malik said.

Getting to his feet, he offered her a hand to help her stand. Iisha swayed with exhaustion as she let Malik guide her back to the campsite. She bid him goodnight and promised that she would be ok before she made her way towards Sethos and laid down to sleep beside him. As soon as her head hit the ground, she was asleep.

Malik watched from a distance. He felt more rested than he had in a long time, having actually slept for several hours. Staring at Iisha, he watched her sleep. Malik knew that what she had chosen to do wasn't just for him, it was for everyone. Taking a seat by the warmth of the fire, he stared at the flames as the others slept.

Chapter Twenty-Five

The air was thick with fog as Uaithiel flew over the stone temple. They observed the locked gate at the front and chose to land in the open courtyard instead. As soon as they touched the ground, a figure appeared in the doorway. The stone archway curved around her, framing her figure. Uaithiel smiled as she stepped into the light. Her violet eyes stared through the angel as she looked them over. Her long black hair fell past her waist, nearly as long as the plain, grey gown that she wore.

"Hello, Jubilee," Uaithiel said.

"Uaithiel," she responded. "It's been a long time."

"Too long, I'm afraid," they responded. "I'm sorry for not coming sooner, a lot has happened."

"I know, we felt it when their power was awakened," Jubilee said. "To be honest, I'm surprised you're here at all."

"I've come to seek her counsel."

"Of course, you have."

Jubilee stepped to the side and let Uaithiel pass her as they entered the hallway. The stonework, though ancient, was pristine.

"You've worked hard keeping up this place," Uaithiel said.

"Someone has to do it," Jubilee responded. "She's in the temple proper right now."

"Oh," Uaithiel paused. "I should wait in the antechamber."

"Of course, it would be rude to intrude on someone else's prayers," Jubilee said with a tone of snark in her voice.

"Jubilee, you know what happened . . ."

"It doesn't matter now, does it?" she cut them off. "It's been what, over a thousand years since it happened?"

"Probably closer to two," Uaithiel said, their voice quiet.

"Exactly, it's in the past," Jubilee turned away from Uaithiel as they entered the large antechamber. With a wave of her hand, she lit a series of candles along the wall. "I'll let her know that you're here."

"Thank you," Uaithiel bowed their head in gratitude.

The angel watched as she opened a set of heavy brass doors and slid through the narrow opening before quickly shutting them behind her. Uaithiel stared at the closed doors as if they could see through them. After a moment, they turned to study the stained-glass windows of the antechamber. Depictions of angels and demons warred in the light. The angel felt their mind slipping back into the past. Shouts of triumph sounded over screams of terror all around them. The angels and demons fighting in the windows now surrounded them, as alive as they could be.

Uaithiel walked through the battlefield, blood coating their sword as they dragged it along the ground. All around bodies lay motionless, both angel and demon alike. A red sun rose off in the distance, as if even the sky had been bathed in the blood of battle. Amongst the noise, Uaithiel heard soft sobs coming from a frail woman. She knelt over a body, a human body. She, too, was human, caught up in the ancient battle by accident. Her bony fingers clasped the too-thin hand of the man before her. He was dead, Uaithiel noticed, and soon she would be too. Blood stained her dress from wounds too numerous to count.

The brass doors slammed shut as Jubilee re-entered the antechamber. Uaithiel jumped slightly at the sound before turning towards the girl.

"Wait here," she said as she turned down a hallway. "She won't be much longer."

"Jubilee," Uaithiel called after her. She paused and turned to face them. "Is there anything you need? Anything I can do for either of you?"

"You should have asked that question ten thousand years ago," Jubilee turned to continue down the hallway.

Uaithiel stood silent and motionless as they watched her turn a corner and disappear from sight. The candlelight flickered as Uaithiel walked towards the far wall. Jubilee had lit ten candles, they realized, one for each Guardian, that each of them might be looked after. They stared at the center, one pure white candle remained unlit. As the angel stared at it, a flame suddenly flickered to life. Uaithiel turned around to find a figure standing in front of the brass doors to the temple. Her black hair was cut to just above her shoulders, framing her narrow face and pointed chin. Long robes of deep blues and purples draped on the floor around her. The angel sketched a slight bow.

"You will forgive her, it hasn't been easy," the woman said.

"There is nothing to forgive, she hasn't done any wrong," Uaithiel said.

"She won't show it, but she does care," she said. "In her own way."

"Of course," Uaithiel bowed their head. "I've come to seek your advice."

"Yes, I imagine you have," she said. "Life is not as easy as it was before."

"No, it isn't," Uaithiel agreed. "And I messed up, again."

"That doesn't surprise me," she said. "But, then again, you weren't the only one who made mistakes."

She turned down the hallway to the courtyard, and Uaithiel silently followed after her. They watched as she emerged into the sunlight. Her skin was so pale that Uaithiel often wondered if she ever spent more than a couple minutes a day outside of the temple. Walking towards a small garden, she motioned for Uaithiel to sit on a bench overlooking it. She sat down beside the angel.

"How many have you found so far?" she asked.

"There are five, no, six of them together now," they said. "But I have lost them."

"What did you do?"

"I was responsible for the death of Malik's brother," Uaithiel said.

The woman clicked her tongue. "That will be difficult to overcome."

"And I lied, I abandoned Yukaio's sister when I promised I wouldn't," they continued.

"Anything else?"

"Not as of yet."

"Well, it's good that you know it won't be your last mistake," she smirked.

Uaithiel stood silently, staring at a spot on the ground.

"Where are they now?" she glanced towards the angel.

"Searching for the remaining Guardians. I think they're quite close to finding them," they said.

"And you don't plan to be there when Malik and Kaidaneir finally have their reunion?"

"The situation is already explosive enough as it is," Uaithiel said. "I feel my presence would only make it worse."

"When do you plan to rejoin them?"

"I've asked Ciara to talk them round, without letting on what she's doing," they said. "I'm hoping by the time they meet up with Bhurak, they will be ready to welcome me back."

"If anyone can convince them, it is Ciara," she said. "It is interesting, though, that you chose her, given what her destiny is."

"I told her."

"You did what?" the woman turned to face the angel. Her expression was blank though her words were filled with rage.

"There were already so many lies and hidden truths, I figured it was for the best," Uaithiel said.

"There is a reason the fates do not share the stories of our destinies with us," she said. "You should not have told her."

"What's done is done," the angel shrugged. "But I don't know what to do now."

"You should pray to the Gods," she said.

"Why?" they asked.

"So that the Gods may give you some guidance."

"I come to you for guidance."

"That may be, but only they truly know where your path will lead. I still pray to them every single day, for myself, and for Jubilee."

"I fear the Gods have forsaken me long ago."

"I do not believe that to be the case."

"Why is that?" Uaithiel turned to face her again.

"Because, in those prayers, I also pray for you, Uaithiel. The Gods have not forsaken you," she said.

"It doesn't change my fate; I've accepted that much."

"Perhaps you accept it a little bit too easily.

"Will you help me?" they asked.

"You know that even if I wanted to, I can't," she said. "Since the day I set foot in this temple, I haven't been able to leave."

"What about Jubilee?"

"She still chooses to stay."

"She's very loyal to you.".

"She does more than she needs to, I think she tries to keep herself busy to avoid thinking about . . . well, you know."

"I do, unfortunately," Uaithiel said.

"The two of you will need each other before the end," she said.

"I can only pray that is true."

"You can feel free to use the temple for that."

Uaithiel turned to face her, as a soft smile graced her face. Uaithiel couldn't help but return it. They sat in silence for a moment, the shadow of the courtyard wall slowly overtaking them as the sun began its descent.

"Will you offer me any advice?" they eventually asked.

"I will give you this - trust yourself as much as you trust the Guardians."

Uaithiel turned away and took off into the air, leaving her alone in the courtyard.

«««○»»»

The woman rose from the bench, glancing towards the garden once more, before going back inside. She found Jubilee sitting in the antechamber, staring at the white candle, the flame flickering in the fading daylight. The woman put a hand on her shoulder, brushing her long hair away from the side of her face.

"They're gone?" Jubilee asked.

"Yes."

"Did you give them any advice?"

"Only the same advice I give Uaithiel every time they visit," she said.

"They should know what you're going to say by now," Jubilee said. "Why do they keep coming back, mother?"

"Because they're hoping for a different answer."

"Well, that's arrogant."

"Is it though, Jubilee?" the woman said. "Isn't that what prayer is?"

"No, prayer is asking the Gods a favour."

"And to grant that favour, you would have them change their almighty plans?"

"You pray every day," Jubilee turned to face her mother. "Are you saying that is just arrogance?"

"I'm saying that it's natural to want to change even the things that are already predetermined," she said. "It's human nature to resist."

Jubilee waved a hand in front of her, and all eleven candles snuffed out, leaving the two women in darkness as even the light through the stained-glass windows gave way to the night.

"If only we were human, though."

Chapter Twenty-Six

Sethos once more awoke to the earth rumbling beneath him. He sprung to his feet as he looked around at the rest of the group. Memories of the dancing tree flickered through his mind. Though the sun had barely graced the horizon, everyone was wide awake. Half the group was gathered around the fire pit, the rest still rubbing sleep from their eyes, likely woken by the tremors. Sethos placed a steadying hand on Mitesh's shoulder as his knees buckled under him.

"What is that?" Sagira asked from the other side of the campsite. "Yukaio?"

"It wasn't me!" he shouted back.

"Can you at least do something about it?" Malik asked.

Yukaio dug the end of his glaive in the ground just as the shaking stopped.

"Thank you," Sagira said.

"It still wasn't me," Yukaio repeated.

"This area must be unstable," Sethos said. "Maybe we should move on."

"But the other Guardians are supposed to be here," Ciara said. "We can't just leave without finding them."

"If this area really is unstable, maybe they've already moved on," Sagira said. "Their location on the map is over two weeks old. A lot could have happened in that time."

"Malik," Ciara pleaded. "They're here, somewhere."

Malik nodded in agreement. He had a feeling deep in his gut, perhaps it was just hunger, but perhaps it was telling him that he should listen. He asked Sagira for the map and spread it out before them.

"There," he pointed to the map. "There's one area that we haven't checked yet. We'll spend one more day here, check that region, and then if we don't find them, we'll continue further east."

"Wouldn't it be better to go north?" Sagira suggested. "We know there are two more Guardians up by the mountains."

"It's been weeks since we got this information. By the time we get there, they might not be there anymore," Malik said. "Every day that passes, there is a greater chance that they will have moved on."

Malik rolled up the map and passed it back to Sagira before barking orders to eat quickly and then pack up. He watched as the group obeyed. Soon the smell of food filled the air making Malik's stomach rumble. Scooping some food into a bowl, he sat alone as he ate. He watched as Kalida, discarding her empty bowl, picked up a bug and placed it on her twin's shoulder. Mitesh screamed and jumped to his feet, wiping it off. Kalida smiling, picked up the bug and began to chase her brother with it. Sethos's voice echoed as he told them not to go too far away.

Mitesh ran, screaming at his twin as she chased him with another bug. Looking back over his shoulder to see how close she was, Mitesh's foot slid into a small hole in the ground. He yelped as he tumbled to the ground. Kalida tossed the bug aside and ran towards her brother.

"Mitesh! Are you ok?" she called out.

"Yea, I think so," he said. "I just tripped."

Kalida sat down beside her brother as Mitesh rubbed at his ankle. She looked off into the distance and could barely see their older siblings. She hadn't realized they had run so far away from the rest of the group.

"I'm sorry," Kalida said. "I know you don't like bugs."

"It's ok," Mitesh said. "I'll get you back one of these days, I promise."

"I'd like to see you try," she smiled, punching him in the shoulder.

As the twins sat there, the ground beneath them shook. Mitesh held his sister close as the rumbling increased. They looked to each other in fear, the shouts of their older siblings barely audible in the distance. A large *crack* sounded from beneath them, and before they knew it, they were falling.

They screamed as darkness enveloped them. Mitesh barely saw the dark mist below them before it vanished. They both landed on a stone-hard surface, surrounded by large chunks of stone and earth. Groaning in pain, Mitesh tried to sit up, looking for his sister.

"Kalida?" he groaned in pain.

"Mitesh, I'm ok," she said.

Firm hands were at Mitesh's shoulders, helping him into a sitting position. Kalida let him lean against her side as she took in their surroundings. The space around them was dark, the only light coming from the gaping hole in the ceiling. She looked up at the spot they had fallen through. An otherwise smooth marble ceiling was jagged where a large chunk had cracked off. Bits of grass and dirt hung limp around the edge.

"Where are we?" Mitesh said.

"I'm not sure," Kalida responded. "Looks like

some kind of hall."

Mitesh staggered to his feet, swaying slightly. His sister stood beside him, helping to steady him. Brushing dirt and dust off himself, Mitesh looked around to examine the hall. Beyond the sparse pillars that reached up to the high ceiling around them, he could only see darkness. He turned and immediately gasped. He nudged at Kalida, who initially pushed him off before she too turned around and let out a gasp of her own.

Rising before them was a magnificent statue of marble. Upon a pillar perched a majestic bird with large, feathered wings and tails that wrapped around the post. Water bubbled at the top of the pillar, gleaming in the light as it sprayed the bird. The twins watched as the falling water ran down the long, curved tails and fell back into the fountain below.

"What kind of creature is that?" Kalida asked her brother. "I've never seen anything like it before."

"Neither have I," he admitted. "But it's beautiful."

"It's more than beautiful, it's magnificent," she said.

Mitesh reached out to touch the stone bird. The marble was cold beneath his fingers as he ran them along the tips of one of the feathered wings. Distant voices stole his attention as Mitesh turned away from the fountain. Pulling Kalida in closer to him, he peered into the darkness. He couldn't make out what the voices were saying, but they began to grow louder, closer. Stepping forward into the darkness, Mitesh called out.

"Hello?" he said. "Hello?"

"Is there someone there?" Kalida asked.

The twins looked at each other as the voice started to become clear.

"Mitesh! Kalida!" it called.

"Hello?" Mitesh said, louder than before. "Who's there?"

"Mitesh!" the voice called again. Mitesh suddenly recognized the voice. He let out a deep breath he didn't even realize he was holding.

"Yukaio!" he shouted! "We're down here!"

"I've found them," he heard Yukaio shout.

The twins looked up to find Yukaio carefully learning over the edge of the hole, looking down at them. A relieved smile was on his face. Moments later, the faces of their older siblings appeared as well.

"Are you two all right?" Iisha called out.

"We're fine, Iisha," Kalida said.

"Can you see a way out?" Sethos called down.

"No, not yet," Kalida answered. "It's too dark down here."

"Just wait a minute, we're going to get you both out," Yukaio promised.

Mitesh looked at Kalida and smiled as the rest of the Guardians gathered above. The twins listened as they discussed what to do next.

Chapter Twenty-Seven

A cloud of darkness shrouded Kai and Saora. Kai felt the air sucked out of his lungs as the darkness engulfed him before it finally dissipated. He let out a gasp as the cloud vanished and looked towards his sister. Her arms were over her head, ready to shield it from the large chunk of ceiling that had broken loose.

"We're ok," he placed a hand on her shoulder.

Lowering her arms, Saora looked around. She blinked rapidly as her eyes tried to adjust to the darkness. Though she couldn't see much, she could see that the room they were in now was definitely smaller than where they had been. She was barely able to make out her brother's silhouette a few inches away from her.

"What happened?" she asked.

"Shhh!" Kai held up a hand.

She watched as he crouched beside an open doorway. He craned his neck to look through while keeping most of his body hidden behind the solid wall. Saora rose slightly to peer around him. In the distance, she could see the fountain where they had been sitting. It was now wholly bathed in light, a massive chunk of the ceiling missing, sun shining through. Littered around the fountain were pieces of marble and earth. Right where they had been sitting, a particularly large chunk had cracked the floor with its impact. Focusing her eyes, she soon saw why Kai had shushed her. Two small figures sat among the debris.

The siblings watched as the figures got up and brushed themselves off. Their voices weren't quite loud enough to make out, but it was clear that they were lost and confused, but not injured. Saora observed as the two noticed the fountain flowing with the water that she had created only hours earlier.

"They must have fallen through when the ceiling cracked," Saora whispered.

"I agree," Kai said.

"Maybe we should introduce ourselves, go say hi," Saora said. "I know it's a long shot, but maybe they know something about this place."

"No, we should wait," Kai said. "Watch them for a while before we decide to do anything."

"They're children, what could they possibly do?" Saora asked.

Kai and Saora froze as the boy took a step towards the room where they were. His voice called out across the hall. Had he heard them in there? As he went to take another step, he paused, and then looked up to the ceiling. Shadows blocked out the light as several people appeared above the hole, looking down at the two figures in the hall.

"They aren't alone," Kai said.

"Maybe they . . ."

"Saora, we've already spoken to everyone in every town and village within a league of here," Kai said.

"But I don't recognize them," Saora said. "Maybe they're not from around here."

"Well then it's even less likely they would know about this city, isn't it?" he asked.

"I suppose," Saora said. "But there's something about them, I think we should investigate."

"You stay here, I'll go," Kai sighed.

"Why do you get to go?"

"Because I can remain unseen."

"Can you keep the shadow up for long enough to observe them?"

"I've been getting better at it," Kai said. "I was able to extend it around you earlier when I moved us here."

"Yes, I've been meaning to thank you for that," his sister said.

"I am good at some things, you know," Kai smiled.

"I know," she said. "Just please be careful."

"I promise."

A shadow emerged around Kai, completely engulfing him. She watched as her brother vanished into the darkness. Saora slapped her hand against her head and shook it as she heard a small thud and a groan.

"I'm ok," Kai's voice said.

"We're doomed," she whispered.

"I heard that," Kai said.

Saora stuck out her tongue in response. She didn't know where her brother saw or if he was even looking, but as a small rock collided with her side, she had a good indication that he saw it. Smirking, Saora slumped back against the wall and sat down on the ground, occasionally peeking her head around the corner to see the new strangers.

«« « ○ » »»

"We've been in the area for days, none of us have seen any other entrance," Sagira said, glancing at the hole in the earth. "I doubt we'll find one nearby."

"She's right, we need to find a way to get them

out here," Ciara agreed.

"Can any of you use your powers?" Terry asked. "Surely some of you have something that can help."

The Guardians all looked to each other. Training together had gotten them all pretty familiar with each other's powers. Most of their eyes eventually fell to Yukaio.

"You have power over the earth," Malik said. "Can you, I don't know, raise up the rocks or summon vines or something?"

"I don't think raising the rocks is a good idea, too risky," he said. "This area is pretty unstable, don't want to make the whole thing collapse."

"What about the vines?" Sethos asked.

"In case it passed your notice, we're in the middle of the field," Yukaio replied. "No vines or roots around here, or else I would."

"Can't you just conjure some?" Sagira asked.

"Again, we're in a field. There's nothing to anchor them too," Yukaio said. "And this field is pretty unstable, I wouldn't want to risk it even if there was a way to anchor it."

"We can't just leave them down there," Iisha said.

"I don't intend to," Sethos said as he peered down through the hole, assessing the distance.

"Wait, Sethos, are you sure that's . . ."

Iisha's sentence trailed off as Sethos crouched down to the ground, placed a hand by the edge of the hole, and then leaped through. He landed on his feet, barely keeping his balance.

"Great, now we have to get three of you out!" Malik shouted down.

"Not unless we can find a way out through . . . Whatever this place is," Sethos said as he looked around. "It was clearly built by someone, there has to be a way out."

"And what if the way out is sealed?" Iisha asked.

"Well, then it might be helpful to have a few others with powers that might be able to break through it," he smiled up at the rest of the group.

Iisha heaved a sigh and looked towards Malik. He considered what Sethos was suggesting for a moment before nodding in agreement. Sethos nudged the young twins out of the way as he watched his own twin copy his movements to jump down through the hole.

"You don't have to come, Terry," Yukaio said to his sister as the other Guardians prepared to jump.

"We're not getting separated again," she said. "Where you go, I go."

Terry didn't give her brother a chance to object as she leaped through the hole. Her landing wasn't as sure as the others, and she collapsed to the ground. She nodded thanks to Sagira, who offered her a hand up. Yukaio landed beside his sister, soft as a cat. They watched as Malik, bringing up the rear, joined the rest of the group in the underground hall.

"This place is incredible," Sagira said, looking around.

"A bit dark, though," Tiergan said. "Ciara, Sethos, anything you can do about it?"

The two Guardians smiled at each other. Ciara raised her palm, and a small fire flickered to light. Noticing a wooden torch among the stony debris, she picked it up, lighting the end, and passed it to one of the others. Sethos, also raising his palms, formed a small ball of light in between his open hands. As the light rose higher, it began to split into smaller lights that shot off in different directions, illuminating the entire hall. Ciara looked from the flame in her hand, to the torch, and back again.

"Well, that makes my tiny flame kind of useless, doesn't it?" she snuffed out the flame in her hand by closing her fist as she looked around the hall.

"Sorry," Sethos shrugged.

"I think we should split up," Malik said. "There's a lot of adjoining rooms and hallways along the walls. Three groups, no one goes anywhere alone, and we meet back here at the fountain in two hours."

"Great, I guess Kalida and I will go with Iisha and Sethos," Mitesh said joyfully.

"I don't think so," Sethos shook his head. "It was the two of you together that got us into this. I think Iisha and Kalida should go with Ciara and Seran."

"That's a good plan," Iisha agreed with her twin as the younger pair groaned and hung their heads.

"Terry and I will go with Sethos and Mitesh," Yukaio said.

"Right, then that leaves me with Sagira and Tiergan," Malik said. "Sethos, can you maintain the lights for that long?"

"I'll be fine," he nodded as he ushered his younger brother away from Kalida and set off to explore the hall.

«««◌»»»

Saora was silent as she watched the group. For a while, she could hear part of what they were saying, making out a few words here and there. Not quite enough to get the gist of what they were saying, but enough for it to be obvious that they all knew each other quite well. When the hall suddenly lit up as small balls of glowing light floated around the great room, her mouth dropped open in shock. The rest of their conversation went unheard. She barely noticed when they dispersed, and a couple headed towards where she was waiting. Ducking back behind the wall, she blinked a few times as her mind processed what she saw.

"Saora, Saora," Kai's voice said as something touched her shoulder. "I have so much to tell you."

"I can't see you, Kai," she said.

Kai's hand touched her shoulder again as darkness surrounded her. Looking up, she saw her brother standing above her, a broad grin on his face.

"They didn't see me at all, but I saw them, Saora. The things I saw!" he exclaimed. "Some of them have powers, just like us."

"Do you know how many of them have powers?" she asked.

"At least two that I saw," he said. "Maybe we should go over and introduce ourselves?"

"I don't know," she said.

"What? A few minutes ago, you were all for it," her brother replied.

"Knowing that they have powers isn't enough. You were right earlier, it's better to watch and see for a bit," Saora said. "There's like a dozen of them and only two of us. Can you keep this shadow around us a bit longer?"

"I can keep us from being seen," Kai said. Saora gave him one of her looks, one of the ones that he couldn't refuse. "I'll do it, but this shadow doesn't stop us from being heard."

He whispered the last few words as footsteps grew closer. Kai pulled his sister away from the doorway so the strangers wouldn't bump into them. The edges of the shadow blurred their vision as they watched four of the strangers enter the room.

"Too bad Sethos's light didn't reach in here too," said a tall woman. "Ciara, maybe you could make another fire."

"Finally, I'm useful again," she smiled as a fire sprang to life in her palms, the light contrasting against the darkness of the room.

A young girl broke free of the grip the tall woman had on her as she ran towards the back of the room. She paused before the set of altars, staring at them and the murals behind them.

"What do you think these are, Iisha?" she asked.

"I'm not sure," Iisha went to join her sister. "They're definitely interesting."

"Iisha, do you see that?" the woman who made the fire said.

"See what, Ciara?"

"Those figures in the murals. There's 10 of them," Ciara pointed to the two groups.

"You're right," Iisha stepped closer. "And look at their hands, each of them is holding an orb."

Ciara pulled the small red orb from her pocket and held it up, comparing it to the ones painted on the wall. The right mural had a female silhouette at the forefront, and though the orb she held was green, it was identical to the one that Ciara had.

Saora had to put a hand to her mouth to keep from gasping at the sight. Her fingers fluttered over her pocket where a deep blue orb resided. Kai looked to his sister, catching her surprised gaze. He lifted a solid black orb and held it out in front of her.

"I didn't notice the orbs earlier," he mouthed the words, afraid to make any sound.

Saora shook her head and placed her finger to her lips again. She turned back to see the tall woman also holding an orb, comparing it to the mural.

"We definitely need to show the others this," she said.

As the others agreed, they exited the small room to continue exploring before meeting up with the rest of the group again.

When the light of Ciara's flame left the room, and the darkness returned, Kai dropped the shadow. He bent over, hands on his knees as he gasped for breath. Saora rubbed his back while he caught his breath.

"That was hard," he said breathlessly.

"You did great," Saora reassured him.

"But did you see them use their powers? She did it so effortlessly, she made it look easy," he said.

"Maybe they've had them longer than we have," she suggested.

"So, what do we do now?" Kai asked.

Saora stepped away from him and up towards the mural on the wall. In the faint light, she squinted to make out the orbs that the figures held. Looking at the left mural, the central figure caught her eye. It was clearly male, and he held a small black orb in his right hand. To the right of the figure, a female was painted holding a deep blue orb. Saora pulled hers out of her pocket and compared it – it was identical!

"Kai, come look at this," she called.

"What does it mean?" he asked, holding his own orb in his hand.

"I don't know, but maybe the book ... The book!" Saora exclaimed.

"What is it?" Kai asked.

"I don't know where that book went," she said as she ran back to where they had been hiding earlier.

"It might have been left behind," Kai suggested. "When the ceiling was falling down on us, I wasn't exactly thinking about the book."

"No, of course not," Saora said. "Any chance you can go and check if it's still by the fountain?"

"Only if you don't mind me being seen," Kai said. "I don't think I could manage a shadow scarf right now, let alone a full blanket of darkness."

Saora nodded and turned to look through the doorway. None of the strangers were near the fountain. They were all exploring the various hallways and alcoves at the ends of the hall. She considered if she could make it there and back in time without being seen, but it was unlikely. And it wasn't worth the risk, not yet anyway. Saora realized that she and Kai would likely have to introduce themselves at some point, but how to do it was important. Walking from the doorway back over to the altars where her brother stood, Saora ran through all the possibilities for their next move.

"Maybe we should have introduced ourselves to a smaller group of them first," she suggested to her brother.

"That makes sense, easier for them and easier for us," Kai agreed. "Too bad they've moved on."

"We could go try and find them," she said.

"We don't want to spook them."

Just then, a gasp from behind them made Saora and Kai turn around. In the doorway stood the young girl from earlier, her mouth open in a wide gasp as she beheld the siblings.

Chapter Twenty-Eight

Zeneviva, carrying her trident at her side, followed Amatheon through the winding halls of the Contenebris Mountain. She barely glanced at the workers steadily mining the materials needed to create the Umbra. One of the overseers bowed to Amatheon as he passed by, and then again to her.

"There had better be a good reason for bringing me here," she said. "This dust is going to be stuck to me for days."

"The darkness has summoned you," Amatheon said. "It would be rude to ignore it."

"Do I look like I care about being rude?" she smirked.

"Do I look like one to be trifled with?" Amatheon asked.

"A little bit, yes."

Amatheon stopped walking and turned to face her, standing only a few inches in front of her. He looked down at her, his expression as bold as if it were set in stone. Zeneviva placed the end of her trident on the floor and shifted her weight to casually lean against it as she stared up at him. In the darkness of the mountain, her taupe skin looked more grey than tan as her lips parted into a wide grin.

"I would suggest you learn to hold that tongue of yours," he said. "The darkness will not take kindly to being spoken to like that."

"Well, we'll just have to see about that then, won't we?" she pushed past him and continued walking down the corridor.

Turning on his heel, Amatheon quick-stepped to catch up and overtake her once more. He easily stepped over the foot she placed out to the side, attempting to trip him as he passed. Reaching the edge of the alcove, he spread an arm across the entryway.

"Even if you will not show me any respect, at least have some respect for the darkness," Amatheon said.

Zeneviva remained silent. After a moment, Amatheon lowered his arm and stepped inside, kneeling before the altar. Zeneviva followed him in and stood to his left. She stood tall as she took in the sight of the altar and the swirling darkness behind it.

"My lord, I have brought her," Amatheon spoke. "May I present to you, Lady Zeneviva."

She inclined her head a bit at the introduction but immediately straightened her posture. Her face was unmoving as the darkness spoke in its ancient tongue. Zeneviva glanced at Amatheon, kneeling on the ground, his head bowed as he listened.

"Yes, my lord," she said as the voice paused. "I am happy to serve the darkness, as long as I am given what has been promised to me."

The ancient voice spoke again, and Zeneviva smiled.

"Thank you," she said.

"Her legions will be very useful, my lord," Amatheon said. "I have already seen one of her beasts in action, and I am confident that, in time, they will help to lead us to victory."

The ancient voice spoke once more, and as it ended, both Amatheon and Zeneviva bowed before the swirling darkness vanished. Amatheon rose to his feet, his glare shooting daggers at Zeneviva.

"I think I rather like the darkness," she said as they exited the small alcove. "Although, swirling darkness, not what I expected. I rather imagined there would be a throne."

"Setting your sights high already?" he asked.

"Don't you worry about my sights," she said. "I know what I need to do."

"Speaking of what you need to do, don't you have an army to raise?" Amatheon said. "And an angel to track?"

"You worry too much," Zeneviva said. "Don't be in such a hurry, this is a marathon, not a sprint. Play the long game, Amatheon, and we will win."

The demon watched as she walked away, fading into the darkness of the mountain.

Chapter Twenty-Nine

Malik ran his hand down a colourful mural along the hallway wall. He looked back into the grand hall, mentally comparing the clean marble stone to the murals that adorned all the hallway walls they had seen so far. Stepping back, he looked at the broad wall. The mural depicted some kind of battle. Different types of monsters that Malik didn't recognize were fighting what appeared to be angels.

"What is this place?" he wondered aloud.

"I have no idea," Sagira said, ducking under one of the floating lights to get a better view of part of the mural. "It looks like it's been here for thousands of years, it's incredible."

"Should we go down a bit further? See what's at the end of the hallway?" Tiergan suggested.

"No, not yet, we should wait for the others," Malik said. "We have to head back to meet up with them soon."

Malik turned to face the wall behind him. The mural there was entirely different. Rather than a scene, it contained an enormous dragon. Its scales were a deep forest green with tones of silver gracing the edges. Malik followed along the massive body up to the front of the head. Its face was turned to face the hallway, making Malik feel like its eyes were following him, staring right through him. The dragon's lips were so red it was as if it could open its mouth and breathe fire at any moment. The creature was perched on one of its long legs, with the other stretched out, pointing downwards.

Malik ran his hand along the dragon's claw right to the tips. The wall felt different there. He furrowed his brow as he felt around the wall with both hands. Beneath the dragon's claw, he could feel four edges forming a box. The stone there was rougher than the rest of the wall. He stepped back to look at it. There was nothing visibly different about it, and the dark paint on the wall made the edges all but invisible to the eye.

"Sagira, come look at this," he said. "Feel right here."

Malik pointed to the wall as Sagira approached. She placed her hand where Malik indicated, and her eyes went wide as she felt the difference in the wall.

"What is it?" Tiergan asked.

"The wall is different there, there are edges," Sagira said. "Maybe there's something in there."

"I think so too," Malik said. "Now, we just need to figure out how to open it."

They each tried placing the edge of their axe blades into the crack to pry it open, but it wasn't wide enough. They moved up and down the wall, rubbing and tapping various places to try and get it to open. Neither was successful. Tiergan stood back, watching the two of them work as he stared at the dragon. He was drawn to the large eyes, moving back and forth, watching how it looked as if they were following him. Stepping closer, he noticed one eye seemed slightly different than the other. He reached up to touch the right eye and found it to be hollow. His fingers curved around the edges of a small hole in the pupil of the eye. He tried to push on the inside of the hole - nothing happened.

"Sagira, can I see your orb for a moment?" he asked.

"What for?" she said.

"You can't really see it, but there, there's a small hole in the right pupil, and I think your orb is the perfect size to fit in it," he said.

Sagira pulled the small purple ball out of her pocket and stepped up to face the dragon. She looked at Malik, who just shrugged and indicated for her to try it. Reaching up, she slid the orb into the eye. Sagira gasped as she realized it was a perfect fit. There was a loud click and then a slow grinding noise. Sagira looked down at the square to find it sliding out of the way. They all peered inside but couldn't see anything except darkness.

"Why don't you stick your hand in?" Tiergan suggested.

"It's your idea, why don't you do it?" Malik said to him.

"I'm not a Guardian, and it was opened by an object only a Guardian would have," Tiergan pointed out. "Maybe it'll be safe for you, but not for me."

"He has a point, you know," Sagira said.

"Great, so go ahead," Malik said.

"You're our leader, and you're the one that found this, you should do it," Sagira said. "Unless you're scared."

"It's your orb in the dragon's eye, what if it's keyed to your power now?" he retorted.

Sagira sighed, realizing she wasn't going to win that battle. Slowly she reached her hand inside, preparing to expect anything. But nothing jumped out at her, and a moment later, she felt a small leather pouch. It jangled as she pulled it out to look at it. Inside were a dozen gold coins, identical markings on each one. Sagira pulled one out of the pouch and passed it to Malik.

"I wonder what these markings mean," he said. "Must be important if it's guarded like that."

"I say we take them with us," Sagira suggested.

"Good idea," Malik placed the coin back in the bag as Sagira pulled the drawstring shut and placed it inside a pocket. "We should head back."

Sagira reached up to pull out her orb, and the panel in the wall shut closed with an echoing boom. As the trio turned down the hallway back to the grand hall, a scream pierced the air. Instantly they took off at a run.

«««◌»»»

"IISHA!" Kalida screamed at the sight of the two strangers in the room that she thought had been empty just a minute ago.

Iisha came running to her sister, putting her arms around her as she looked into the room. She gasped in shock at the sight of the duo standing by the altars. Pushing Kalida behind her, she stepped forwards.

"Who are you?" she asked as Ciara and Tiergan filled in behind her.

"I'm Kaidaneir Kunzakie, and this is my sister Saora," the male stepped forwards.

"Kaidaneir?" Iisha repeated.

"Yea, although you can call me Kai," he said. "It's what everyone calls me. Actually, I don't even really like being called Kaidaneir, I prefer just Kai."

"Then why did you introduce yourself that way?" Kalida asked, tilting her head to look around her sister.

"I . . . I really don't know," Kai said. Behind him, Saora resisted the urge to shake her head.

Iisha and Ciara looked at each other and smiled.

Iisha stepped forward and extended a hand.

"My name's Iisha, this is Ciara, Kalida, and Seran," she said. "It's nice to finally meet you."

Kai eagerly shook her hand, grinning.

"What do you mean 'finally'?" Saora asked as she stepped forward.

"Ah, it's a little bit complicated, but suffice to say we've been looking for you for some time now," Iisha said.

She turned around at the sound of rapid footsteps approaching. Malik, Sagira, and Tiergan were running towards them.

"We heard a scream," Malik said. "Is everything ok?"

"Everything's fine, Malik," Iisha said. "Actually, there's a couple people we want to introduce you to."

"Introduce us?" Malik asked, confused. As Iisha stepped to the side, he could see two people standing in the small room, the light barely hitting them.

"Malik, meet Kai," Iisha said to him, and then turned to the other. "Kai, meet Malik."

Kai waved to him, but Malik only stared. A long, tense moment passed before Malik finally spoke.

"It's good to meet you," he said.

Again, rushed footsteps stole the group's attention. Sethos had finally made it from the other end of the hall and quickly went to his sisters to make sure they were ok. After assuring him that they were fine and that Kalida had just been startled, they introduced Kai and Saora.

"Seriously?" Sethos said. "We've been looking for them for days, and we find them down here, by accident."

"That's the Gods for you, I suppose," Sagira said.

"So . . . Do all of you have powers?" Saora asked

cautiously. "We saw a couple of you use powers."

"Saora!" Kai said to his sister. "Are you sure you should be asking that?"

Saora looked from her brother to the group now gathered in the doorway, blocking out most of the light. Their silhouettes painted an odd picture of a mix-matched group.

"I think it's ok," she faced Malik, standing at the forefront of the group. "Do you?"

"No, not all of us," Malik said. "But most of us."

As he spoke, his attention drifted to the mural on the wall behind Kai and Saora.

"What is that?" he asked.

"We were going to tell you all about that once we met up again," Ciara said. "I think it's us."

"Us?" Kai asked. "What do you mean, that's us?"

"Those of that us have powers, we're known as the Guardians," Malik said, stepping towards Kai. "We were granted these gifts by the Gods to protect the inhabitants of this world."

"Yea, way to not give them too much information at once, Malik," Yukaio said sarcastically.

"Well, if he's going to be the leader, he needs all of the information sooner rather than later," Malik said.

"Leader?" Kai exclaimed. "I'm sorry, what?"

"Apparently, in addition to just giving us these powers, the Gods chose who would be our leader, and apparently it's you," Malik explained.

"Malik, maybe you should slow down a bit," Sethos urged.

"I think it's for the best he finds out everything now, make sure he's up to the task," Malik said, then turned back to Kai. "What powers do you have?"

"Watch this," Kai said as he willed the darkness around him. Though every muscle in his body barked in protest, he pushed through. A shadow passed over Kai, and as it dissipated, he vanished.

"Oh, so you can disappear, impressive," Malik rolled his eyes. "Any chance you can make that permanent?"

"That's not all," Kai said, reappearing.

He reached his hand out in front of him, and a cloud of darkness appeared before him. Kai took a step into it, and a moment later emerged behind Malik, tapping him on the shoulder. Malik whirled around to find Kai directly beside him.

"Ok, I'll admit that's a bit more impressive," he said.

"What can you do?" Kai asked Malik.

"I can create lightning, not really something that would be advisable in here," Malik said.

"Yes, I would have to agree with that," Kai said.

"And you, sorry, what's your name again?" Malik asked.

"Saora," she crossed her arms over her chest.

"Right, Saora, and what can you do?" he said.

"You see that fountain out there?" she said, to which the group nodded. "I did that. The water I mean, not the carving. I can create and control the waters."

"Another elemental Guardian, nice!" Yukaio said. He continued when Saora gave him a confused look. "I can control earth, Sagira can control air, and Ciara can control fire. It's all the basic elements."

"Elemental . . ." Saora said. "I remember reading something about that."

"Reading it? Where" Sethos asked.

"We found a tome yesterday, had a lot of information in it, but I don't have it right now. I think it got left by the fountain, did any of you happen to see it?" Sagira asked.

"No, sorry," Sethos shook his head.

"I'll go get it, be right back," Kai said. A cloud of

darkness appeared before him, and he vanished as he stepped into it. A minute later, another cloud appeared beside Saora, and Kai emerged. As he did, he bumped into Saora, tripping over her feet, sending both of them to the ground. "Sorry, still working on that."

Malik stared wide-eyed at their supposed leader. He recalled the burden he'd felt when he was told to lead the others until they found Kai and the relief he anticipated when he would get to pass on the title. But that relief hadn't come. As he stared at Kai, now scrambling back to his feet with a silly grin on his face, he wondered how the Gods thought that this could be the best decision.

Standing upright again, Kai caught Malik's glance. At the stare that the other man was giving him, Kai passed the tome to Saora, not ready to be judged yet. As Saora placed the tome on one of the altars and began to search through it for information, Kai approached Malik.

"So, if I'm leader, are you, like, second in command then?" he asked.

"Something like that," Malik said. "I was told that until we found you, I'm in charge."

"Well, you've found me now," Kai said.

"Doesn't necessarily mean anything, though."

"What do you mean?"

"The one who told us that you're supposed to be in charge isn't a part of our group anymore, they haven't been for a while," Malik explained. "And I've done a good enough job leading them so far. I'm not sure you'd be up to the task."

"You've known me for all of five minutes," Kai said in disbelief.

"Yes, and in those five minutes, I've seen you act impulsively and then trip over your own feet and fall. We're supposed to be fighting a war."

"Actually, I tripped over my sister's feet."

"Not helping your case."

"Look, we've just met. I don't know about the rest of you, but there's still a lot that Saora and I don't know. Plus, I'm starting to get a bit hungry," Kai said. "So, let's finish reading that book, get some food, and when we're all a bit calmer, we can try again."

Kai turned before Malik could respond and strode over to his sister. Malik stared at the back of his head, throwing mental daggers. After a moment, he resigned himself to joining the others.

«««○»»»

Zeneviva knelt along the shoreline of the ocean, one hand with a firm grasp on her trident, and the other waving in the water. The coolness nipped at her fingertips, filling her with vigour. A rumbling beneath the water rippled along the surface.

"Soon, my dear, soon your time will come," Zeneviva said.

Rising to her feet, she stepped into the water. Waves lapped around her as she strode in deeper and deeper. She paused as the waves caressed her midsection. Wrapping both hands around the staff of her trident, she lifted it high into the air above her.

Creatures of the deep, hear my summons,
Arise from your slumber, find your voices,
Come forth and walk on the land,
Take what is yours by rights,
Rise and join my fight

She thrust her trident into the water, the staff thudding against the ocean floor. A wave rippled outwards in all directions before the waters went still. Zeneviva stared into the silent depths. She let out a breath she didn't realize she had been holding as a single bubble rose to the surface of the water and popped. Slowly, another bubble surfaced, then another, and another. Water splashed as a scaled head and torso emerged, water dripping off its green-grey body. Green scales glinted in the moonlight as the Yacuruna extended its arms, clawed hands reaching up into the night. A roar pierced the night air as the creature beheld Zeneviva. All around the Yacuruna, the water bubbled and broke as dozens after dozens of creatures rose from the waters. The Yacuruna approached Zeneviva, smirking, and nodded as it strode past her onto the beach. Watching her force grow before her eyes, Zeneviva couldn't help but smile.

Chapter Thirty

Kai shoved another handful of nuts into his mouth as he looked at the group around him, squinting in the now dim light. Sethos's lights had faded hours ago when he was unable to keep them lit any longer. He observed Sethos lying on the ground, sound asleep, exhausted from maintaining the light for so long.

"So, let me make sure we've got this right," Saora said. "There's this angel named Uaithiel and he- "

"They," Sagira corrected.

"Right, sorry. And they told you that we're all destined to save this world from a war against the darkness?"

"That pretty much sums it up," Sagira nodded.

"Ok then," she said. "Where do we start?"

"That's it?" Yukaio asked.

"What else is there to say?" Saora shrugged. "If this is our destiny, who are we to fight it?"

"I understand that, I just figured it would take a bit more explaining. It's a lot of information," Yukaio said.

Saora smiled. "Then we better get started."

"First, we need to find a way out of here. I take it the two of you know your way around?" Sagira asked.

"Yes, I can get us to the exit passage," Saora confirmed.

She looked up at the fountain, the water still

bubbling around the great bird. Despite how eager she had been to leave this place, it had started to grow on her. Especially this room, there was something about the great hall that just felt right. Saora looked at Malik, leaning back against the side of the fountain, reading through the tome. He angled the book so the light coming through the hole in the ceiling illuminated the pages. Saora shifted in her spot, deciding to move closer so they could talk about the book.

"Have you found anything interesting yet?" she asked as she sat down beside him.

"A lot of it is written in a language I don't understand," Malik said. "But it seems to be the history of this place."

"Anything about us?" Saora said.

"There's a section here, near the back, that I think is about us," Malik flipped through the pages. "It talks about Gods-blessed children with different powers."

"That sounds like what you described based on what the angel told you," she said.

"Yes, but here's the odd bit," Malik said. "it goes on to refer to these blessed children as Gods themselves."

"Gods?" she asked.

"Well, technically, it's described as demi-Gods," Malik explained.

"Kai and I read about the demi-Gods earlier, but we weren't sure what they are," Saora said.

"I suppose a demi-God is what we are, whatever that means," Malik said. "But that's . . . I don't know. It seems outrageous to think."

"Well, think about it, have you ever met anyone else who can summon a lightning storm to destroy hundreds of Umbra?" she asked.

Malik whipped his head around to stare at her.

His wide-eyed confused expression made her smile.

"Terry told me about it," Saora explained. "I'm so sorry about what happened."

"It's my own fault, really," Malik said, his voice barely a whisper.

Saora placed a hand on his shoulder. "I know we can never replace your brother, but you're not alone, ok?"

"Thank you," he said.

Saora watched his expression as Malik's gaze turned from her back to the book. His eyes barely glazed over the page, obviously still somewhere off in a distant part of his memory. Absent-minded, he flipped through the pages.

"Stop," Saora said suddenly. "Look at that."

Malik focussed on the image. It was an identical, albeit smaller, version of the mural in the room with the altars. Saora took the books from his hand, silently thanking the Gods that the page was in the common tongue as she read the page aloud.

"The ten Gods-blessed Guardians of Madeira each hold a sacred power in their meamina, or soul. This base of power is crucial to their ability to defend our world from the growing darkness. While each Guardian has their own power and is unique, they can be divided into two main groups, the elemental Guardians and the celestial Guardians. The elemental Guardians derive their power from the physical world, whereas the celestial Guardians derive their power from the metaphysical world. The below image is a representation of the Guardians and their meaminas."

"We were never told that much," Malik said.

"It is interesting, but does it mean anything?" Saora asked.

"I don't know," Malik shook his head.

"Hey, come look at this," Saora called.

She laid the book on the ground in front of them as the others gathered around.

"Oh, those are the same murals as in the antechamber," Kalida exclaimed.

"It says that there are two groups of Guardians, the celestial and the elemental," Malik explained. "But we don't know if it means anything."

"Does it say which of us is which?" Iisha asked.

"No, but I think we should be able to figure it out," Saora leaned over the image. "There's five in each group . . ."

"Earth is definitely elemental," Yukaio said. "And so are water, air, and fire."

"What's the fifth one?" Sagira asked.

The group looked at each other, each shaking their heads.

"Well, darkness has to be celestial, right?" Kai asked.

Sethos nodded. "Time, too."

"So that leaves light and lightning," Ciara said, looking at Sethos and Malik. "Which one would be elemental? Maybe lightning?"

"Did Uaithiel say what the other Guardians powers are?" Saora asked.

Yukaio shook his head. "If they did, I don't remember."

"Wasn't one of them ice?" Sagira asked.

"Oh, right," Yukaio said. "Would ice be elemental?"

Kai pulled the book closer to him and squinted. Saora instinctively reached towards her brother but pulled back. Kai smiled as he looked at the image. "I don't think we need to worry about the text at all, look at the image."

"What about it?" Malik asked.

"Well, these are supposed to be us," Kai said, pointing at the lead celestial figure. "That meamina, it's black, like mine. We don't need to try and guess, we can just look at the image."

"That's really smart," Sagira smiled. "I can't believe we didn't think of that sooner."

Kai grinned and shrugged. "It's all being part of a leader."

He pulled the meamina from his pocket and held it out, the others all following suit. Saora leaned over the book, looking back and forth between the book and the meaminas. "So, we were right about the four elements. But it looks like both Sethos and Malik are celestial Guardians, and so is Iisha."

"So, I guess the last two that we have to find, one is elemental and one is celestial?" Yukaio said.

"I wonder what their powers are," Kai said. "The celestial one looks green, and the elemental one is kind of off-white."

"I guess we'll figure it out when we meet them," Iisha said.

"This is all well and good, but does it mean anything?" asked Sethos.

Malik gasped as a thought popped into his head. "We need to look something else up."

"What is it?" Saora asked.

"Sagira, do you still have that satchel?" he asked.

"Oh right! Of course," Sagira said.

She reached into her pocket and pulled out the small leather satchel. Undoing the drawstring, she dumped some of the contents into Malik's palm. He nodded in thanks and spread out the coins on top of the open pages of the book.

"We found these earlier," he explained. "They were hidden in a secret compartment in the mural down the hall that opened when we used our meamina."

"Used it, how?" Kai asked.

"We placed it in the eye of the dragon, and the compartment popped open," Sagira said.

Saora rotated one of the coins in her hand. The edges had even ridges all the way around, and the face of the coin was intricately detailed. Whoever had made them had put a lot of time and effort into it. Looking back and forth between the coin and the book, she flipped through the pages.

"Nothing," she said.

"Nothing?" Malik repeated. "But that book has everything else about this place, why not these?"

"I don't know. Maybe it's in the part of the book written in that other language," she suggested.

"Maybe," he conceded. "But we should definitely take it with us when we go."

«« « ◯ » »»

The night was dark as the crescent moon moved through the sky. Although there was little light in the grand hall, the reflection of the stream of moonlight off the statue was magnificent to behold. It was as if the bird had come alive at night. Saora stared at the fountain, her bag already packed and at her feet. Despite the sleep that still lingered in her eyes, she had accepted it was time to move out. Though the sun wasn't even up yet, Malik had suggested they move out early as Kai and Saora said it would take a few hours of walking to find the city exit.

"Best not to lose the daylight," he had said.

Kai hung his bag over his shoulder, eyeing Malik. They hadn't mentioned their conversation to anyone else, nor had they discussed it again. Kai pushed down the feelings of doubt for his own abilities, trying to convince himself that he was just as capable as Malik at leading this group. He held out a torch for Ciara to light with her fire as he made his way to the front of the group.

"That tunnel there will lead to an older part of the city. From there, we will have to circle around a few side chambers because some cave-ins blocked the direct path," Kai explained, trying to hold his voice as steady as possible. "If we head out now, we should reach outside shortly after sunup."

He started to walk towards the tunnel, his sister falling into step beside him. He resisted the urge to look back and see if everyone was following him silently, or if they were grumbling about it. Instead, he looked at his sister, who gave him a reassuring smile.

Turn after turn, Kai led them through the labyrinth of the underground city. There were few conversations as they walked through, a silence falling over them like a blanket. Kai noted each mural on the wall as they passed, remembering the way to the exit. Before long, quickened footsteps appeared beside Kai, and he turned to see Malik matching his steps.

"What direction are we going?" Malik asked.

"Up ahead, we take the next left," Kai said, pointing at the corridor.

"No, I mean what direction, like on a map," Malik said. "North, south, east, west?"

"Oh," Kai said. "I'm not sure which direction we're facing right now, but I know that the exit is a fair bit north of that hall."

As Malik was about to comment, a deep groan sounded in the distance. He stared down the hallway as a second groan sounded, and then a grinding noise. Malik looked to Kai, whose face had gone pale as he halted his steps.

"What is that?" Malik asked.

"Gargoyles," Kai said.

"What are gargoyles?" Yukaio asked.

"Great stone monsters, very strong, and very protective of their home," Saora explained.

"Have you faced them before?" Sethos asked. "What's the best way to fight them?"

"Yes, we've faced them," Kai said. "But the best way to fight them . . . there really isn't one."

"How far to the exit?" Malak asked.

"Not that much further now," Kai said.

"Run?" Malik asked.

"Run," Kai agreed.

He drew his sword in one swift motion and set off at a running pace. This time he did look over his shoulder to make sure that everyone was following him. They were moving too quickly for him to do a headcount, but it looked like everyone was staying as close as possible. As Kai turned down one hallway after the other, the sounds of the gargoyles coming to life grew closer.

Kai came to a sudden halt. Malik slammed into him, stumbling back.

"What are you doing?" he shouted.

"We aren't going to make it," Kai said.

He turned to face the group. In the darkness behind them he could see the silhouettes of the gargoyles approaching. The stone wings groaned as they flew through the dark hallway, the sound echoing all around. Kai raised his sword, ready to fight.

"The rest of you keep going," he said. "Saora, show them the way out."

His sister didn't argue. Taking over his place at the lead of the group she beckoned for them to follow. Kai stood firm as he watched the rest of the group run. He allowed himself a brief sideways glance. Malik stood beside him, his hands gripping his bhuj.

"Are you sure it isn't best to just keep going?" Malik questioned him.

"No, they're gaining on us too quickly," Kai said. "You should get out of here with everyone else."

"And leave you to get all the glory? Not a chance," Malik said.

"There's at least five of them that I can see."

Malik followed Kai's gaze down the corridor. He squinted against the darkness, unable to make out anything. How Kai could see them he didn't know. Malik gasped as Kai ran forwards into the black. As the sound of his sword clanked against stone, Malik joined him.

When they were finally close enough for him to see, Malik held his breath to keep from gasping in shock. The gargoyles were indeed pure stone. From their deep inset eyes to the horns jutting out from their head to the giant wings that somehow carried them through the air, they were pure stone. He watched as Kai's sword bounced off them, barely making a dent.

Malik ducked as one of them swiped at him. He turned and swung his bhuj. It ricocheted off the gargoyles head, propelling the Guardian back. For a moment he admitted that Kai was right to send the rest of them away.

"Any ideas?" Malik shouted in between attacks.

"No, you?" Kai responded, his breath near panting.

"One, possibly, I don't even know if it will work," Malik said. "Do you think the others have made it out yet?"

"Saora knows the way, I'm sure they're almost there," Kai said.

"Ok, because this might be a bit dangerous."

"More dangerous than what we're already doing?"

"Fair point. Get back."

Darkness swallowed Kai and he vanished, reappearing beside Malik as the two men backed away from the gargoyles. Kai watched as Malik quickly sheathed his bhuj and raised his hands. Lightning cracked at his fingertips, sparks flying outwards, striking one of the gargoyles. It groaned as it soared backwards into another, knocking them both to the ground.

Kai watched as fissures formed along the gargoyles chest where it had been struck. Malik raised his hands, striking again. As the lightning bounced off the walls and ceiling, stone cracked, and the gargoyles groaned in agony.

At least four of them did.

The smallest of the group turned and raced through the lightning, narrowly avoiding being hit. Kai didn't have time to raise his sword as the stone creature rammed into him, knocking him to the ground. Malik pivoted and aimed once more. Before the lightning could strike, he was on the ground, his back aching where stone impacted it. He rolled over in time to see the gargoyles fly overhead and land directly between them and the path to the exit.

"So much for your plan," Kai said as he regained his footing.

"I don't see you coming up with a plan," Malik retorted.

Kai looked up at the ceiling. Large cracks ran through it already. Another strike would likely send it crumbling to the ground.

"Strike the ceiling," Kai said.

Malik followed his gaze upwards. "You know we'll be trapped, or possibly crushed," he said, the lightning already sparking at his fingertips.

"I know," Kai said, sheathing his sword.

Malik nodded. As the gargoyles lunged towards the two men, Malik struck. The lightning hit its mark on the ceiling, the large cracks spidering outwards, groaning and rumbling. An avalanche of stone began to fall. The gargoyles beat their stone wings, trying to escape, but to no avail.

The two men watched as the ceiling fell, crushing the gargoyles one by one. As the last of them was trapped beneath the stone, Malik breathed a short sigh of relief. But another crack made him look up again. The cracks continued to spider along the ceiling above their heads. He didn't have time to make a sound as the stones began to fall. Darkness overtook him.

And then he breathed a deep breath. The shadows peeling back from his eyes revealed a shocking scene. The collapsing ceiling continued down the hallway, but he was now on the other side of it. He looked sideways at Kai, bent over his knees panting.

"Did you . . ." he started.

Kai wordlessly nodded, still catching his breath.

"You had that planned all along, didn't you?"

"You're not the only one with plans," Kai said. "Let's go."

Kai turned and started towards the exit once more. His hand drifted over his side, still reeling from the exhaustion of using his powers again so soon. Rounding a final corner, a speck of light at the end of the hallway shone like a beacon. Kai ran as fast as he could towards the exit, clambering up the few steps to get to the ground level. He turned to offer Malik a hand to help him up the steps. Malik ignored it, making his own way up. Kai closed his hand into a fist and pursed his lips as he looked at the group. No one else seemed to notice what had just happened.

"Are you alright?" Saora rushed towards her brother.

"Yes, those gargoyles won't be bothering us any time soon," Kai smiled.

"Should we seal that entryway?" Sethos asked.

"The gargoyles have an aversion to sunlight, they won't come out here," Saora said. "We're fine."

"But what about anyone else that might try to venture in?" Sethos said.

"Considering there's a gaping hole into one of the halls now, maybe we should leave this way open, so no one gets trapped," Yukaio said.

"Not only that, but they're also probably all dust by now," Kai said.

Kai noticed that Malik actually looked impressed for a moment before his expression changed back again. Malik motioned for Sagira to get out the map so they could get their bearings.

"What are all those X's for?" Saora asked as she leaned over the map.

"Those ones are where we were, and that was where we were told we could find the two of you," Sagira explained. "And those ones up there are where we think the last two Guardians are."

"Where were you when you fell through the hole?" Saora asked her. As she watched Sagira point at the map, she mentally calculated how far they had gone. "We were about . . ."

"You were probably here," Kai said, pointing to the map. "Just about a league or so away from that lake. Say, why does that lake have a big mark over it?"

"You want to avoid that lake, trust me," Ciara said. "I haven't heard any good things about it."

"Ok, so then we'll circle around the western side

of it and up into the mountains there," Malik traced a finger along the map.

"Shouldn't I be declaring that?" Kai asked as Malik stared at him. "I am the leader."

"Really? Because I'm not so sure you're up for it," Malik said.

"I lead us out of the underground city, didn't I?" Kai crossed his arms over his chest. "Not only that, I did just save you from being crushed."

Malik stepped up to Kai, staring him in the eyes. The battle of their wills silently playing out. "The only reason I would have been crushed was because of your plan."

"I only needed that plan because your first one didn't work."

"Well maybe if you would have reacted quicker, it could have."

"I did just as well as you down there, it not better," Kai said. "Besides, wasn't I chosen by the Gods?"

"Supposedly," Malik said. "But I don't really think that matters right now."

"So, you would defy the Gods?" Saora stood beside her brother.

"Where have the Gods been?" Malik asked. "Where were they when my brother died?"

"Malik, I understand you're upset, and you have every right to be, but it wasn't the Gods that were responsible for your brother's death, that was Uaithiel," Ciara said, trying to calm him.

"Right, it's the angel's fault. And who was it that told us that Kai should be in charge?" Malik looked at each of the Guardians. "That's right, it was the angel. I don't think we can trust any decision Uaithiel made."

"I'm sure Uaithiel was just doing their best," Ciara said.

"You have no idea what you're talking about. You

never met them," Malik snapped at her.

Ciara opened her mouth to respond, but then closed it. She dragged her toes through a soft patch of dirt, making small circles while pondering how to respond. Uaithiel had said that she would know when the right time was to mention their encounter. Looking from Malik to Kai, she could see the tension between the two men. Now definitely was not the right time.

"You have no idea what it's like," Malik continued shouting, again directing his words to Kai. "I have led this group for weeks now. We just met you, we don't know anything about you yet."

"But Malik," Iisha said when he paused for a breath. "Didn't you say you were going to be happy to pass over the role of leader when we found Kai? That it was such a burden?"

"That was before we met him," Malik said. "Look at him, do you really think he would be capable of leading us?"

"I think we owe it to him to give him a chance," Sagira said. "We gave you a chance when we first met you."

"We could put it to a vote," Yukaio suggested. "Each of you makes a case for why you should be in charge, and then we'll vote."

Iisha, noticing the tension growing, quickly nodded in agreement. Malik shoved his way in front of Kai and began to speak. He spoke about how they had spent time together and grown not just as friends, but as family. They had trusted him this far, and he asked them to continue to trust him a bit more. When Kai stood up, he struggled to keep his voice from shaking. Malik's confidence in himself had unnerved Kai, but he was determined not to let it show. Kai spoke about destiny, how if they hadn't fallen through a hole, they would have never found each other, and how it's worked out for the best. He told how he truly believes that it's his destiny to become the leader the Gods chose and that he wants the chance to live up to it.

"Do we all vote? Or Guardians only?" Mitesh asked once both men had finished speaking.

"I think Guardians only," Sethos said. "No offence, but we're the ones that are going to be following someone into battle."

"Ok, so split up," Saora said. "If you support Kai, come stand by him, or if you support Malik, go stand over there."

Saora took a step closer to her brother. She watched as Sethos and Iisha exchanged a look, and both went to stand beside Malik. A warm hand laced through hers, as Saora felt Ciara move beside her. The girls exchanged a look, hoping for the best, before finally being joined by Sagira. All eyes turned to Yukaio as he looked from one to the other.

"I'm sorry," he said as he strode over to stand beside Malik.

"A tie," Saora sighed.

"Maybe we should let the siblings vote, just to be a tie-breaker," Kai suggested.

"No, we agreed this is how it was going to be done," Malik said as he counted the siblings. If they each voted with their own family, it would give him the victory. But it wasn't the siblings that would be following him into war – it was the other Guardians. It was them that he needed to win over. "There are still two more Guardians that we need to find."

"Two more would give us another even number and another chance at a tie, then," Ciara pointed out.

"Then the next one will be the tie-breaker," Kai

said. "Uaithiel told us that the last Guardian was going to be the hardest to convince to join us, I doubt it will make a difference which of us is in charge when we approach her. So, let's find Bhurak, and he will be the tie-breaker."

Malik nodded. "Agreed."

Chapter Thirty-One

The wind bit at Kai's skin as he wrapped his arms around himself in an attempt to stop shivering. The group had been making their way north for days now, each day growing colder and colder. As bad as the days were, the nights were worse. Ciara worked herself to near exhaustion to make enough fires to keep everyone warm through the night. After the first night, most of the group had forgone trying to save face and huddled together in small groups to sleep.

"How much further north is it?" Kalida asked, her teeth chattering.

"About another day or so," Sagira said. The map was tucked safely in her pocket. She had memorized their route when her fingers started to get too cold to keep taking it out to check they were on the right path.

"You're positive the last Guardian is up this way?" Saora asked.

"It's where the angel said they last felt him," Sagira said. "Unless he's moved on, but hopefully he hasn't."

"He probably has, it's freezing up here," Sethos said.

"But Uaithiel said that his power is ice," Sagira reminded them. "Maybe he doesn't get cold like we do."

"Then maybe he can share that ability," Yukaio

laughed.

The group fell silent. Beneath Yukaio's joke was a desperate desire for warmth they all shared. His bones ached with the cold. Kai looked at the young Guardian, shivering as they walked through the mountain range.

"Maybe we should try and find some shelter for the night," Kai suggested. "There might be somewhere along the base of the mountains that we can set up where the wind will be blocked."

"We should go over there," Malik motioned with his chin, his hands too cold to take out of his armpits. "There looks to be good tree cover along the rockface. We might get lucky and have the wind blocked on two sides."

As the group walked towards their chosen site for the night, Kai strode up beside Malik, speaking in a low voice. "Malik, can I talk to you?"

"I don't suppose I can stop you," he said.

"I have an idea, but I don't think everyone will like it," Kai said. "I want your support for it before I say anything."

"I'm listening," Malik looked sideways at Kai. The two men had barely spoken at all in the last few days, only exchanging words long enough to argue about what their course of action should be.

"Every day we go further north, it gets colder and colder," Kai said. "I think that everyone that isn't a Guardian should turn back."

"Really?" Malik asked.

"Yes, just hear me out," Kai turned to face him. "We've been extremely lucky these past few days not to be attacked by the Umbra, or anything else. But this cold can be just as dangerous. If it's true that the Gods are watching over us, then we should be fine, but what I've heard about what happened with Uaithiel, maybe the Gods aren't watching over everyone else the same way. Maybe they should turn back."

"And go where?" Malik questioned.

"I don't know, maybe back to the underground city?" Kai suggested.

"With the gargoyles?" Malik raised an eyebrow.

"Well, they don't necessarily have to go into the city, just in the general area," Kai shrugged. "Although the marble hall with the fountain was pretty safe when we were there."

"Other than a collapsing ceiling," Malik said.

"Ok, well then, do you have a better idea?" Kai said. "I'm just trying to think of something to keep them from freezing to death up here."

"No, I don't have a better idea," Malik admitted. "And I hate to say it, but think you're right, I think that they should turn back."

"You do?"

"Yes, but it isn't going to be a popular opinion."

"That's why I want you to be united with me on that decision. It'll be easier for everyone to accept it that way," Kai said.

Malik nodded. "We'll tell them after supper that in the morning everyone who isn't a Guardian is going to turn back and wait for us near the ancient city."

««« ○ »»»

Kai stared at Malik as the silence lengthened. They had been right - suggesting half of them turn back was not a popular idea. Barks of protest came from every single member of the group. Malik announced that the non-Guardians would turn back, and that was the end of the discussion. Many of them turned to Kai, who just shrugged and said that he agreed with Malik's decision. Despite having full bellies and the warmth of the fires around them, tensions remained high.

"Kai, you can't seriously be taking his side on this," Sagira said.

"Actually, it was his idea to begin with," Malik interjected.

"Kai!" Ciara exclaimed.

"Look, I think we all knew that we would have to split up from them at some point. Our mission is to fight in a war, and it wouldn't be right to bring those without powers into it," Kai said. "Whether we split up sooner or later, it is going to happen eventually."

"I won't leave my siblings," Sethos said with determination. "Iisha and I agreed to this to keep them safe."

"Leaving them will be the best way to keep them safe, Sethos," Malik said.

"If they go back, then so do we," he placed a hand on Iisha's shoulder, who nodded in agreement.

"Sethos . . ." Malik started but paused as Kai held up a hand.

"Look, we can't make you come with us, if you really want to turn back to be with Kalida and Mitesh, I'm not going to stop you," Kai said. "But I will ask you to consider not just your brother and sister, but everyone else's. And I don't just mean in this group, I mean in this world. You're all lucky to have each other, to look after each other and take care of each other, but what about everyone else? What about those younger sisters who don't have someone to look after them? What about the younger brothers who don't know how to fight? We can help them, too."

Sethos met Iisha's gaze. Neither could deny what Kai said, but they weren't ready to admit anything. Iisha placed her arm around Kalida's shoulders, pulling her in closer to her side.

"Don't answer right now," Malik said. "Take the night and think about it."

"I can do that," Sethos said as the group tucked in for the night.

"Thank you for your help," Kai said to Malik.

"I'll admit I was impressed by that speech you gave," Malik said. "Maybe you aren't *completely* hopeless after all."

"You've known everyone longer than I have, do you think any of them will actually leave?" Kai asked.

"I'm not sure," Malik shook his head. "Sethos is very protective of Mitesh and Kalida. I think he would go insane if anything happened to them. Getting them to split up isn't going to be easy, but I think he and Iisha will decide to do the right thing."

Kai nodded as he moved closer to the fire to go to sleep for the night. He looked back at Malik, who remained sitting, his knees pulled up into his chest, poking one of the fires with a long stick.

"Aren't you going to sleep?" Kai asked. "I thought you took watch last night."

"I don't really sleep much," Malik shook his head.

"How come?" Kai asked.

"I'd rather not talk about it," Malik said flatly.

Kai didn't push him. They had made a lot of progress in the last few hours, and it was more than they had spoken to each other without yelling the entire time since they met. Kai waved Malik good night and rolled over to try and get some sleep.

Malik watched the others as they drifted off to sleep, wishing that he could do the same. There were a couple of nights he asked Iisha to do the time bubble so he could sleep, but he saw how it exhausted her. Malik reached his hands out towards the fire, his fingertips practically in the flames.

They tingled as the heat melted away the cold that had settled inside of him. As the warmth spread throughout his body, Malik felt relaxed. His eyelids grew heavy and drooped closed before springing back open. But after a few minutes of drooping, they shut tight as his head lolled onto his shoulder.

As he looked around, Malik was back in the forest by the river, Umbra roaming around. He turned away, but the scene shifted, and he was again facing the action. No matter which way he turned, the battle appeared before him. Malik covered his eyes with his hands.

"No, no, no," he whispered.

"Hello, again, Malik," Amatheon's voice sounded behind him. He had heard it enough times now to know it without looking. "It's been quite some time since I've seen you. Tell me, how have you been?"

"Just leave me alone," Malik said, his voice lifeless.

"Your group has gotten bigger, I see," Amatheon continued.

"Just stop," Malik said.

"You're up to eight Guardians now, that's impressive," Amatheon said. "Oh, and you've finally found Kai. How did it feel to hand over control of the group to him?"

Malik could feel Amatheon's grin as he taunted him. Shifting his hands from covering his eyes to his ears, he closed his eyes, squishing them as tight as possible. The sounds of Amatheon's voice still echoed between his fingers. Malik muttered under his breath, asking him, begging him to stop. After what seemed like an eternity, there was silence. Malik lowered his hands and opened his eyes.

"Malik," a voice said from behind him.

His eyes widened. It wasn't Amatheon's voice, the voice he had grown so used to in his nightmares. It was a different voice, but just as familiar. He turned around.

"Tariq," he said.

His brother smiled at him, standing there, full of life.

"No, no," Malik shook his head. "You're dead, you're not here."

"But I am here, Malik, and I don't have to leave," Tariq said. "Not if you make the right choice."

"This isn't real," he said.

"Of course, this is real," Tariq stepped towards his brother. "I've missed you."

"I miss you too," Malik looked up at his brother.

"You're doing so great, you know," Tariq said. "I'm so proud of you!"

"It's hard without you," he said.

"You lost a brother but gained a whole family."

"I would trade it all to have you back."

A smile flashed across Tariq's face for an instant before it vanished.

"You could, you know," Tariq told his brother.

"No, it's a lie Amatheon is trying to feed me, you shouldn't listen to him," Malik said.

"Who else should I listen to then? The angel that got me killed?" Tariq asked.

"No, of course not," Malik shook his head.

"Then why are you listening to them?"

"I'm not."

"Yes, you are," his brother said. "Every moment you let Kai be in charge, you're doing exactly as Uaithiel told you to do. What they forced you to do by killing me."

"I might have misjudged Kai," Malik admitted.

"You haven't," Tariq said. "I've been watching. You're clearly much more capable of being a leader than that . . . child."

"I . . . I . . ."

"You need to take what is yours!"

"How?" Malik asked.

"Show him that you're in charge, don't just ask for command, take it," Tariq said. "Take it."

Malik watched as his brother stepped back and began to fade away.

"No, wait!" he shouted, reaching towards Tariq.

"Take it, Malik," he said as he disappeared into nothingness.

«« « ◌ » »»

Malik opened his eyes and was startled to see a figure hunched over him. Blinking a few times to clear his vision, he recognized Kai, grinning that stupid smile of his.

"Sorry," Kai said, backing up a bit. "I thought you said you don't sleep?"

"I said I don't sleep *much*," Malik corrected.

"Well, if you're always shaking like that in your sleep, then I can see why," Kai said.

"What are you talking about?" Malik asked.

"Just before you woke up, you were shaking and muttering a bit under your breath," Kai said. "Were you having a nightmare or something?"

"Definitely *or something*," Malik said, looking away from him.

He was silent all throughout breakfast, as many of the group said their goodbyes to each other. Iisha and Sethos had decided to stay with the Guardians, realizing that what Kai had said the previous night was right. Malik watched as they hugged their younger siblings tight before letting go. While the young twins just waved to Malik, Terry approached him before departing. She wrapped her arms around him in a giant hug.

"You're going to be ok," Terry said.

"You too, kid," Malik said.

"You know he's not really gone," she said.

"What?" asked Malik.

"Tariq, he isn't really gone," she repeated. "He's always right here with you, in your heart."

She placed a hand on Malik's chest. Malik cupped it with his own before returning the hug she gave him.

"Take care of yourself," he said as she turned to walk away.

Terry walked past the young twins, stopping to make sure they had all their stuff as she went. Mitesh shoved her off as he continued to talk to Yukaio. The young twin blushed as Yukaio laughed.

"I'm going to miss you," Mitesh said.

"Same here," Yukaio agreed. "But we will see each other again."

"I know, but it might be a while," he said.

"Yea, but just think, you get to go hang out in that cool underground city," Yukaio said. "Just try not to fall through any ceilings this time."

Mitesh laughed as Sethos shoved a sack into his arms, knocking the wind out of him. Mitesh looked up at his brother, unsure about leaving. He and Kalida had spoken about it through half the night. It was for the best; they both knew that. But Mitesh wasn't worried about himself or his twin – it was the Guardians that he worried about as he slung his bag over his shoulders and set off with the others back down south.

Chapter Thirty-Two

The cold air whistled as it soared through the mountains. Uaithiel's wings felt as if they had long ago turned to ice. Pushing against the bitter cold, they flew through the night into the northern mountains. They landed softly on the ground when their wings got too cold to continue in the air. Tucking their wings in tight to their back, Uaithiel felt a bit warmer as they continued on foot. Pausing every so often, they reached out to sense the Guardians. They were close now, closer than they had been in weeks. Uaithiel felt a surge of pride as they realized how many of them had joined together.

The angel's hands were stiff with the cold as they grasped the rocks, pulling themself up onto the rock face. Crouching down at the edge, they peered over the side. In the distance far below, the glow of campfires broke through the night's darkness. Uaithiel watched the Guardians sleep, curled up together in the cold night. They resisted the urge to approach, to be there when they woke up. *The time isn't right yet*, they thought.

Uaithiel sat at the rock edge through the rest of the night and into the morning. The rising sun warmed their wings, melting away the night's cold grip. They watched as the Guardians stirred and began to pack up their belongings. When the Guardian's siblings began to head south, Uaithiel gasped. Though they knew it was the right thing for the group to do, Uaithiel wondered who it was that had suggested sending their family back to safety. The young humans walked at a brisk pace, eager to get out of the cold mountains and back to the warmth of the south. In the opposite direction, the Guardians set out, searching for their next member.

Uaithiel rose onto their feet and prepared to take off, planning to stay far enough behind the Guardians not to be noticed. But something pulled at their heart. They turned to watch the humans going south. Pushing off the rocks, they rose high into the air, higher than human eyes would be able to distinguish, and headed south. An internal battle waged inside the angel. Their duty was to the Guardians, to protect and watch over them. But these humans were their family, and they cared deeply for them. Despite the fact there would be nothing Uaithiel could do to protect them should anything happen, perhaps just watching over was a good way to start.

As the long hours passed, the angel silently flew above the humans, watching as they talked and laugh, so carefree, so innocent. Uaithiel couldn't help but imagine Tariq walking with them, laughing at their jokes, helping them build a fire in the evening. By the time the sun was starting to go down, the group had nearly exited the mountain range. Unburdened by not having to search for the other Guardians, they were able to move at a much quicker pace than what they had done on the way north. As the sun set, the moon gleaned in the sky when the group stopped to rest for the night. Uaithiel landed in the thick of a tree and sat on a branch, their legs dangling below.

The crackling of the fire made Uaithiel long to be down there, feeling its warmth. Without warning, a sharp pain shot through Uaithiel's head. They leaned forward, placing their head in their hands, closing their eyes. The angel gasped for air as the pain radiated through their mind. After a moment, it began to lessen. Uaithiel opened their eyes and looked around. Nothing appeared to be out of place. They looked down at the group of humans by the fire. *So pathetic*, they thought. *What's the point in even being here?*

Uaithiel shifted to a standing position, placing a hand on the trunk of the tree. They stretched out their wings, preparing to take off. One last glance towards the humans had them reconsidering. *No, I promised to watch over them, no matter how little it might mean.* The angel sat back down on the branch and leaned against the tree truck, settling in for the long night.

By the time the sun eventually rose over the mountains, Uaithiel's entire body was stiff. They stretched their arms and wings on either side as far as they could go before relaxing them. The tension eased somewhat as they rotated side to side, also stretching their back. They stood up and prepared to take off as the group set out again. Uaithiel was thankful that the air grew warmer the further south they went.

The sounds of talking and laughter only just reached Uaithiel as they followed, remaining unseen. Soon another noise began to arise in the east. The group below fell silent as they listened, trying to determine the sound. Uaithiel watched, unsure of whether to intervene, as they turned and began heading towards the noise. Deciding to scout ahead, Uaithiel picked up the pace, wings beating as hard as they could. Reaching the edge of a cliff face, Uaithiel landed and looked down, horrified at the sight below.

An army marched through the mountains, dozens if not hundreds strong. Uaithiel knew them by the greenish-grey tone of their skins, their claws and teeth, but it was their scales that definitely gave them away. Shimmering scales in various shades of green covered their bodies. *Yacuruna.* The angel watched as they marched by, row after row. He didn't need to see Zeneviva to know that this was her army – only she could command a legion such as this.

The scraping of feet against rocks sounded behind Uaithiel, and they startled before realizing it was only the humans. *The humans!* Uaithiel realized and considered whether they should leave. They wouldn't be able to protect the humans from the Yacuruna if they were spotted. Before they could make up their mind, the group was upon them.

"Uaithiel, we heard a . . ." Terry started, meeting the angel's stare. "Wait, what are you doing here?"

"I assume the same as yourself, Terry," they said. "I came to investigate."

"Investigate what?" Kalida said, making to rush forwards.

"Not so fast," Uaithiel held up a hand to stop her. "It isn't safe for you to be here. You should turn back."

"Oh, so now you care about our safety?" Terry crossed her arms over her chest.

"Terry, you know that my powers to protect anyone that is not a Guardian are extremely limited," Uaithiel said.

"Yet here you are," Tiergan said.

"What is it that you don't want us to see?" Mitesh asked.

"Better yet, how did you know we were here?" Terry asked.

"A little over a day ago, I found the Guardians again, just before the lot of you departed from them," Uaithiel admitted. "Instead of tracking them, I decided to follow you to make sure that you got out of the mountains safely."

"Why?" Tiergan asked, a firm expression on his face.

"I have done wrong by many," the angel said, looking at Terry as they spoke. "I wish to try and make up for that in any way that I can."

"Prove it," Terry said. "Tell us what's down there."

"Below that ridge, there is an army moving north, they are servants of the darkness," they said.

"Umbra?" Mitesh asked.

"No, fortunately not. Although, I'm not sure if this is better or worse," Uaithiel turned to glance over their shoulder as the army continued to march, unaware of their presence up above.

"What are they, then?" Kalida asked.

"They are creatures of the deep waters," the angel said. "Yacuruna."

"What are you going to do about it?" Terry asked.

"I am going to warn the Guardians," they said.

"Then get going," Terry suggested.

"But not yet," Uaithiel continued. "First, I am going to make sure that you lot are out of harm's way."

"Why?" Tiergan asked.

"Because I owe it to the Guardians to do what I can to help all of you," Uaithiel looked at each of them.

Their eyes landed on Seran, standing a bit away from the rest of the group, eyes wide with shock. It occurred to Uaithiel that this was the first time they had met since awakening. Terry noticed the angel's stare and followed it towards Seran. She stepped towards the young man and took his hand.

"Seran, this is Uaithiel," Terry said, and then turned to the angel. "I take it you already know him the same way you knew the rest of us?"

"Yes," Uaithiel said, breathless. "Seran, it's good to see you again."

"From everything I've heard, I'm not sure I feel the same way," he said.

"I understand, I am trying to change that," they said.

While Uaithiel focussed on Seran, Terry slipped past them and crouched by the edge of the cliff. Her eyes widened at the sight of the army before her. She scanned the rows of Yacuruna marching through the passage below before turning to Uaithiel.

"There has to be a hundred of them," she said.

"Yes, which is why it is not safe for you to be here," Uaithiel said. "The sooner you leave, the sooner I will be able to warn the Guardians."

"We were planning on going back to this underground city we found a while back," Tiergan said. "It's about another day or so south of here."

"Dahkra," Uaithiel said. "That's a good choice. Though the ancient city is abandoned now, it will provide you with refuge until something more permanent is found."

"If we go, will you go warn our siblings now?" Tiergan asked.

"First, I will see you safely to the city," Uaithiel said.

"We don't need you to hover over us," he said.

"Then I will watch from afar if you prefer," they said. "But I will not abandon you, I promise."

"I've heard that one before," Terry turned away from the rockface and continued back down the path towards the city.

Kalida and Mitesh rushed past Uaithiel to each

peak at the army before Uaithiel placed a hand on each of their shoulders and turned them away. Tiergan took over for Uaithiel at guiding the young twins down the path, leaving the angel behind. Seran stood still, staring at Uaithiel.

"If you have something to say to me, then, please, say it," Uaithiel said.

"There's nothing to say," Seran shook his head as he ultimately turned around and followed the others.

With one last glance back towards the army, Uaithiel took off, following the young humans down their path. Their pace had quickened, and their laughter had died since seeing the army that now marched to face the Guardians. Stopping only to eat, they pushed themselves to their limits as they walked all day and through part of the night. At long last, they paused before the stone entryway and the stairs leading down to it. Uaithiel landed on the ground beside them as each of them sat on the ground, panting, and recovering their strength.

"We're here, now go," Terry said.

"I just wanted to give you my word, I will look after the Guardians," they said. "All of them."

"Well, they aren't here," Terry said.

"Please, stay safe, all of you," Uaithiel turned from them and shot back into the sky, racing to meet the Guardians before the army. "You may not be Guardians, but you are still important. Your family would be lost without you."

Chapter Thirty-Three

The snow stuck to the ground, blanketing the earth in a layer at least a foot deep. Kai's footsteps pressed deep into the snow, leaving clear tracks behind him as he led the group further north in the mountains. His teeth chattered as he stuck his fingers under his armpits, trying to save any warmth that he had left. Slipping on an icy rock, his feet went out from under him, hands catching himself on the cold ground. He shook off the soft snow and wiped his hands on his pants, sticking them back under his arms.

"Are you ok, Kai?" Saora asked beside him. Her short black hair was plastered to the sides of her face, wet with melting snow.

"I'm fine," he nodded his head.

"This might be a bit easier if we had someone who knew exactly where Bhurak was," Ciara said from the back of the group.

Kai paused and looked back at her, then at Malik, who shook his head.

"I don't disagree with you," Kai said. "But it doesn't matter now anyway, we don't know where the angel is."

"Even if we did, I wouldn't trust them," Malik said.

"I agree," Yukaio said.

"Look, did they make some bad decisions? Yes, of course," Ciara said. "But, they thought that they were doing the right thing."

"Killing an innocent person is the right thing?" Malik turned to face her, his blood rushing.

"No, of course not," Ciara said. "But whether we realize it or not, this is a war, and there are going to be casualties. We need to accept that. I doubt that by the end of this any of us will be able to say we didn't make any mistakes."

"Ciara, I understand what you're trying to say," Sagira said. "But you weren't there when they looked us right in the face and admitted that they were responsible for Tariq's death."

"It must have been incredibly difficult for all of you," she said. "But their guilt now is just as strong as their conviction they were doing the right thing then."

"How do you know that?" Sethos asked.

"What?" Ciara said, realizing her mistake.

"How do you know what Uaithiel is feeling?" Sethos repeated.

Ciara looked down at her feet, dragging one foot to push some of the snow around. "I met them," she admitted. "Before I met all of you."

"You what?" Malik screamed.

"When I was out gathering firewood during that thunderstorm, they found me," Ciara explained. "They told me that I was destined to meet all of you, to be a Guardian, and . . ."

She trailed off and looked away from the others.

"You didn't think to mention any of this?" Iisha asked.

"Uaithiel said not to," Ciara continued. "They said it would be best if I didn't mention it unless necessary because of the hurt that they caused all of you."

"You shouldn't have kept this from everyone," Kai said.

"It isn't Ciara's fault," Sagira said. "Uaithiel should never have put her in that position."

"Speaking of them . . ." Yukaio sighed as he pointed to the sky.

In the distance, a winged figure flew through the air, dark against the bright sky. As they soared through the air, a dark cloud began to grow, as if following them.

"Is there a storm coming?" Yukaio asked.

"No, that doesn't look like a storm . . ." Malik said.

"Umbra!" Sagira exclaimed.

"Do you think Uaithiel can outrace them?" Ciara asked, concerned.

"I . . . I don't think that's Uaithiel," Iisha said.

As the winged figure grew closer, they could see that it wasn't the angel approaching them. The figure's dark robes billowed in the wind as black wings carried him through the air.

"Who is that?" Kai asked.

"Amatheon," Malik answered.

"We need a plan, and quick," Sethos said. "Whatever bullshit the two of you have going on needs to end, now."

Malik and Kai stared at him as they both nodded, the colour draining from their faces. Malik barely heard Kai's voice as he stared at the approaching wave of Umbra. In his mind, he was back in the forest, erupting into a storm of lightning. A hand at his shoulders, shaking him, pulled him back to the present. He turned to see Kai staring at him.

"Malik, are you listening?" he asked.

"I'm sorry," Malik said.

"I need you to focus," Kai said. "I've never faced this many of them at once before."

"We . . . we . . ." Malik stuttered.

"Light and heat are their weaknesses," Sethos stepped forwards. "Also, the only thing that can destroy them are our weapons. They were forged by the Gods."

"Ok, how many arrows do you and Iisha have?" Kai asked.

"Don't worry, we have enough," he said. "When our magic is strong, they tend to replenish themselves."

"Handy," Kai said. "So, the two of you should take the flanks and . . ."

"Kai!" Saora cut him off. "You need to see this!"

Kai looked to his sister, standing on a large boulder. She reached down and offered him a hand, pulling him up beside her. As Kai steadied his footing, he looked off into the distance where his sister was pointing. Below the Umbra that eclipsed the sky, an army marched on the ground. The light above them was snuffed out as they approached, their gleaming scales turning dark. The two turned to face the rest of the Guardians.

Kai took a deep breath. "Ok, new plan."

«««◌»»»

Uaithiel pushed as hard as they could against the biting wind. They could feel the Guardians nearby, the eight of them still together. Reaching out their mind a bit further, Uaithiel found the ninth Guardian. He was barely a league away from the others. As Uaithiel neared, a darkness filled the sky ahead. *Umbra!* Though they were still a fair distance away, their presence was unmistakable. *And if the Umbra are there, then . . .* Uaithiel's thought trailed off, not wanting to think about the army marching on the ground. Fighting on one front would be hard enough, but on two?

Howls and screams filled the air as the clanging of metal echoed below. Uaithiel nearly froze mid-air at the sight they beheld. The eight Guardians had fallen into a battle formation, one quite like what they had used thousands of years ago, the angel noticed. They stared at the two gaps where the remaining Guardians should have been fighting alongside their companions.

Kai stood at the forefront of the Guardians, swinging his blade at the approaching army of Yacuruna as he dodged teeth and claws. A calm had come over him as he focused on the battle, on keeping his friends safe. Saora and Yukaio flanked either side of him, also fighting the ground army. Behind them, Sagira took down any that got through their line. Further back, Sethos and Iisha crouched behind a pair of large rock formations on either side of the battlefield, arrows flying at the Umbra in the sky. Malik stood by Sethos, summoning lighting to strike down any Umbra that got too close; Ciara stood by Iisha, taking down Umbra with her flames.

Uaithiel watched as the Guardians fought as one unit, just as they had always done. But seconds felt like eternities as the Guardians grew weary. The angel watched as the lightning strike became less frequent, as the sword and axe strikes missed their targets more often than not. Flapping their wings as hard as possible, Uaithiel soared forwards, over the battlefield and off into the mountains.

Hurry, hurry, hurry.

«««○»»»

Saora's breath caught in her throat as she swung her sais. The creature dodged her attack with ease, bearing a grin that was all teeth. The rows of sharp points gave Saora pause as she took a step back. Gathering herself, she lunged forwards, and the

Yacuruna made to strike her, but Saora reacted faster than he anticipated. He croaked as her sai went through his open mouth and out the back of his head. Yanking her weapon back, he fell to the ground, dark blood puddling in the snow. Without a pause to catch her breath, she turned to face the next one, and the next, and the next. After slashing one across the chest, spraying blood everywhere, she stole a moment to look to her brother. Kai looked more composed than she had ever seen him, as if he was born for this. *Perhaps he was.* She worked her way closer to her brother.

"How are you doing?" she asked between strikes.

"They just keep coming," he said, glancing towards her. "Stay in position."

Saora nodded and moved back towards where she had been, drawing some of the creatures away from Kai and Yukaio. Behind her, Sagira swung her axe as hard as she could, cleanly severing a scaled head, watching as it rolled through the snow. A howl emerged behind her as an Umbra rushed down and passed through her. Sagira screamed as she fell to the ground. Saora's own cry echoed as she watched her fall. Pushing her way through a pair of beasts, she tried to fight her way towards Sagira.

Scaly green hands wrapped around Sagira's arm as sharp claws dug into her skin, pulling her up off the ground. Her axe slipped out of her hand as she tried to swing it in defence. Her eyes widened in fear as the Yacuruna holding her raised a clawed hand, poised to strike. Before its blow could land, dark blood sprayed from its neck, coating her in the warm liquid. Its hand loosened, dropping Sagira, who fell to the ground, as the scaled creature collapsed beside her. Looking up, Sagira saw Saora standing above her, holding out a hand. Sagira wrapped one hand around the handle of her axe, and the other around Saora's arm, letting her help her up.

"Good timing," Sagira said.

"Of course," Saora responded.

The two stood back-to-back, weapons coated in blood, poised to attack. Despite the growing number of bodies around them, the forces kept coming.

"There's too many of them," Sagira shook her head.

"We can do this," Saora said, trying to hide the uncertainty in her voice.

As one, they each stepped forwards and resumed the fight. The howls of the Umbra above filled the air around them. A swarm moved closer to the Guardians as a flash of lightning passed just over their heads, striking down the shadows. Saora turned to see Malik standing there, panting, as he nodded to her. She turned back to keep fighting.

Malik's knees wanted to collapse under him, especially after sending out that last bolt of lightning. How he had missed the Umbra getting that close, he didn't want to think about. Raising his hands again, another bolt of lightning burst forwards, striking an Umbra, showering the ground in ash. He leaned back against a boulder, his chest heaving.

"Malik, don't forget to breathe," Sethos said as he fired an arrow.

"I'll be ok," he said.

"Liar," Sethos replied.

"Just focus on your shooting, archer," Malik forced a smile.

"Can you see Iisha?" Sethos asked.

"She's doing fine," Malik reported. "Ciara's fire is keeping the Umbra away from her much better than the rest of us."

"Good," Sethos said, loosing another arrow.

"How are you doing?" Malik turned to his friend.

"I'm not sure how long we can keep this up," Sethos said. "There's just too many of them."

"I know what you mean," Malik said.

The howl of an Umbra grew closer. His arm was as heavy as lead when he tried to lift it to strike with his lightning. The electricity shot from his hand and bounced off the ground, sparking far below the Umbra. Malik screamed as he lifted his axe with all his might and swung it. The umbra vanished with a *whoosh,* and a pile of ash was left smoking at Malik's feet.

"You can't keep this up," Sethos said. "Get over to where Ciara and Iisha are, they can provide back up for you."

"I don't think I can make it that far," Malik said. "Besides, I'm not going to leave you."

"I'll cover you as you go, and then once you make it, the lot of you can provide cover for me," Sethos said. "Ok?"

"Ok," Malik gasped for breath. "On three?"

"Get ready," Sethos began to count. "One . . . two . . . three!"

As he shouted the last number, Malik pushed off the boulder and ran across the battlefield as fast as he could. Arrows whizzed past his head, vaporizing Umbra as he ran through a shower of falling ash. Malik collapsed as he reached Ciara. She stepped in front of him, blocking him from an attack.

"We need to cover Sethos," he panted.

Ciara nodded to Iisha to redirect her aim and waved a hand to signal Sethos to start running. His long legs carried him through the field, his feet trying to keep their grip on the slick ground. Reaching his sister, Sethos ducked down beside her, readying his bow once more to resume firing.

"How are the others doing?" Iisha asked.

"I wasn't able to get a good look," Sethos said. "But I imagine not much better than us."

The archer strung another arrow and took aim at the ever approaching darkness.

Chapter Thirty-Four

Yukaio's feet flew out from under him as the icy ground began to melt with the heat of the smoking Umbra ash. He thrust the end of his glaive into the ground, steadying himself. While he was distracted, a beast lunged for Yukaio. The young Guardian ducked as the Yacuruna flew over him, crashing into the ground. Yukaio raised his glaive and swiped the blade through the creature's midsection. Looking up from the fallen creature, he saw another half dozen swarm around him.

Covered in dark blood, Yukaio fought his way through towards Kai. From the corner of his eye, he could see Sagira and Saora doing the same on the opposite side. The four Guardians stood back-to-back as the Yacuruna surrounded them.

"There's too many," Yukaio said.

"We have to keep going," Kai said. "We have to."

"Kai . . ." Saora panted. "Maybe retreating . . ."

"I doubt they'd let us just run away," Sagira said. "We'd have to fight our way out of here."

"We're stronger together, we can do this," Kai said. "I have to believe we can."

"I think I can muster up one more attack," Yukaio said. "What about the rest of you?"

"Once more," Saora said. "Together."

"Together," Sagira echoed.

As one, the four Guardians let out a battle cry and surged outwards. Weapons raised, they pushed back against the beasts surrounding them. Kai swung at a pair of Yacuruna who dodged his attack. The breath was knocked from his lungs as one collided with his chest. The other administered a swift kick to his side, sending him to the ground. His fingers scrambled for the hilt of his sword, searching through the mix of ash and bloody snow that now covered the battlefield. Looking up, he watched as the beast approached, a knife in his clawed hands. Just as Kai prepared to take the blow, a wave of power reverberated around him, and an icicle impaled the Yacuruna, sending it to the ground.

The Guardians looked to the edge of the battlefield as a male figure stood there. His shoulder-length hair was as white as snow, and his skin pale enough to imagine that he had never been in the sun. Ice blue eyes gleamed as he raised a hand, and another icicle sprang forward, taking out another creature. Drawing a long, thin katana from its sheath, he ran towards the Guardians. The blade sliced through the Yacuruna with ease as he made his way across the battlefield.

"Are you alright?" his hollow voice said as he approached them.

"We are now," Kai said as he got to his feet. "Thank you, Bhurak."

He stared at Kai for a moment, before nodding in response.

"I have a plan, come with me," he said.

Kai looked at the others for confirmation. Their silent glances told him enough - this was their chance. Bhurak sprinted across the field, continuing to clear a path for the other Guardians. They raced after him, taking out as many foes as they could on their way.

"Wait! What about Malik and the others?" Saora

said as they reached the edge.

Bhurak paused and looked back, glancing between the approaching foot soldiers and where the other Guardians still battled the Umbra. He thrust his sword into the ground and got down on his knees, placing his hands on the ground. He closed his eyes and focussed his power. A wall of ice emerged between the Yacuruna and the Guardians, spreading down the battlefield, creating a path for the others.

"Malik! Ciara! This way!" Kai shouted.

The two signalled to the archers behind the boulder. Sounds of ice cracking filled the air as the Guardians ran down the cleared pathway. As they approached, Bhurak turned and ran down a pathway through the mountains. The rest of the Guardians wordlessly followed him. Behind them, the cracking ice grew louder until it eventually exploded as the ice shattered, Yacuruna rushing through, and Umbra following overhead.

"I hope you know what you're doing," Sethos said.

"I know these mountains and paths better than anyone," Bhurak said.

He skidded to a halt in front of a large lake, chunks of ice floating on the surface, stretching as far as they could see on either side.

"You were saying?" Sethos said.

"Trust me."

Bhurak placed his hands on the edge of the lake, ice forming beneath them. The ice stretched out to the other side, creating a bridge.

"Go, go, go!" he screamed.

The Guardians moved as fast as they could across the ice, feet slipping on the slick surface, arms reaching out to each other to help balance. Bhurak brought up the rear, moving across the ice with ease. Looking back, he saw the army gaining distance on them and urged the Guardians forward. As they reached the other side, he turned around to face the army. Bhurak panted, his breath coming in heaves, the ice in his veins dissipating. Teeth filled grins spread across the remaining army as they started down the ice bridge.

"We need to destroy it," Ciara said. She raised her hands, embers of fire dancing around her fingertips.

"Wait," Bhurak held out a hand. "Not just yet."

"What?" she asked.

"Wait, wait . . ." Bhurak watched as the army grew closer and closer. As the last of the creatures entered the bridge, he said, "Now!"

Ciara gripped her mace tightly, swinging it around, engulfing it in flame. With all of her might, she struck the edge of the bridge. Ice melted and cracked under the impact of the flaming weapon. She pulled her arm back, ready for a second strike, sending reverberations down the whole bridge as the ice collapsed beneath the feet of the army. Tossing her mace aside, she sent a wave of flames from her hands towards the beasts. Most dodged the flames by jumping into the water, the rest ducking to the ice, clinging to the remaining chunks as they melted away.

"That's not going to do anything," Sethos said. "They live in the water."

"Unless I do this," Malik raised his arms up.

The sky opened up, and lightning filled the air, striking the lake. Screams erupted as the water boiled, electricity surging through the body of water. One by one, the bodies of the Yacuruna floated to the surface, unmoving. As the lightning ceased, Malik collapsed to the ground.

"Malik!" Sethos said, kneeling by his friend.

Sethos gently lifted his head and propped Malik up against his knee. Slowly his eyes fluttered and opened again.

"Did it work?" his voice was hoarse as he gasped for air.

"Yea, it did," Sethos smirked at him before turning to the rest of the group. "He's ok."

The howling and shrieking of the Umbra grew as they formed a blanket blocking out all the sunlight. The Guardians watched as beneath them a winged figure approached, long black robes flowing.

"Well, well, Guardians," Amatheon said. "I have to say I'm impressed."

"You won't defeat us," Sagira shouted.

"Perhaps not today, but one day you will meet your end, and I promise it will not be a pleasant one," he said.

Amatheon spread his arms wide. The Umbra spread apart, streams of light breaking through their blanket of darkness. Black lightning sparked through the air as the umbra dissipated. The lake exploded, showering the Guardians in water and ice. A rumbling crack sounded above the Guardians as black lightning struck the mountainside, ice covered rock breaking off, falling. Iisha stepped forwards and raised her arms up, freezing the falling boulders.

"Move!" she shouted.

The Guardians ran, Sethos and Kai supporting Malik, who was still near unconscious. Iisha walked backwards towards the others, and, once she was out of the way, lowered her hands. Ice shattered as the boulder crashed into the ground where they had just been standing. Splinters of ice poked at her skin as she shielded her face from the debris. Bit by bit, the sunlight returned as the Umbra disappeared. The Guardians breathed a collective sigh as many of them collapsed to the ground.

"Thank you for your help, Bhurak," Kai said, holding out a hand.

"Of course," he said, avoiding eye contact but shaking Kai's hand.

"How did you know we were in trouble?" Ciara asked.

"A friend of yours told me," Bhurak said. "A Guardian angel."

Kai turned to the rest of the group. Behind them, the angel emerged on the other side of the lake. Their white wings blended in so well with the ice and snow coating the mountains that Kai found himself wondering how long the angel had been standing there. Kai looked them in the eye as they dipped their head in approval. After exchanging glances with the other Guardians, Kai returned the gesture. Uaithiel spread their wings and soared over the waters that had once again calmed. They landed beside Kai and Bhurak.

"Kai," they said. "I know you don't remember me yet, but I'm . . ."

"Uaithiel," Kai finished the sentence. "I've been told a lot about you."

"And?" the angel asked.

"And if you hadn't brought Bhurak to us right when you did, we might not be standing here," Kai said.

"This doesn't change what happened, Uaithiel," Malik said. "I will never forgive you for what you did."

"I don't expect forgiveness," Uaithiel turned to Malik. "Only that you understand that it was not an easy thing for me to do. I do regret what happened, but at the time, I felt that it was necessary."

Malik opened his mouth to respond but closed it. He was too exhausted to argue right now. There was a part of him that was grateful to the angel for finding the ice Guardian. Malik looked at Bhurak – he appeared to be right at home in the ice. Not a single bone in his body shivered despite the cold.

"Just a suggestion, but maybe we could move somewhere a bit warmer?" Malik asked.

The rest of the group agreed with a great deal of enthusiasm. Sethos and Kai again helped Malik to his feet as they followed the rest of the group. Kai turned back to see Bhurak, standing in the same spot.

"Are you coming?" Kai asked.

Bhurak looked at Uaithiel, who motioned for him to follow the group. Bhurak dragged his feet across the ice as he caught up with Kai and the rest of the group.

Chapter Thirty-Five

The crackling of the fire was the only sound that filled the air as the Guardians sat in silence. Exhaustion had taken its hold on all of them. Bhurak had suggested a cavern that would provide shelter from the cold where they could spend the night safely. Uaithiel had promised to stand guard so each of the Guardians could sleep and recover after their battle. Other than scrapes and bruises, there were no serious injuries on any of them. Uaithiel was quick to point out how lucky they had gotten in that regard. Saora ripped up some cloth to make bandages to help cover a few of the wounds.

"This battle could have easily gone bad very quickly, Uaithiel said.

"But it didn't," Ciara pointed out.

"Yes, and for that, I am very grateful," the angel said as they rubbed their temples.

"Are you alright?" Clara asked.

"Hmm, yes, I'm fine," Uaithiel said. "Just a headache."

The angel strode towards the mouth of the cave, the warm fire at their back. When they were sure the Guardians couldn't see, they closed their eyes and rubbed them. The pain pierced through their head, blurring all their other senses. Uaithiel looked back at the Guardians, exhausted, and felt the drain on their powers. *A pity they aren't stronger,* they thought. They turned their back on the Guardians and watched the fields and sky as the day faded into night.

"Kai," Malik said, motioning for him to come over. "I want to talk to you."

"You should get some rest, Malik," he said. "We can talk tomorrow."

"No, now," Malik insisted.

"Alright," Kai agreed, sitting beside him.

"You did well today," Malik said.

"So did you."

"No, I didn't. I froze."

"What are you talking about?" Kai gave him a look of confusion.

"When we first saw the armies approaching, I should have helped plan the formation, but I froze," he said. "All I could think about was the last time I faced that many Umbra, about . . ."

His voice trailed off. Malik looked down at the ground as memories rushed through his mind. Kai understood what he didn't say.

"Being a leader is difficult," Kai said.

"I know," Malik agreed. "You might need my help here and there."

"Me?" Kai shook his head. "After today, I was thinking maybe you should be in charge."

"No way," Malik said. "We need someone who won't freeze when an important decision needs to be made."

"Are you sure?" Kai asked. "You know I'm more than willing to do this, but I thought that you wanted to be in charge. I thought we were going to get Bhurak to be the tiebreaker for our vote."

"It's not so much that I wanted to be in charge, but more I didn't want *you* to be in charge," he admitted. "And I still don't really like the idea of it, but you aren't completely useless."

"Thank you, Malik," Kai said. He held out a hand,

and Malik shook it.

Kai stood and turned to go, his foot colliding with Ciara's mace. Losing his balance, he fell to the ground. He reassured everyone that he was alright amongst Ciara's apologies for leaving her weapon out. Malik rubbed his forehead with one hand and wondered if this really was the right decision.

«««○»»»

Zeneviva lounged in a tall black chair, her feet hanging over one of the arms, as she rested her head against the back of the chair, eyes closed. She didn't move at the sound of a door opening, then slamming shut, and the hurried footsteps that approached her. The sound of Amatheon tapping his foot impatiently didn't cause her to stir.

"Zeneviva," he said after a while.

"Yes, o impatient one?" she smirked.

"I think you have some explaining to do," Amatheon said.

"I rather think I don't," she countered.

"Where were you today?" he asked. "You were absent on the battlefield."

"I just said I don't have anything to explain to you," she repeated.

"Perhaps you would care to explain it to the darkness instead then?" Amatheon suggested. "Your forces got slaughtered today."

"Oh, I'm well aware of that," she said, finally opening her eyes.

Zeneviva swung her feet down in one fluid motion and stood, turning to face Amatheon. She flicked her long hair back over her shoulder with a sweep of her hand as she sauntered up to the demon.

"There is nothing that happened today that I am

not already aware of," she said.

"So then, you must be aware that your plan failed, miserably," Amatheon said.

"And what was my plan exactly?" she tilted her head inquisitively.

"To kill the Guardians," he said.

"Well then, I would say that you failed at that too," she said. "Although, that little temper tantrum of yours with the lightning and the falling rocks sure was a spectacle."

"How do you know about that?" he asked.

"You really need to start paying attention, I'm getting tired of repeating myself, Amatheon," she said. "There is nothing that happened today that I didn't know or plan for."

"I thought the goal was to kill the Guardians?" he said.

"Hmm," she laughed. "Long term, of course, that's the goal. But what was the goal for today?"

"Why don't you enlighten me?" Amatheon said tersely.

"I merely wanted to see the Guardians in action," she said. "I had already been vanquished to the depths by the time the final battle happened. And now I know the limits of their powers."

"And you couldn't have mentioned any of this before?" he asked.

"No, because then you wouldn't have gone at them with your full force, and I wouldn't have seen their true limits."

"At least that explains why you were nowhere to be found. But I still don't understand how you know what happened," Amatheon said.

"I didn't need to be there," she said. "I saw it through the eyes of another."

Zeneviva smirked as she turned away, returning to her chair. She picked up an old leather-bound book from a small table by the chair and began to leaf through the pages. Amatheon stared at her, barely comprehending what she had just said. He thought back, and his eyes widened with realization.

"The angel?" he said.

"Very good, I was starting to wonder if you would get it on your own or if I would have to spell it out for you," she said.

"Your insolence will not be tolerated for long," Amatheon warned.

"We will see about that," Zeneviva said. "Once I make my move, you will see that patience can be the key to victory."

"I'll believe it when I see it."

Amatheon turned on his heels and walked out of the room, slamming the door as he went. The *thud* rumbled the room, but Zeneviva remained unfazed. She swung her feet back over the arm of the chair and continued to flip through the book in her lap. Pausing on a page with a picture of a young woman on it, she stroked her fingers over it.

"Soon," she said. "Soon, you will be mine."

«« «◌» »»

Bhurak watched as the rest of the Guardians sat close to the fire, basking in its warmth. But he sat furthest away, the icy wind whistling through the cave didn't bother him. The ice that ran through his veins helped him feel at home in the cold. He looked at a bowl of porridge that someone had handed him some time ago. Though it was good, he didn't have much of an appetite. He looked up as Kai approached and sat down beside him.

"Not hungry?" Kai asked.

"Not really," Bhurak said. "But I appreciate it."

"Well, we appreciate you coming to our rescue," Kai said. "We wouldn't have lasted much longer without you."

"I'm sure you would have been fine, I really didn't do that much," Bhurak shook his head.

"Are you kidding? You were amazing out there yesterday," Kai exclaimed. "I, for one, am glad that you're a part of this team."

"Are you sure you want me?" Bhurak asked.

"Is there a reason why we wouldn't?" Kai said.

"I saw all of you fighting when I got there, you're all so strong and skilled, and I'm . . . well, I'm not. What you saw today was about the limits of what I can do, it took everything I had inside," he explained.

"Look, what I saw today was incredible. You came up with a plan in a matter of seconds and executed it, saving all of us in the process," Kai said. "Your powers are just as strong as any of ours."

"I was only able to do that because I know these mountains well," Bhurak said. "I just don't think I'm good enough to be a Guardian."

"You know they're making me the leader of this group, right?" Kai asked as Bhurak nodded. "Between you and me, I don't know how to lead a duck to water. I'm used to being told what to do by my little sister, ok? So, if I can step up and take control, you can do this too."

"I don't know . . ." Bhurak said.

"Ok, fine," Kai said. "The weapon you have there, those blades?"

"My kunai? What about them?" he asked.

"Where did you get it?" Kai said.

"I've had them for as long as I can remember," Bhurak shrugged.

"They were given to you by the Gods. They forged and blessed them and for you to use to protect this world," Kai said. "Do you really think the Gods would have chosen wrong?"

Bhurak stared at the bowl of porridge in his lap as he shook his head. He looked up at Kai, who gave Bhurak a slap of encouragement on the back.

"Eat up, we need to head out soon," Kai said as he departed.

Bhurak brought the spoon to his mouth, inch by inch, and took a slow bite. He still wasn't sure about all of this, but if Kai genuinely wanted him to be a part of the team, then he would do his best not to let him down.

«««○»»»

"Remind me again why we aren't going back down south?" Sethos asked.

"There is a lot of work to be done before all of you are ready to fight again," Uaithiel answered as they led the group over a rocky plain.

"Mitesh and Kalida are back down south," Sethos continued. "We need to go back, find them."

"I assure you they are perfectly safe," Uaithiel said. "I made certain that they arrived back at the city of Dahkra and that they agreed to stay there. They will be safe, I promise."

"I doubt your promises," Malik said.

"I have to agree with Malik," Yukaio nodded. "Last time you made a promise to look after my sister, you abandoned her."

"I do not expect forgiveness for that, but I do need you to believe me now," the angel said.

"So, where are we going then?" Kai asked. "Is it to find the last Guardian?"

"Yes . . . and no," they said.

"What the hell is that supposed to mean?" Malik asked.

"Elbridith has always been a bit . . . temperamental," they explained. "Approaching her needs to be handled gently and in the right way. There is a residence we can use near the forest where she has been these past few weeks."

"And then what?" Sagira asked.

"And then I will observe her and determine what the best approach will be," they continued.

"Why is she so temperamental?" Iisha asked.

"She has had a difficult life, not that any of you have had it easy, of course, but there are some scars that not even time can heal," Uaithiel said.

"Like what?" Iisha asked.

"That is a discussion for another time," the angel said. "It's just a bit further now."

"Uaithiel, are we still going east?" Sagira asked as she held the map in her hands.

"Yes, we are," they said.

"Aren't we getting quite close to the Contenebris mountain?" she asked.

"Unfortunately, yes," they answered. "But we will be staying far enough away so as to not draw any attention to ourselves."

The Guardians looked to each other with uneasy glances. As they continued, they could feel a sense of dread grow in the back of their minds, the power of the darkness looming ever closer. They breathed a collective sigh of relief when Uaithiel said that they had arrived. The sight of a stone building jutted out behind the trees. Though it was not large, it was intricately crafted. Uaithiel opened the large brass doors and led the group inside.

"This is one of the nine temples of Madeira," they explained. "Most have long since been abandoned, even though they are still standing."

"Why were they abandoned?" asked Yukaio as he looked up at a series of stained-glass windows.

"The priests and priestesses were driven out by the darkness long ago," Uaithiel said. "No one knows if any of their descendants even remain after all this time."

Uaithiel gave them a quick tour of the courtyard and the sleeping chambers before departing. They warned the Guardians not to wander too far from the sanctuary as there were many dangers that lurked in these woods. Malik locked the doors from the inside, as Uaithiel instructed, as the angel could always return by flying over the walls and landing in the open courtyard.

«««○»»»

"Porridge again?" Yukaio whined as Sethos passed him a bowl. "Don't we have anything else?"

"Sorry, Yukaio," Iisha said. "It's all that we have left right now."

"We've had it for the last four meals in a row, five if you count this one," he said.

"I'm sick of it too," Ciara said.

"You know, when we were walking here, I did see what looked like an orchard not too far away," Kai said.

"Uaithiel said not to leave," Sagira reminded him. "It isn't safe."

"Well, technically, they said not to wander too far away, not to not leave at all," Kai said. "The orchard shouldn't be too far. I could be there and back in an hour, maybe two."

"Kai, are you sure?" Saora asked her brother. "Uaithiel warned us for a reason."

"Yes, it could be dangerous," Sagira chimed in.

"More dangerous than fighting two armies at once?" Kai asked.

"Well . . . probably not, but . . ." Saora said. "We

are kind of close to Contenebris."

"It'll be fine, Saora," Kai said. "I think I can handle gathering some apples."

"If it means we can get some flavour in our food finally, then I vote yes," Yukaio said with enthusiasm.

"Maybe you should wait for Uaithiel to get back first," Saora suggested.

"They've been gone over a day now, who knows how long till they get back," Kai said. "Keep the door unlocked for me?"

Saora scowled at her brother as he set aside his porridge and grabbed an empty sack. Swinging the straps over his shoulders, he made his way toward the doors. Sethos followed him to the exit, unlocking the doors and holding them open for Kai.

"I'm going to leave them open until the sun goes down," Sethos said. "That should give you about three hours."

"Plenty of time," he smiled.

"Make sure you get back in time," Sethos rested a hand on the side of the door. "I won't risk the safety of everyone else in the dark."

Kai nodded as he exited the sanctuary. The cool air caressed his skin as the wind blew around him. It was definitely warmer than the mountains were, but still quite chilly. He followed the path leading away from the sanctuary, hoping that he was going the right way. Before long, the thicket of green trees reddened with fruit. Kai slid the bag from over his shoulder and placed it on the ground, opening it wide.

His fingers began to ache as he twisted the apples off the branches, tossing them into the bag. Smiling, he bit into a juicy apple with a loud *crunch,* juices ran down the side of his mouth, savouring the flavour of something other than porridge. *This is definitely worth it*, he thought to himself. Kai moved down a line of trees, gathering as many apples as he could. His mind drifted away with the sweet flavour as he took another large bite. A twig snapped somewhere behind him, pulling him back to the present.

Kai dropped the bag of apples and turned around. Looking around, he drew his sword as a cool wind sent shivers down his spine. The only movement he could see was the rustling of the branches in the wind. He considered that it might have just been his imagination, that there wasn't anything out there. But in the back of his mind, Uaithiel's warning stuck like glue. Keeping his sword in one hand, he half-turned back to the tree, using his free hand to pluck more apples and toss them in the bag. As he looked at the apples, a shadow moved in the corner of his eye. Whipping his head around, Kai saw a figure move quickly through the trees. He followed it.

He watched as the figure moved through the trees, dodging roots and rocks with ease like they knew where every single one was. Kai picked up speed as he entered a small clearing. He studied the figure paused on the other side, a woman. Her long, pure white hair fell past her waist, swaying in the wind. She was shorter than Kai, but with a solid build. Kai was surprised to notice her feet were bare as she stood in the grass. Her left hand wrapped around a wooden staff that was just about as tall as she was. Slowly, she turned her head to peer over her shoulder at him. Her piercing green eyes glanced over him before focusing elsewhere.

"And who do we have here?" she asked.

"My name is Kai," he said firmly. "Who are you?"

"None of your business," she turned to fully face

him, clicking her tongue. "I suggest you leave before you regret it."

A knot twisted in Kai's stomach. "I don't think I can do that until you tell me who you are."

"I will give you one more chance to walk away with your life," she said, sliding one foot back into a fighting stance, angling the wooden staff towards Kai.

"I should warn you, I'm a lot stronger than I look," Kai said as he raised his sword, preparing to defend himself.

Without warning, the female lunged towards him, raising her staff to strike. Kai barely ducked in time to avoid her strike. Before he had a chance to even raise his sword, she had turned and struck again. This time Kai wasn't able to move out of the way. The staff collided with his abdomen, knocking the wind out of him. He staggered back, trying to catch his breath. The girl took a step back, twirling her staff in one hand as she took up another attack position. Kai dove forwards, somersaulting and popping up directly in front of her, striking with his sword. A swift flick of her wrist had her staff blocking the weapon. The pair attacked and parried back and forth, neither gaining any ground.

Kai raised his foot to kick her side, but she anticipated his attack and moved out of the way. Kai stumbled as he tried to regain his balance. He swung his sword at her, but she blocked with her staff. The sharp metal sword bounced off the wooden staff, not even leaving a dent. She raised her staff once more, knocking Kai's sword out of his hand as he tried to parry her attack. He watched as the sword fell to the ground a few feet away. Backing up slowly, he held up his hands in front of him. He tried to make eye contact with her but noticed that her eyes were practically closed.

Kai dove to the side, aiming for his sword. As his fingers grazed the hilt, her staff collided with his back with a loud *thwack!* Kai let out an agonizing scream as he fell to the ground. Looking over his shoulder, he saw his foe bringing the staff down again, aiming for his head. He rolled out of the way as the staff hit the ground. Before he could reach his sword, a foot landed on his chest. She pushed down, knocking the wind out of his lungs as she bent over to pick up his fallen sword. Raising the blade, she held the point at his throat.

"Wait . . ." Kai said, breathless. "Please . . ."

A rustle in the bushes distracted the girl. Though she looked away, the blade didn't move an inch. Kai tilted his head to try to see what caught her attention. He could see the faint outline of a tall, winged figure. *Uaithiel!* He thought, mentally sighing in relief. His head buzzed as adrenaline continued to rush through his veins. He couldn't make out Uaithiel's words, nor could he focus on what the girl with the sword at his throat was saying. Cold metal poked his throat as she moved the blade closer to him. He felt a small trickle of warm blood run down the side of his neck. Kai saw Uaithiel take a step backwards as she released some of the pressure holding him to the ground.

Without warning, Uaithiel spread their wings and soared forwards. The girl lifted her foot off Kai, dropping the sword beside him. Kai coughed as the air rushed back into his lungs. He looked up in time to see her running off into the trees as Uaithiel knelt beside him, helping him up.

"Who was that?" he gasped.

The angel stared at the empty path.

"That," Uaithiel said. "Was Elbridith."

Chapter Thirty-Six

Kai sat on the floor of the sanctuary as Saora fussed over the cut on his throat. Uaithiel stood off to the side, and though they didn't show it, Kai could tell that they were unhappy. He tried to reach for the bag of apples that he had made Uaithiel go back for - after all that had happened, no way did Kai want to leave behind the spoils of his adventure. Saora slapped his hand away as she finished dressing the wound.

"You're lucky," she said. "It isn't that bad, probably won't even scar."

"Thank you, Saora," Kai said. "What about my back?"

"You've got a few nasty bruises, *those* will take some time to heal," she said.

Kai avoided looking at Uaithiel as he put his shirt back on. His arms were heavy as he tried to lift them above his head. The group was silent, the tension in the room thick enough to cut with a knife. Kai looked over to see Yukaio silently eating chunks of apple mixed in with his porridge.

"So, Yukaio, how's the apple?" Kai asked.

"Don't try and change the subject," Uaithiel glared at him. "I gave you one order."

"Yes, and it was 'don't go far' not 'don't leave,'" Kai said.

"I also said that dealing with Elbridith would have to be done carefully," the angel said.

"So, technically, that's two things you told us," he said.

"That is not the point, Kai," Uaithiel said. "You are supposed to be a leader, an example for the rest of the Guardians to follow."

"I'm sorry," Kai said. "She snuck up on me and then attacked me."

"And she very likely might have killed you had I not showed up when I did," Uaithiel pointed out.

"Thank you for saving me," Kai said.

"Where do you think she went?" Malik asked, finally deciding to join the conversation.

"I'm not sure, I'm going to start over tracking her again," Uaithiel said. "Hopefully, she doesn't go far."

"Do you think Kai spooked her?" Saora asked.

"Trust me, she was anything but spooked," Kai said.

"She prefers to be on her own," Uaithiel explained. "Even before, she was always a little bit more independent than the rest of you."

"So how bad did I mess all of this up?" Kai asked.

"Pretty bad," Uaithiel said.

"Is there anything that any of us can do to help?" Sethos asked.

"Stay here," Uaithiel said as they turned to leave.

Kai stared at the ground, flinching as he heard the slamming of the doors, then the lock clicking shut.

"They can't just expect us to sit here and wait, can they?" Sethos asked.

"Uaithiel seemed pretty angry," Iisha said. "I don't think we should do anything."

"They were probably angrier that you almost got yourself killed," Malik said. "What would we have done then?"

"They never said that Elbridith would actually attack one of us," Kai said. The group fell silent for a moment.

"The apple is delicious," Yukaio said. Kai smiled as he reached into the bag and pulled one out, taking a large bite.

"Worth it," Kai said, his mouth full of delicious fruit.

«« «○» »»

Elbridith rested her staff against the rocky wall of the cave as she sat down on the hard ground. Though the battle today was easy, it was one she hadn't expected to have. Her throat burned with thirst as she tried to relax. Closing her eyes, she attempted to control her breathing, falling into a deep meditation. She felt her heart slow as the adrenaline left her system. Her muscles slackened as the tension floated away. Elbridith felt her mind expand, leaving her body, searching through the forest. Racing through the thicket of trees as if she were physically there, she searched for the angel. Their words lingering in her memory distracted her as she searched.

"Elbridith," they had said her name as if they had known each other for years. There was a sense of familiarity that she did not share. "Please, think about what you're doing."

"Who are you?" she demanded.

"Think, you know who I am," Uaithiel said. "Try to remember."

"I don't know you."

"You aren't alone," the angel said. "I am a friend, and so is he."

She turned to look at the male lying on his back as she held his own sword at his throat. Now he did have a sense of familiarity as she fought him.

"You are a Guardian of Madeira," the angel said. "Please, put down the sword and listen to me."

"I don't think so," she pressed the blade deeper into his skin, a small trickle of blood ran down the side of his neck. She could taste the smell of blood in her mouth.

Uaithiel took a small step forward. "Elbridith, put down the sword."

"No."

"If you come with me, I can explain everything," Uaithiel said. "I know you're missing some of your memories, you're confused about some things. I can help you."

"I very much doubt that," she said.

"I need you to trust me. You don't want to hurt him, let us help you."

"If you want him so bad, you can come and get him."

The angel, spreading their wings and soaring forwards, caught her off guard. Giving up, she dropped the sword as she retreated into the forest.

She forced her mind to move past the memory and to continue searching in the present for the angel that had tracked her down. How had they known where she was? She would have to be more careful in the future. Her mind reverberated back into her skull as she hit a stone wall. Refocussing, she looked more closely at the stone structure. A small building with large, ornate doors stood in the middle of the forest. Some type of temple that her mind couldn't enter. She felt the energy around and inside of it. They were in there, not just the angel, but that human that nearly became her prey. The energy emanating from the sanctuary was strong enough to indicate that there was likely more than just the two of them in there.

Elbridith pulled her mind back through the forest and into the small cave. Reaching out a hand, her staff rushed through the air, her fingers closing tight over it as it landed in her hand. She ran her fingers over the grooved wood that twisted into burls and knots. There were no new marks anywhere along the wood. It had held up against his sword far better than she expected. Placing the end of it against the ground, she pulled herself to her feet and fastened a cloak around her shoulders. She pulled the hood over her head, obscuring most of her face, and stepped out of the cave into the night.

«‹«‹○›»›»

Uaithiel slipped back through the courtyard doors as the sun began to rise, shutting them without making a noise. They walked into the main antechamber outside of the temple, expecting it to be empty, and paused when they saw Kai sitting on a small stool in the corner staring at one of the stained-glass windows.

"Did you get any sleep?" Uaithiel asked.

"A little bit," Kai said. "It actually hurt to lay down."

"I can imagine," the angel said. "Although it serves you right for acting like a fool."

"I know," he said. "Were you able to find her?"

"Yes, I did. She's moved on from where she was, but she's still close by," they said.

"Do you have a plan?" Kai asked.

"Honestly, no," they admitted. "I was hoping that you might have an idea."

"Me? Why me?" Kai said.

"Well, you are the leader of the Guardians, you know more about each of them than anyone else does," Uaithiel said.

"But I can't remember any of it," Kai said.

"Can you remember any of your training? Do you remember learning to use a sword?" they asked.

"No, not at all," he said.

"Yet in the battle the other day, you were able to hold your own against not one, but two armies. You don't remember learning to fight, yet you were able to wield your sword with skill. You don't remember leading the Guardians, but you were able to organize them and form a battle plan," Uaithiel explained. "You don't remember Elbridith, but you knew her, some part of you, deep down, still knows her. Trust your instinct. What does it tell you?"

Kai looked away from the angel and stared at a spot on the ground. There was something familiar about her when he saw her. *Her eyes*, he thought. No way would he ever forget those eyes, the stunning green as vibrant as every leaf and blade of grass in the forest, the way they looked through him as if he wasn't even there. He tried to remember anything else about her, but his mind was blank.

"We should go together," Kai said after a long silence.

"When do you want to go?" Uaithiel asked.

"No, I don't mean just us," Kai explained. "I mean all of us, all the Guardians."

"Why?" the angel said.

"I don't know, you're the one that said to trust my instinct," Kai shrugged.

"Very well," Uaithiel agreed. "We will set out after breakfast."

Kai watched as each of the Guardians rose and ate some food. Despite all of them scolding him last night for nearly getting himself killed, each and every one of them took a large helping of fruit that morning. He explained the plan as they ate. They would all set out from here and find Elbridith. Together they would welcome her to their group.

"What else can you tell us about her?" Malik

asked. "Anything that might help us."

"This won't so much help you, but it is a good thing to keep in mind," Uaithiel said. "Elbridith has psychic abilities."

"Is that her Guardian power?" Saora asked.

"No, these psychic powers were something she was born with, they run in her bloodline," they said.

"So, what is her power then?" Sethos asked.

"Though all of your powers are great, hers is also a burden," Uaithiel explained. "Elbridith holds power over life and death itself."

"What?" half of the group exclaimed.

"She can bring people back from the dead?" Sagira asked.

"The short answer is yes, but it isn't anywhere near that simple. The person's soul must not have crossed into the afterworld yet in order to be brought back to life. Also, the amount of energy it takes her to do so severely drains her own life force. She essentially has to exchange a portion of her own life force to bring anyone back," Uaithiel said.

"This is the type of information that would be good to know," Kai told Uaithiel.

"I know, I'm sorry. Sometimes it's hard to remember that none of you have any memories of the past," they said.

As they finished eating one by one, Kai began ushering them out the door. He wanted them all to have as much daylight as possible to find and convince Elbridith to join them. The journey through the forest was silent as they followed Uaithiel. The angel decided to forgo flying and instead walked at the head of the group so they could follow along easier. After what seemed like hours of walking, Uaithiel held up a hand to pause the group. Kai looked up at the angel as they signalled that Elbridith was nearby. Kai moved forward, his steps silent as he looked through the branches. Elbridith herself was crouched in the same position, likely watching something in the distance that Kai couldn't see.

"Trust your instincts," Uaithiel whispered.

Kai stepped out from behind the branches, purposefully snapping a twig under his foot. Elbridith whirled around to see him approaching. A cloak and hood covered most of her figure, her piercing eyes barely visible beneath the shade.

"Come back for another round?" she asked.

"I'm not here to fight, Elbridith," he said. "I'm sorry I didn't know who you were yesterday."

"So that angel has been talking to you too, then?" she said.

"Not just me, but all of us," Kai said, motioning for the rest of the Guardians to come forwards.

Elbridith continued to stare forward as the Guardians filled in around Kai. No one drew their weapons. Kai had told them to appear unthreatening, but to still stay alert.

"Can't take me on your own, so you brought back up this time?" she smirked.

"No, we aren't here to fight," Kai said. "We want to talk to you."

"I have nothing to say."

Kai took a step forward. "Then, just listen. You are one of us, you're a Guardian."

"I'm nothing like you," Elbridith shook her head.

"Elbridith," Bhurak said, stepping up beside Kai. "You are one of us, can't you feel it?"

"The only thing I feel right now is hungry," Elbridith said. "And you all just scared away my dinner."

"You have one of these, right?" Bhurak held out his meamina.

Elbridith's hand fell to her side, brushing over

something in her pocket.

"It's your soul," Bhurak said, taking another step forward. "It connects you to your powers, it's your life force."

"It's just a trinket," she said.

"No, it isn't," he said. "Just come with us, and we can show you."

"Bhurak . . ." Kai whispered as the ice Guardian took another step forward. Something twisted in Kai's stomach.

"Trust us, Elbridith," he continued forward. "You are one of us."

Elbridith turned to face Bhurak and made to step towards him. Bhurak relaxed, placing his meamina back in his pocket as he reached out a hand to Elbridith. Kai didn't even have time to blink as Elbridith pulled Bhurak's arm, spinning him to face the rest of the group. Grabbing a small knife hanging from a belt at his side, she held the blade to his throat. Bhurak's face paled as he took a deep breath.

"What are you doing?" his voice shook.

"Shut up," she said to him before facing the rest of the group. "Here's what is going to happen. You are going to let us walk out of here, and you are not going to follow. Understand?"

"We'll let you leave if that's what you want, of course," Kai said, holding his hands before him. "Just let Bhurak go."

"He's my assurance that you're going to leave me alone," Elbridith said. "If you follow me, and I will know if you do, he's dead."

Kai screamed for her to stop as she stepped backwards, retreating into the trees. The Guardians stood there in shock as they watched Elbridith and Bhurak disappear.

Pronunciation Guide

The Guardians
Yukaio Roex – yu-kay-oh roe-ex
Sagira Konen – sah-gear-uh co-nen
Sethos Nerri – seth-os ner-rye
Iisha Nerri – i-shaw ner-rye
Malik Ishta – mal-ick ish-tah
Ciara Mish – see-ar-uh mye-sh
Kaidaneir (Kai) Kunzakie – kay-da-neer kun-za-kee
Saora Kunzakie – say-or-uh kun-za-kee
Bhurak Harnda – bur-ack harn-dah
Elbridith Genotau – elle-bruh-dith gue-nah-too

Other Characters
Terry Roex – ter-ree roe-ex
Tiergan Konen – teer-gan co-nen
Kalida Nerri – kah-lee-duh ner-rye
Mitesh Nerri – muh-tesh ner-rye
Tariq Ishta – tar-ick ish-tah
Seran Mish – sear-an mye-sh
Uaithiel – you-ae-thee-elle
Amatheon – ah-mah-thee-on

Places
Madeira – mah-day-ruh / Madeiran – mah-day-ren
Contenebris – con-ten-uh-bris
Dhakra – dock-ruh

About the Author

Amelius Marin has been creating the world of Madeira for over a decade. They enjoy rainy evenings and warm cups of hot chocolate. Amelius lives in Niagara Falls, Ontario with their three cats, Merlin, Arthur, and Morgana.

For updates on the Madeiran Guardians, visit Amelius's blog.

www.ameliusmarin.com